HUNTINGTON PASS

BY VICTOR SMITH

authorHOUSE®

AuthorHouse™
1663 Liberty Drive
Bloomington, IN 47403
www.authorhouse.com
Phone: 1-800-839-8640

First published by AuthorHouse 7/6/2011

ISBN: 978-1-4634-0864-0 (sc)
ISBN: 978-1-4634-0863-3 (e)

Library of Congress Control Number: 2011908729

Printed in the United States of America

For Mary, Jesse, and Leda who provided
spiritual support and unconditional love

And

For Alan Catlin who provided intellectual support
and much-needed critical motivation

PART ONE

NOVEMBER 5™

VE, AVE, BE careful, you're a little excited now. Remember **. . . A***what they say about the future: be careful what you fish for. Sometimes things don't turn out the way you th...*anks, I say, hauling the stuff of my priceless life from the back seat of the sedan. I tug on the strap of my duffel bag, dragging it out across the vinyl, dropping it on top of the skis, poles, boots, and unicycle next to the car.

Sure you don't want a beer? I ask again, my bluejean pockets flush with fives and singles, a couple-three twenties. The rest I keep in the duffel. You did me a real favor getting me up here like this, you know.

He shakes his head and says he's got to get to Oneonta by dinner time. Dinner time, yeah...you go eat, now. He drives off spattering gravel, waving his hand around, opening windows even though it's cold. You'd think he didn't enjoy my company, or something. Me? Buck Avery? Everybody loves Buck Avery.

NOW, HERE I STAND NEXT to the bridge at the bottom of the access road to Huntington Pass, it's getting dark, and the wind is blowing out of the northwest like it's fixing to drop a foot tonight. Early snow. What better way to start out fresh. Good sign.

I wonder if I can carry all my stuff on the uni. I'm pretty

1

used to carrying all kinds of baggage around, so I throw the duffel over my shoulder and begin picking up my stuff, piece by piece, until I look like a porcupine with skis and poles sticking out in all directions. I look around and get the feeling, but only for a second, that I'm all alone. Then it all comes back to me, why I'm here in the first place, and I whistle up a little rock 'n roll as I think through my next couple of moves.

The access road looms long before me, snaking up the hill to the lodge and ticket booths. I've been here before, some years ago. And now I'm back. Return of the Kneissl Kid. They'll know who I am. I pull my trench coat closer to my throat and button it using the hand holding only my poles and boots; a pretty good trick, but I'm pretty good at a lot of things. I look down at the uni through the jumble of steel, wood, and leather I'm holding, and decide that I'm probably carrying one thing too many for this load. So I carefully drop it all again and begin looking around for an alternative.

Change. Choices. Life is full of them, or should be, anyway. This is one right here. An alternative to squalor, a change in seasons, a new beginning. Leave Utica behind, forget the back rent, and live the life you've dreamed. You have to make change happen, that's what I say. Make change happen.

Well, how about this? I'll just stash my stuff under the bridge for a bit until I get my bearings, have a beer, and find a place to crash for the night. I try to do it in one trip around the guardrail, down the embankment, but it's kind of slippery and I end up quite a way below the bridge, up to my ankles in the cold water, mud all over my hands. So I drop to my knees and start to cr...*All right, Ave, real nice. You have enough trouble just walking with that leg of yours, why do you always have to ma*...ake three trips around the guardrail, finally getting all my stuff hidden real nice, just underneath the bridge, right up tight to the edge of the bank.

Well now, it's time to bust open a cold one. I climb back around to the guardrail, up and over, then I pick up the uni. I set it just so between my legs out in front of me and hooch myself back into the saddle. Back in the saddle again. Back where balance is a friend and where I'm maybe the best there ever was. I spin my way down toward town, stretching my arms overhead in a big yawn. I'm thinking I probably could have carried my stuff after all, but, hey...I got a good spot for it until I'm ready to move in somewhere later tonight.

I walk into the bar at the Klondike, a dimly lit dive that's just as empty as the ski trails over the top of the roofline, up on the northeast ridge facing town. I set the uni against a table, careful to get the saddle wedged just right so it doesn't wheel out from under itself. I turn toward the bar and pick out a good stool from the empty line along the scratched mahogany. The uni crashes to the floor. I whistle to get the bartender's attention away from the black-and-white TV on the shelf up in the corner. He doesn't seem to hear me, so I whistle again. He turns slowly, I mean real slow, and just looks at me for a minute.

Hey, ho, Mr. Barkeep, I say, a good opening being a thing of value anywhere you go these days. Any chance you got a beer back there somewhere?

He stands there looking at me, then slowly walks over to the corner and reaches up to turn off the TV.

"Closing," he says, wiping his hands on his apron.

Whaddaya mean? I ask.

"Closing," he says, walking back into the kitchen.

Well, Jesum Crow, I'm thinking, I'll just take my money somewhere else, somewhere there's a human behind the bar.

Oh, Mr. Barkeep, I yell back, picking up the uni, I want you to remember one thing, just one thing. I scooch up onto the saddle and ride it around the inside of the bar, between tables, only knocking over a couple of chairs. I'd probably knock over a few just walking to the door. I ride a lot better than I walk. You just remember some day, maybe next year some time, you just remember how you...

He comes back out from the kitchen, wiping down a big French chef's knife, and walks the length of the bar. Since this has actually happened to me before, I've got a pretty good idea what comes next and I spin toward the door. Balancing with my feet horizontal on the pedals, I wave goodbye and reach for the door handle. I pull it open and bump up over the threshold. I turn back as I close the door.

See you later, masturbator.

So I ride down the block a little further until I see the lights are still on at Sam's Dinette. I've been to this little diner before. And it's not bad, not bad at all. I'm having trouble getting the door open so I hop off the uni and set it up against the wall. I pull the handle and walk in, turning back to grab the uni. Don't want anybody stealing something valuable like that, I'm thinking.

You got any beer? I ask, knowing the answer, just trying to be friendly.

"No, sir," says Sam, a huge man with a belly that he can't seem to keep his apron tied up and over. "Got coffee, though."

Hey, ho, I say, Bring it on.

It's not beer, but it's not bad. I chug it like a beer just to see what Sam thinks of that. I can't really tell what he thinks, though, since my eyes are closed and my tongue is doing the Hully Gully, trying to scrape the pain off the inside of my mou...*How nice, Ave, now really! Is this your way of making a first impressi...*Shit, I say, 'Scuse my French, wiping tears off my face.

Sam brings over the carafe and pours from two feet above the cup without looking; filling it to the rim, spilling nothing.

How do you do that? I ask.

"Do what?" he asks.

4

I hunker down on the counter, both hands around the steaming cup. I guess I'll take my time with this one. I order a couple of cheeseburgers and fries, which come in less time than it takes to get the coffee past my throbbing tonsils. Sam sets them down in front of me and I drain the cup.

Refill? I ask.

I eat the first burger in three bites and down my third cup of coffee. I wolf half of the second burger and dip a fry in the pool of ketchup half-covering my plate. I tip back my head, hold the fry up at arm's length above my cavernous mouth and drop it. It hits a tooth and falls sideways up against my nose before dropping to the floor. Sam frowns.

Usually pretty good at that, I say as I slide off the stool to retrieve the fallen spud. I pick it up and pop it in my mouth, regaining my perch at the counter. I take a dozen paper napkins and put them in my pocket.

Cut these yourself? I ask, wiping ketchup off my nose with the back of my hand.

"Frozen," Sam says.

Refill? I ask.

I DECIDE TO TAKE A circuit of the town before going back to get my stuff, before I try to find a room. I'm buzzing so bad that I have a little problem with balance, even though I'm maybe the best there ever was, anywhere. I bump up onto the sidewalk and pedal east, feeling each crack, pumping my arms like I'm running a marathon or something. Everything is closed and it's getting dark, real dark. I pass the Alpine Lace Ski Shop. Its windows are full of the most expensive women's jumpsuits and high-heeled ski boots, fur-trimmed après ski boots, the newest and flashiest of the little, short-shit skis they all use today. I pass the Troubadour, a theater, a drug store, Gus's Gas, a line of little ticky-tacky cottages that just have to be seasonal rentals, and a cozy-looking laundromat. I'll just have to check them out in the light of day, I guess.

I pedal down to the very end of town and turn back in front of the dark windows of Momma's, which has a sign like a bar but appears to be somebody's house. Halfway back through town, I stop at Gus's and pull some change out of my pocket. I drop a couple of quarters into the soda machine and hear the root beer drop into the chute below. I open the door, pull it out, and crack it open. Not beer, but not bad, I'm thinking. I tilt back my head and take the whole bottle. Man, does that ever ta...*Ave, you should know what happens when you do tha...*at all without taking my feet off the pedals, without holding onto things. Like I say, I'm maybe the best there ever was.

I get back to the bridge and realize that I'm now buzzing like a swarm of yellowjackets, which makes me laugh right out loud because that's what they call the instructors here at Huntington. I sit balanced on the uni, one foot up on the guardrail, wondering just how good life can get. I decide that I might just as well save a night's worth of money by sleeping under the bridge, which seems like a pretty good idea seeing that everything in town is closed. I step up and over the guardrail and pull the uni over behind me. I skid more carefully down the embankment with my other leg downhill this time, and clamber up under the protection of the bridge as a light snow begins to fall. I open my duffel in the dark and pull out my four blankets, laying them out on as flat a spot as I can find on this embankment. I tuck my blankets in under the stink of my socked feet and settle my head on the cushioned saddle of the uni.

So, I'm thinking, this is one great way to end the first day of the rest of my life. Life is just so priceless. Some people don't understand how important it is to be alive, no matter what they've got going on. Mom, Dad -- both gone. Where? Who knows? Dead, just like it said in the paper, far as I can see. Gone. But not forgotten: the one thing, the only thing that ever scares me. If you're not still alive in somebody's brain, you're deader than shit, 'scuse my French. And empty as a flushed toilet.

But, whatever else happens in this priceless life of mine, I won't be flushed out and forgotten. You can bet anything you've got; change is coming – lots of it - and people are definitely going to know who I am.

So I snuggle down into my four blankets and close my eyes to jagged flashes of color streaking out of nowhere from deep inside my buzzing brain. I sleep on and off, mostly off, grinning as my intestines trumpet out the coffee, root beer, and beef fat in three-part harmony. A 'sweet Welsh air', as Dad would say, floating above the water music burbling below.

NOVEMBER 6ᵀᴴ

WHO WOULD THINK a young guy like me could feel so old and stiff? Criminy. Must be the slope of the bank making me tighten up like this. I laid up a couple-three good rocks on the downhill side. You'd think that'd keep me from rolling, let me relax.

Time for coffee. Yes. It's not beer, but it's not bad. I stuff my four blankets back into my duffel and shake off the cold. I make sure all my stuff is pushed up tight under the bridge and out of sight. Then I scrabble around and up the embankment, little stones splashing into the creek below. Which way, the lodge or Sam's? It's 6:30 and on a good day they should both be open. Maybe not the lodge, though.

I set the uni out in front of me and pedal off, my arms flapping to generate faster warmth, not speed or balance. I don't need to think about balance because I might be the best there ever was. I was probably born balancing on something or other, Mom would always say, just sitting there smi...*my little monkey on skis, my little Ave. Just look at him wiggle, just a lit...*til one day I hear some jerk say I look like a monkey on the uni. Screw him, I'm thinking. He's probably getting up to some kiss-ass little job this morning while I'm up here in Paradise. Who's the little monkey now, huh?

The lights are on at Sam's so I pull up and flip the uni out from underneath me, grabbing it from behind - Buck-style - like I always do. I bring it inside, and take a seat at the booth next to the kitchen door. A harried-looking waitress, introducing herself as Marie, slides onto the bench opposite me in the booth and plops down an order pad. She flips pages over the top until she gets to a blank one.

"So, whaddaya want this early on a cold morning, Hon?" she asks. She looks up from the pad, skewering me with her baby blues, leaning over to one side on her left elbow, chin cupped in her hand. She is maybe thirty, with more lines than dimples, but still cute as a button. I wonder how many kids she's supporting and whether she's got a hubby back home to shake her springs.

Whaddaya got? I ask in return, wondering if a cool answer might get her wondering if there might be something else she'd rather bring me.

"Need a menu?" she asks, digging into an apron pocket. "Got one here somewhere."

Start with some coffee, I say. It's not beer, but it's not bad, I'm thinking. I'll be awake enough to order once you get back.

I stretch my muddy legs out on the bench, leaning up against the side wall of the booth to take stock of the place. There's a "No Admittance" sign above the double swinging doors into the kitchen, and two doors labeled "Buck's" and "Doe's" to its right. Just my luck, I'm thinking, my own personal pot to piss in, 'scuse my French. I'll just have to take a picture of this. I may not have a camera, but I've got a pen that works, and my words are worth a thousand pictures.

Pictures...there's a double row of framed and autographed pictures along the opposite wall, all with Sam in his greasy apron and a bunch of guys in ski jackets that I figure are famous for something or other. I'd sign mine right across the bottom, kind of to the right and slanted up a bit, making sure not to cover my face or anything. Buck. Buck Avery, the Kneissl Kid.

I decide there's things I need to remember about this place so I pull a napkin out of the dispenser and flatten it out in front of me. I reach into my shirt pocket and pull out my girlie pen. It's a wide-barrel job with a clear plastic case full of baby oil and fake snow that falls lightly when I shake it. And it falls on a buxom babe in a bikini, who holds her upper arms tight to her torso and bends forward at the waist, pressing her little titties together, shivering. When she shivers, they spin around and around. Crack me up. You just gotta love snow.

Marie brings a steaming mug of coffee, a spoon, and a little basket full of creamer and sugar packets.

No cream? I ask, glancing down at the basket.

"Where do you think you are," she asks, "The fucking Moulin Rouge?"

And I am instantly in love. I feel a glow rise up from my unmentionables to the bottom of my chin, where it spreads out across my cheeks like that hot wax Mom used to paste all over her face at night. I go from wondering about a spring-shaking hubby to whether I, myself, might find a squeaky bed somewhere in this town to sweat up this foul-mouthed maiden of the steam table. I think hard for a witty response, but noth...*Think, Ave, you know what happens when you get too excited. You know you're no...*Not really, I say.

Marie walks away without taking my order, but I don't need to be out of here fast anyway, at least not today. I shake a packet of creamer and rip the top off roughly with my teeth, glancing up to see if Marie might be watching, which she is not. I hold it up over my coffee, tapping it, watching the off-white powder spread out across the blackness. I stir it slowly until I realize that Marie is again sliding in the booth across from me.

"Here," she says, as she pushes the menu across at me. "Eggs, hash, pancakes, bacon, sausage, toast, three kinds of cereal, biscuits, gravy, and sticky buns. Your call." I order scrambled eggs and white toast, thinking I'll save a little money this morning.

"Refill?" she asks.

Oh, yeah. I say. It's not beer but it's not bad. Marie leans hard right and slides out of the booth, leaving behind a lingering scent of some perfume I can't name. But then, I can't name any of them.

I wave to Sam behind the counter and he nods back. I yell over, gesturing at the wall of pictures with my thumb, Those guys have these same pictures at home with your name on them?

"Yeah," he says, "And Santy Claus is coming to town."

Not for a month or so, I say, winking large, as Marie brings back the carafe of coffee. She pours and I leer, wishing the buttons on her shirt faced the other way this morning.

"Your eggs'll be right up," she says.

I leave a tip that will definitely make her remember me, but most people seem to do that anyway. I pocket my pen and add the napkin to the roll in my pocket, carefully securing it with my rubber bands. I pull the uni out from under the table and wheel it to the door.

See you soon, I say, waving to Sam.

"Not if I see you sooner," he responds with an exaggerated wink. I straddle the uni and head back toward the bridge, my arms churning up more speed in the briskness of the cool morning air. I pass a line of houses, The Mortar and Pestle Pharmacy - which I instantly dub the Mortar and Pestilence, turning it over and over and over and ove...*ve, Ave, Ave? You know you have to th...*in my mind until I see the little sign sticking out in the middle of the next block. Hedwig's.

BUCK, BUCK AVERY, I SAY, sticking out my right hand at belly level toward the old lady. Shake, spear, kick in the rear. The impulse is always there, right below the surface ever since junior high school. But instead I just take her hand as it comes my way and, bowing slightly at the waist, bring it up for a kiss on the back of her bony knuckles. Pleased to meet you, I say.

Hedwig's looks just fine. The sign fronts a two-story frame house sheathed in roofing shingles, with bleary-looking plastic stapled over the windows. Two afterthought dormers stick out of the roof, shingled in more modern stock. I look around the foyer as if it were expansive.

"I keep it just the way it was when Mr. Pbrofonski passed away." she says. And I can see that, looking through the open door to the cluttered sitting room. "Ten dollars a night, week in advance," she continues.

I'll take it. I say, digging deep into my pocket for my larger bills.

"There's two other young gentlemen sharing number One, you'll be in Three," she says, re-counting my crumpled wad of fives and tens. "No girls in the room and no food."

No food? I ask.

"I hate the rats," she says, "I can't touch them. Mr. Pbrofonski always took care of them."

Rats? I ask.

"Rats," she says, "Just don't bring in any food and you'll be fine. The bathroom's down the hall and to the right, first door."

I follow Hedwig upstairs and down the dark hallway to the door with the perky, little mouse holding a 3 that looks like it's made of Swiss cheese. The door creaks as she opens it, exposing a dingy, curtained window illuminating a single bed, dresser, nightstand, and a half-dozen pegs sticking out of cowboy-and-Indian wallpaper. A ragged throw rug is tacked to the floor, covering a hole, maybe somebody's bad carpentry or something.

"This was Billy's room before he left for the Army." she says, bustling about, straightening, sweeping at dust with the back of her hand, real busy so that I can't ask anything about him. "Mr. Pbrofonski thought it was better for us to rent it out."

Well, I say, I'll keep it nice. I can always move into another room when he comes home to visit. I can usually tell when it's better not to ask questions.

I stand here after Hedwig's abrupt and snuffling departure, thinking that this will be just right until I find a job and move into a bigger pad, something I can really call my own. Downstairs I hear the civilized sound of a toilet flushing and I realize that I can probably count on one hand the times I've trickled in a real toilet since I left Uti...*Come on, Ave, is this really important? Should you be wasting your time on stupid, little things li...*I smell cabbage cooking.

I skip happily down the stairs two at a time and hear Hedwig acknowledge my cheery wave from the doorway: "Too much noise!". I grab my uni from the umbrella stand in the foyer and head back for the bridge.

I CASUALLY LEAN THE UNI against the guardrail and step over the embankment and back under the bridge. My stuff is all where I left it, ready for a new home under a roof this time. I gather it up into my duffel and drag it out next to the guardrail. I drag out my skis, boots, and poles and I lay them next to the duffel and the uni. I know I can do it this time.

I throw the strap of the duffel over my left shoulder and swing it around so its bulk lays against the small of my back. I tie together the inner laces of my ski boots and drape them around my neck. I take my skis and set them upright, leaning against the guardrail. I hold my ski poles in my left hand and straddle the uni, holding my position with the poles. I get my balance with both feet on the pedals and snatch the Kneissls with my right hand, swinging them up and over my shoulder, pedaling off before the skis even leave the ground. I am flying.

Several cars beep as I pedal down the street toward my

new home, children craning around to watch me out the back windows. A man on the sidewalk raises a hand to wave as I pass; I would generally slap him five going by, but my hands are full at the moment. Squirrels scamper out of my way, cats race up trees, and a Police car slows. I would wave, but my hands are full at the moment. The patrol car passes me and stops just up the street, waiting for me to go by again. But I stop at Hedwig's before I reach the cruiser, tossing the skis and pulling the uni out from under myself, Buck-style.

I carry my stuff upstairs in two trips after trying to do it in one. "Too much noise," Hedwig yells from the kitchen. I bring up my skis and the uni on my second trip. I close the door and spin through 360 degrees, surveying the cramped surroundings of my new home. It's time to unpack.

I start sorting through my stuff, setting it up around the room, and it feels like the first time in months; it is the first time in months. My four blankets come out first and go limp on the bed. I stand the uni up against the dresser, then change my mind and hang it on the wall from a peg sticking out of an Indian's eye. I take my ski boots – good, stiff buckle boots of fine Italian leather, with inner boots laced in parachute cord - and hang them from a peg beside the uni. I hang my ski poles by the straps on the same peg. My skis, my classic Kneissl Red Stars, go up on the wall horizontally, across the top of four pegs, looking like a million bucks.

I paw down further into my duffel and pull out two pair of tattered Levis, three tee shirts, another wool shirt just like the one I'm wearing, two pair of underwear that clearly need washing, a Swiss Army knife, five socks, a long scarf, a mitten, two dog-eared notebooks, a hash pipe that hasn't seen a match since Marcy State, a knit watch cap, a sweater, two packs of Luckies, my pocket watch, an oversize mason jar full of coins wrapped up in the sweater, six pencils and a spare pen bunched together inside a dozen rubber bands, a twice-read copy of *On The Road*, a fork, another sweater, two pair of holed waffle-weave longjohns, another hat, a condom that's that's been laying around around longer than the hash pipe, another tee shirt, a Huntington Pass brochure, my wad of paper napkins wrapped with rubber bands, five sugar packets, an empty film container that still smells like hash after almost a year, sunglasses in two pieces, another pack of Luckies, and a lighter with about twenty wraps of duct tape around it that will come in handy when I decide to fix the glasses. I carefully arrange the clothes in the three drawers of the dresser and set out my other stuff in good order on top of the nightstand and dresser.

Life is good, I'm thinking. I pick up the Huntington Pass brochure, lay back across the bed, and look at a picture of the spiderwork of trails laid out across the face of the bowl. "Biggest vertical drop in the East!", "Over 400 acres of snowmaking", "Night skiing", "Complimentary cocktail with three-day packages", "Annual Huntington Cup Race February 6th". I close my eyes and link my fingers behind my head, elbows out like I do sometimes when I ride the uni. I think about my early years coming up, the first pair of used Kneissls my Daddy bought me when my voice was changing - right after our little talk about the birds and the beast - and the way they turned me into a legend before I was eighteen. Jumps, bumps, freezing my tongue to the safety bar, screaming straight-line down the middle of Tamarac through clots of terror-stricken beginners, my first kiss on the lift night-skiing. All this finally coming together into a new life, complete with a new home to call my own. All I need is a job.

"AND WHAT BRINGS YOU TO Huntington, Mister...Let's see, Mr. Buck?" she asks.

Buck, Buck Avery, I say to the woman behind the desk. She is short and perky-looking, with cropped dark hair and glasses perched on top of her head. Her name is Mrs. Kistler, according to the cheap, plastic name tag pinned askew just above her left tittie. She wears a thick ski sweater and stretch pants with heel stirrups disappearing into a pair of very sexy-looking, high-heeled boots that I can see each time I peek under the modesty panel.

Actually, it's writing, I say, But I've got some free time. You got a job, I got the skills. I can teach anybody to ski, even a crippled-up moron. But I never got certified or nothing. I stare deeply into her eyes, leaning forward across the desk to appear interested.

"I'm sorry, Mr. um, Avery, is it?" she says, "We don't have any openings right now."

You can call me Buck, Ma'am, I say, trying to make her feel more at ease in the company of a legend. I know how hard it can be.

Well, there's plenty of other things I can do until an instructor job opens up, I add, giving her a good opportunity.

"I'm sorry, Mr. Buck, but we have filled all our positions for the season," says Mrs. Kistler.

It's just Buck, I say, correcting her gently so as not to antagonize her, Mr. Buck runs a drug store back home in East Utica. I used to work for him back in, oh, March of 196...*sick, Ave, is that what you want her to think? When there's something important that you want, you have to foc...*cause we had to, like, count out all those little pills, and all. She rolls her eyes, probably has some kind of grit or something in one of them. I'll take anything that comes with a season's pass.

"I'm sorry, Mr. Avery, but we have nothing available," she insists.

Okay, then, I say, Guess it's time to speak with your supervisor. This always seems to work for me.

"I'm sorry, but I handle all personnel decisions for Mr. Barnacre and I don't think you want to talk to him right now."

I decide to push the issue. I'll wait for Mr. Barnacre, if you don't mind, I say. I settle comfortably into my chair and cross my legs like a civilized person.

"I can call Mr. Barnacre, if you'd like," she says, "But here's what he'll tell you. Your hair is too long for Huntington and you have a beard. There are no men with beards working at Huntington and none with hair past their ears or collar. That's what Mr. Barna...*Christ, Ave, you know you have to think these things thr...*who you are when he hires you."

Well, Jesum Crow, I'm thinking. He's got no right. That's discrimination, and this is 1979. That's discrimination, I say, You can't get away with this in 1979.

"And your clothing is not in keeping with the image Mr. Barnacre seeks to project," she continues. "I'm afraid we have nothing for you."

Whaddaya mean, I ask, All your lifties, snowmakers, and garbage tossers have crew cuts and have to salute this guy?

"I'm sorry, Mr. B...Mr. Avery," she says, looking down at my application, "I have things to do."

Well, Mrs. K...K...Kistler, I say, leaning in, leering wide-eyed and tongue-length from the nametag on her left tittie, Is it too much to ask to sit in your bar and have a goddam beer, 'scuse my French, or do I need a stupid-looking haircut first?

"I'm sorry, Mr. Avery. You'll have to leave."

SO, THERE'S OTHER BARS IN town. And I've got good, dependable transportation. On the uni, everything's in balance. I don't even have to think about anything, because I'm maybe the best there ever was. I spin down across the bridge and onto Main Street where I pass Hedwig's and head for the Troubadour. There are three cars in the parking lot, probably about right for a late Thursday afternoon before the season starts. I'm still upset, but I know that'll change with the first beer going down. I pop my feet off the pedals and dismount,

Buck-style, right in front of the stairs to the porch. I swing the uni up under my arm and walk on in.

I take a stool next to a tired-looking woman at least ten years my senior who seems like she's been here for a while. I order a Utica Club and light up a Lucky. I look over to find she is staring at me, not something I was necessarily looking for.

"You new in town?" she slurs, eyelids hiding the upper half of her iris on either side, "Or do you just look different today?"

I look her over pretty carefully, the pause being a fairly cool way to set myself up for the likes of her anyway. Then I glance away and take a long drag on the Lucky. I slowly turn her way with a whole lot of nonchalance and blow out a perfect smoke ring. I look up at the ceiling as the smoke ring begins its rise, losing its identity in the cloud above, when a little bubble of mucous - as best I can figure - drops out of my nose and down my windpipe. A strangled cough bursts out just as I raise my glass of UC to further extend the pregnancy of the pause, blowing foam across the bar and startling the woman back a little closer to sobriety. I slam the glass back down on the bar, hacking and pounding my chest. She gets into the act, patting my back until the snot is expelled and my lungs stop their heaving.

Well, Criminy, I'm thinking. So much for nonchalance. I wipe the tears out of my eyes and sit here, chest heaving, my voice box useless for the moment.

Thnks, I say, or at least I try to, I dn't knw wht jst hppnd.

"Well, Hon, I don't think I've ever seen a man move like that before," she says, eyelids back where they belong for the moment.

Jesum, I say, Something went down the wrong way, I guess.

"No such thing as going down the wrong way," she

says. "And I've never seen a man's tongue stick out that far before, either," she continues, eyes now bright with interest and anticipation. She turns 90 degrees on the stool to face me directly, knees poking against the side of my thigh. "You okay?"

I get my first complete view of her at this point. She has at least ten, maybe twelve years on me, and a lot of those years had to be pretty rough, from the looks of it. Her face is lined, but still kind of child-like and sincere. She has the skinny body and legs of a chain-smoking alcoholic, but she is wearing a sweater that clings to her magnificent chest like saran wrap. The hair on her head is a henna red that doesn't look like it came with the original package, but her feet are stuffed into stiletto pumps that look like she's had them on all her life.

Well, I'm thinking, this is complicated. I'm still not sure she isn't one of those hookers Huntington is famous for, but I get the impression she's too drunk to be doing business either way.

Think so, I say, finally getting control of my breathing, looking to see what's left in my beer glass.

"Hon, how'd you like to buy a lady a drink?" she asks, eyeing my cigarettes.

What are you drinking, I ask, a little worried that she might be looking to swipe my new pack of Luckies.

"What are you buying," she asks.

I'm drinking UC, you can have whatever you want, I say, pulling the Luckies over to a safer spot on the bar. My mind's eye crawls into my pocket to see if I have anything but singles left. I decide to offer her one cigarette to keep her from stealing the rest of them.

"Thanks, Hon," she says, taking one and tamping it against the bar, "I gave them up quite a while ago. They started scaring me. I never light them anymore, but I still love the way they feel between my fingers like this."

She brings the cigarette up next to her cheek, wrist cocked back, eyes boring into mine. She wiggles a little mambo move with her shoulders and winks large, just like I do. "I'm pretty hot, smokin' or not, don't you think?" she says.

Oh, yeah, I say, looking away and dragging long on my Lucky. I point it over at her glass and raise my eyebrows, blowing smoke up and away from her this time.

"I believe I will have another Manhattan," she purrs, tapping invisible ash.

I signal the bartender and repeat the smoky gesture toward her glass, immediately wondering if this repeat of nonchalance might put me into another fit of some kind. He takes it and mixes the cocktail quickly and without comment, like he's done it before, and I'm sure he has. He sets it in front of her and counts out three singles from the little pile in front of me.

"Where's home, Hon?" she asks, and I wonder if she means immediate home with a squeaky bed involved, or where I was actually born. I'm so taken with the fact that I now have an actual home again that I just have to tell her a nice story.

I'm kind of between things right now, I say, I'm renting a little house down the street until I find something bigger to buy. I've got my eyes on thi...*see what you're doing, Ave? Just why are you talking to this woman? She's not what I'd call your type, and I can't imagine why you would need to impress her with your little sto*...recently, I say, within walking distance, which is a priority for me.

"Married?" she asks.

No, you? I ask.

"Was," she answers, drawing long on the unlit Lucky.

Kids? I ask, pretty sure I know the answer.

"County took them," she answers, verifying my assumption, and adding some real flavor.

See them much? I ask, the only thing that comes to mind at the moment.

"County's back in Montana," she answers, taking half the Manhattan in a gulp. "But that's just as well."

So she tells me about waking up drunk after coming in late after being out making big money one night. She went home to bed, had a smoke to wind down, and there was a fire, I guess. She says something about how they had to go back in after getting her out because she forgot to tell them the kids were in bed. Well, I'm thinking, now I'm safe. This should drop her into a deep hole of depression that's too narrow for the both of us to crawl into, hopefully.

But she spins my way again and rubs her knees back and forth against my leg, reaching over in front of me, rubbing a tittie against my shoulder as she squashes her Lucky in the ashtray, just like it was lit or something. I signal for another beer and notice that she's staring at me again.

Well, the best defense is a good offense, they say. So I figure I'll just scare her away. I turn toward her and knock knees a couple of times getting one of mine in between hers. This ought to do it.

I begin to think this might be a bad idea when I see the bartender roll his eyes toward the ceiling. But I know this is a bad idea when she squeezes my knee real tight and stares into my eyes. I reach for my beer, nearly knocking it over with the back of my hand. She squeezes again. I drain the beer and pull my watch out of my pocket.

Uh, oh, I say, holding the watch up, I've got to be getting on home.

"Not just yet, Hon," she says, gripping my knee tighter, patting it with her free hand. "I don't know who you are. My name's Andrea."

Buck, Buck Avery, I say, feeling the knee lock tighten as her eyes go gooey, probably thinking about rhyme and motion.

"Pleased to meet you," she says, "Can you give me a ride home?"

Nope, I say, I don't have my car up here yet.

"Wanna walk?" she asks, and I get a wrenching feeling in the pit of my stomach. I weigh the possibilities and decide that this is an entanglement I might not want to get involved in this quickly. I mean, I've only been in town a day and, with my entire life stretching out in front of me, I should probably be watching my beh...*Ave, that's much better, now. You're starting to thi...*into bed with some aging babe's got kids in Montana. Strong, skinny legs, though, Bet she can ski.

Sure, I say, my out-of-nowhere answer startling me, scaring me, arousing me. I unlock my knee and slide off the stool, grabbing the uni leaning up against the mahogany.

"What's that?" she asks, eyeing the simple contraption, grabbing my shoulder for balance.

It's a uni, I reply, it's short for unicycle. And it strikes me that I don't really have to clarify that, but then it strikes me again that I probably do. We walk out the front door and down the steps.

"You ride that?" she asks, her face all puckered up with liquor and disbelief.

Sure do, I say, Watch.

I lay it out in front of me and set my left foot in place, then I roll it under and pedal off down the sidewalk. I go about twenty feet or so, do a 180, and start back toward her. I stop in front of her and grab the front of the saddle with my right hand. Holding it tight to my crotch, I jump it up and down three or four times like a pogo stick, to show her that I'm maybe the best there ever was, anywhere.

"Whoa," she says, "Don't that hurt your dick?"

Balancing here in front of her, I'm taken totally off guard by the question and have nothing to say. So I nonchalantly reach back to grab the saddle, to dismount Buck-style. Again, nonchalance gets the better of me because I guess I'm having a bad day. My heel catches a crack as it goes back to take my weight, throwing me off balance and forcing my other leg out to break my fall. The uni flies forward, bouncing into the street as I jump backwards to regain my balance.

No, I say, kind of sheepishly, Never seems to be a problem.

We walk - actually, she walks and I ride - to the end of Main Street where we take a left in front of Momma's, which is closed. She tells me all about Montana as I circle around her to keep upright at this slow pace. It sounds like a nice place, except for the social services people and one particular ex-husband. I tell her about my novel, which is all bundled up in a rubber-banded wad against my chest at the moment. Andrea is all bundled up in a big coat against the growing cold, but I can still see the outline of her chest in the fall of the fabric. We walk another block toward the creek that turns Brookhaven Place into a dead-end and Andrea motions toward the third house from the little cul-de-sac.

"My place," she says, "At least the room at the head of the stairs, anyway." We come up the driveway and I hop off the uni, Buck-style. She laughs.

"You want to leave that out here, Hon?" she asks.

No, I say, Where I go, it goes. I feel cool and in charge, kind of like a cowboy, saying it. Must be my new wallpaper.

She takes out a key and opens the door to a room that is the size of mine but much nicer. There are no street lights glaring through the curtains, and the walls are painted a comfortable beige, not blazing with gunfire and flaming arrows. She opens her coat and I feel something getting stirred up in the bottom of my cup, if you know what I mean.

"Want a drink?" she asks.

You got a bar here? I ask. She pulls a half-full bottle of Peppermint Schnapps from her dresser drawer and holds it up at eye level. It's not beer, but it's not bad, I'm thinking.

"I only have one glass," she says, rummaging in the

second drawer, coming up with a little rocks glass stolen from the Klondike.

That's okay, the bottle's glass, I say, wondering if this makes any sense at all to a drunk. She coughs and laughs, though. Andrea pours herself a hefty dollop and hands me the bottle.

"Cheers," she says, and takes the dose in a chain of swallows. I upend the bottle, which glugs five times.

"Hey, Hon, she says, "That's all I got."

Hey, Babe, I reply, I'll buy you two more.

She holds out the glass and I pour in another couple fingers of syrupy clearness. I finish off the bottle and toss it into the wastebasket, which tips over and rolls.

I prefer a fireplace, but I use whatever's handy, I say, though I'm pretty sure this one doesn't make any sense to her at all.

Andrea downs half the glass and saunters over, throwing her skinny arms around my neck, slopping Schnapps down the back of my shirt.

Hey, that's going to get sticky, I say.

"Hon," she says, "That ain't the only thing." She plants her syrupy and sweet-stinking lips over mine and snakes out a playful tongue, carelessly setting the glass on the dresser. My own tongue finds this pleasurable enough, but quickly finds that she is missing a molar and an upper right eyetooth. Andrea has apparently learned that people don't see these things when sitting to her left, the side I must have been on. I begin to get a little nervous when she starts groping and reaches for my butt, wiggling her fingers in under my belt. But I begin unbuttoning her blouse, figuring second base is a pretty good hit for your first time up in a game like this. Then I hear the zip and feel a hand inside my pants.

"Oh...my...God," she exclaims, her mouth pulling back from mine, her eyes opening wide as those little plates they put under the coffee cups over at Sam's. She drops to the bed, her fingers a blur as she struggles to unbuckle my belt. I stand here in a growing panic, looking down to see that her roots are growing out in gray and that her arms flap with waddles as she works. I pull back just as she bites fiercely into my belt, snarling like that famous lion at the Utica zoo. The belt snakes out, its end snapping through belt loops like machine-gun fire as she rears back. She grabs a handful of shirt and bites at my waistband, groping around with her other ha... *Ave, you weren't raised in a barn, were you? Do you know that you left the front door ope...*enormous unmentionable flops free.

"Oh...my...fucking...heart!" she says, her eyes practically bulging out of her head, "Where did your Momma hide you all my life?"

I am now very agitated, my face is burning, and I feel ready to run right past second base and off the field. This is turning into a game I'd rather not be part of. She grabs and I spin quickly away from her, my unmentionable flopping over across my right thi...*I never! Ave. You have to leave right now, you have to go this very mi...*in there? Whoa, Sweet Jesus!" she yells, reaching around me from behind with both hands now, biting at my butt right through my Levis. I take a deep breath and bump her backwards so she loses her balance, falling over into a heap in the middle of the floor. I fold myself back into my pants and buckle my belt.

Andrea doesn't even try to get up. She sits there with one tittie exposed, beginning to cry. I reach down to help her up, but she pushes me away without a word. I stand here, speechless myself, as she turns from me and adjusts herself back into her bra. She is trembling in a different way now, more heaving than vibration. She looks over her shoulder at me and her eyes are kind of glazed over, with a streak of tears winding around her cheek and down along a vein on her twisted neck. She boosts herself to get up and falls back again, the Schnapps beginning to mix with everything else she's been drinking. I grab her around the waist and hoist her to standing, her back against my stomach. She quakes in silent sobs, bent forward as I hold her close.

"It's just...it's just," she says between sobs, "I can't..."

I turn her around and she buries her face in my shoulder, continuing to quake and shudder. I can see that I have entered a very different world since walking up those stairs on my second night here in this town, and I'm about ready to head back down to something that feels a little more like reality.

She finally looks up at my face, her own stained with tears and cheap make-up heading chinward, dripping onto my shirt. She looks into my eyes for a moment, then drops her arms and turns away.

"I'm sorry," she sobs, "I'm just really sorry."

It's my fault, I answer, rubbing her bony back, It's something I shouldn't have started in the first place.

"No," she says, "I started it and it's my fault you think I'm a just a no-good whore now."

I stroke her graying hair and tell her that I shouldn't have treated her with such disrespect back in the bar, giving her the wrong message like I must have done. She has gone from looking red-hot and dangerous to dead-drunk and vulnerable, and I think I like her better heading downhill like this.

I pick up my trench to go. I shove in my left arm and turn around to get it over my shoulder, seeing her looking at me again.

"Don't leave me," she says. "Stay here tonight, I swear to God I won't touch you. I'm just...just."

I drop the trench in a heap on the floor and hold her, swaying, feeling her breathing slowly return to normal.

NOVEMBER 7TH

I WAKE UP AND wonder where I am, something that is certainly not new to me. A drifter has to get used to this feeling in a hurry. Looking up from the floor, I miss my own wallpaper and, especially, the deep softness of my new bed. The floor is level and hard as the Bonneville salt flats, nothing like the deep furrow of my own mattress. A "safety bed", Mom would call it; couldn't fall out of it if you had to.

I shudder as a half-baked memory of last night begins to rise, allowing a first guess at why I am here. Andrea - I think that's her name - lies snoring in the bed pretty much fully clothed, and it all starts coming back. Splayed out and sleeping like this, it's easy to imagine her hard-scrabble history, but I also think I see a happy ending in there somewhere, with somebody -- just not me, hopefully. I'm feeling pulled in two directions: lucky at avoiding an obsessive and unnecessary entanglement, but drawn somehow to the pain and weakness of this aging babe of the barstool. Lying there with her face relaxed in sleep, she looks the fallen angel, but another five or so years older than my first guess back in the dimness of the Troubadour.

I look around and see the uni leaning safely in the corner next to the door. I can probably get up and out without waking her, but I wonder whether this is the right approach, whether she might be thinking of hurting herself or something. So

29

decide to wake her up first. I stumble up from the floor and smell the sickening sweetness of Schnapps as I tuck in my shirt. Andrea snuffles loudly and half-turns to the wall in her sleep. I pick up my trench and gently shake her shoulder to check on her, to say goodbye. She opens crusty eyes and stares up at me for a long moment without thought or recognition.

Buck, Buck Avery, I say.

"I know, Hon," she says, staring without expression.

Thanks, I say, I've got to get going.

"I'm sorry," she says.

I fidget around with my coat buttons, shuffle my feet, and continue, Well, I'll probably see you around, not going anywhere fast around here.

"Yeah," she says, coughing twice, "Me neither."

I turn to go. I pick up the uni and bounce it twice on its cushy balloon tire.

"Buck," she calls hoarsely as I open the door, "I'd sure love to do something with that dick of yours someday."

Maybe someday, I answer, flushing red, my shoulders shuddering under the trench as I close the door behind me, Maybe someday.

I PULL MY POCKET WATCH which tells me it's almost 7:00. I straddle the uni and take to the street to avoid the fine coating of last night's snow that has stuck to the sidewalk. It's much colder this morning, and I button my trench to the throat as I pump my way toward Sam's. I pocket both hands, though I know from a couple of falls a few years back that this is not a safe thing to do.

Sam's is empty except for two deer jackers sitting at the counter, drinking coffee and talking in whispers. They are both in full camo and tell Sam that they are up from New Jersey scouting before the season opens. I know better, because I saw the scoped rifles lying on the back seat of the Camaro out front, the smear of blood they forgot to wipe off the rear bumper. I take my regular booth and wait to see if Marie is working this morning. My heart almost breaks through my wool shirt as I see her curvy butt bang backwards through the swinging kitchen doors. She is carrying two plates of scrambled and sausage, looking around for the right table. I wink large, but she doesn't see me.

But soon Marie slides into the booth across from me and slumps forward in exaggerated exhaustion, her forehead on her crossed arms.

"Jesus," she says as I gently raise her head and wave my hand in front of her face, "What a fucking night."

I'll say, I say, without elaboration.

"I go to bed around 10:00 for a change," she continues, "and I get these strange, strange dreams that just won't stop. There's this guy in all of them, and he's got this wicked bulge in his bilge, if you get my drift."

I do, I say, leaning forward with genuine interest, I do.

"So, I'm trying to get at this guy, as you might imagine," she continues, "and he's playing this hard-to-get shit, turning away from me every time I make a move."

Yes, go on, I say.

"So, this goes on and on, I wake up a couple times, but it comes back each time. Then I finally go back to sleep. And an hour later, here I am."

Must have been me, I say, shivering all over despite the big gas heater next to the booth.

"In your dreams," she says, "Start with some coffee this morning?"

Sh...sure, I say, as she slides out of the booth with her pad. I watch the curve of her calves with a brand new sense of wonder as she trots back to the counter to get the carafe. I grab for a napkin and my girlie pen. Oh, Marie!

WITH A FULL STOMACH, I begin another day of the rest of my life. The brisk air is full of the future, telling me I've made all the right choices in coming here. I look up over Sam's roof and see that they have begun to make snow on the upper reaches of the mountain's north face, the muffled sound of compressed air and water like music to my ears. Two weeks and I'll be skiing again. All I need is a job and a pass, preferably a job that comes with a pass. But my prospects at the mountain are pretty slim at this point and I certainly don't plan on cutting my hair anytime soon.

I could try my hand at bartending again, I suppose. Got fired from the last job in Utica, but that's another story. Up here they don't know about those details, and I'm certainly not talking. Trip over one bottle, spill one tray of drinks; who gets fired for that anymore? I don't know a thing about sports, except skiing. I never watch a world series or football, couldn't tell you who plays what. What good's a bartender who can't spout that drivel. I'm too ornery to wait tables. Somebody asks me how's the Beef Wellington, what am I supposed to say? It's on the menu, isn't it? Would we sell it if it sucked? I don't know.

I decide to make some rounds over the next couple of days, to see if anybody has a decent job they need done the right way. I ride down the street to Huntington Hardware, figuring I can sell nuts and bolts, paint, and rat poison as well as the next guy. No dice; he just keeps staring at me, nodding his head as I tell him I can sell anything that ever got made, maybe even nails on speculation. I laugh and look down at the rows of little bins running down the aisle. I scoop up a handful of fasteners and say, Wanna screw? I got nuts. Crack me up. I laugh again and tell him I can sell anything he's got, just try me. He glances down at the uni, back up at me, back down at the uni. I'm thinking that if he'd just pay a little more attention to what I'm saying, if he could just keep his mind focused, he'd mayb...*be something, Ave, I'd always* *hoped. But I think it's time to leave right no...*no dice. I guess it's just as well. So I leave quietly.

I check out the Mortar and Pestle - a good prospect, I'm thinking, since they only have one pharmacist back behind the counter and I've had comparable work experience. But I guess he doesn't understand the whole thing about how much fun it would be to answer the phone, Mortar and Pestilence, may I help you? Just cracks me up every time I think about it.

"I'm afraid we don't have any openings at this time," he says. I'm afraid we don't have any openings, I repeat back to him, aping his tight-ass attitude and diction. He says nothing, just looks at me funny and I kind of know I don't have a job here; not today, not any day. I'm afraid, I'm afraid, I say, All I can say is...*six deep breaths, now Ave, don't do anything you mi...*ight have a real nice opening for you, sir. And he picks up the phone, but I leave, still tall and proud.

I ask about a position cooking short-order at the Klondike, but the day barmaid doesn't seem to do the hiring. All they have is an after-hours, part-time job pushing broom and doing various slop-bucket work until some guy gets back from Utah or somewhere. Excuse me, but the Kneissl Kid does not do slop-bucket work. With no bites here either, I pull up a stool and order a beer instead. Then two, three more. At 12:30 or so I leave to continue my job search, maybe get a little lunch somewhere.

I ride down Tuttle Street to get back to Main where most of the action is. I pass the Little Indian Ski Shop and make a mental note to stop in after lunch. Halfway up the next block the patrol car pulls up alongside and cruises next to me, same speed, with Dudley Dooright looking right at me. I salute. He picks up his microphone and this booming loudspeaker right next to my ear tells me to please pull to the side of the road. Totally unnecessary.

Dudley Dooright steps out with his flashlight even

though it's just past noon. "Good afternoon," he says, "Never seen one of these in town before."

Never got stopped on one before, either, I say, looking him over. He is tall and gaunt, muscular and ramrod-straight, cheeks hollowed from sucking on the cigarettes I can smell on his gray uniform. He has no hair visible around the underside of his Smokey the Bear hat. He is a local constable, according to the seal on the side of the beat-up sedan. The loudspeaker and flashing lights are bolted on a gutter-mounted wooden canoe rack. His name tag says Cotterly, and he has a gun. Cop, I figure.

"So, what brings you up here to Huntington?" he asks.

Same thing that brought you here, sir, I say.

"I was born here," he says, looking irritated now.

Like I said, I say, Same thing. Life, change. Life brings me up here. I swing my arm around to indicate the vast expanse of vibrant beauty looming above and beyond the sleepy little village, and Officer Cotterly flinches like I just tried to slap him or something. He holds his flashlight up over his shoulder, nonchalantly scratching at a spot just behind his right ear. But I know all about nonchalance, and I can see he's holding it like that so he can whack me with it. I jump back quickly and trip over the uni, dancing a little to keep from falling.

"Are you okay?" asks Officer Cotterly. "Anything I should know about?"

I think for a second or so, wondering why this is happening to me. I wonder what he needs to know about.

Maybe you should know that I'm the Kneissl Kid? I say, half-asking, half-telling. He looks surprised at this, which doesn't really surprise me since it happens to a lot of people the first time they meet the Kid. And they generally remember the day it happens.

"Can you fly?" he asks, looking genuinely interested now.

Can the Pope shit in the Vatican? 'Scuse my French, I say, puffing up my chest in pride. I'm thinking he must have heard of me before.

"Have any ID?" he asks, shoving the flashlight under an armpit to leave both hands free.

Buck, Buck Avery, I say, extending my shaking hand. Officer Cotterly flinches again and I stand here with my hand out. Don't have any ID on me, sir, but you definitely won't need any to figure out who I am once the snow flies.

He walks around to the driver side of the car and opens the door, leaning around the front of the windshield to ask me if I could "just stay right there for a minute, okay?" He gets in and keys the microphone. I can't hear what he's saying, but he seems to be telling somebody the news. He's here, right here in Huntington, would you believe?

I'm standing here, just like he asked, listening to the snow guns up on the north ridge. Won't be long now, I'm thinking. I'll be flying, swooping, doing my little chop-hops down the steeps. They'll all know who I am real soon now. I take out my girlie pen and a napkin to kill time, using the roof of a parked car as a desk.

Officer Cotterly gets out and comes back around, no flashlight this time. "What's that?" he asks. I show him the pen, shaking it, smiling.

"Are you on any medications?" he asks.

Do I look sick to you? I ask, again answering questions with questions. Healthy as a horse, I say, You just take a little ride up that hill in a couple weeks, you'll see if I look sick or not.

"Mr. Avery, do you have a job?" he asks.

Not yet, I say, I am a man of means at the moment, but I may choose to secure something in the future. He looks me over slowly from head to toe.

"Do you have a place to live?" he asks.

I am temporarily lodged at Hedwig's, I say, gesturing

down the street. Officer Cotterly flinches again. But only until I find a suitable home to purchase.

Officer Cotterly shakes his head and slowly walks back around the patrol car. He stops and looks over the roof at me, just behind the canoe rack. "How long have you been drinking, Mr. Avery?"

Buck, I say, You can call me Buck. Mr. Avery is my father. He asks again, and his skinny face does not smile. Since Labor Day, I say, adding, 1967, maybe?

NOVEMBER 10ᵀᴴ

SURE, THE BED sags, and the wallpaper is more appropriate for a child of seven. But it's under a roof, and that's all that really matters. I lie here waking up in stages after a long night at the Klondike; smelling Hedwig's stewing cabbage, listening to the toilet flush, watching floaters slowly cross the ceiling until I blink and send them skittering. I hear the two young men down the hall in Number One arguing over something, probably money.

I reach blindly to the right, pawing at the nightstand for my Kerouac. I open it to the Huntington Pass brochure separating page 124 from 125. As I insert the brochure between two back pages I realize that I'm too hung over for heavy reading. I also notice the banner across the top of the brochure announcing the rates for the coming year:

Daily Rates

Adult weekend - $28.00
Student weekend (with ID) - $20.00
Under 5 - Free
Senior Citizens - $15.00 (Over-70 Ski
Club free) Adult weekday - $25.00
Student weekday (with ID) - 17.00
Ladies Day Wednesday - $20.00

1979 - 1980 Season Pass Rates

Adult Season Pass - $350.00
Student Season Pass (with ID) - $225.00
Early Bird Adult Special* - $189.00!!!
(*available through November 10'th)

Another wave of nausea washes over me, along with the passing thought that I have no job and no prospects, I have a lot less money than I arrived with, and I don't know what day it is. Without a job, I never seem to worry about what day it is. But today something is chewing at me, something is telling me that I have to figure it out.

I put the book back on the nightstand and rock myself up and out of my safety bed. I stretch and yawn, twice, then pull on the same jeans and wool shirt I wore yesterday and the day before. I stare across my stuff, organized in rows and columns on the nightstand, and catch a glimpse of myself in the mirror. I smile and salute the bearded face surrounded by the shaggy mane of hair I have not yet grown out to my full satisfaction. A scar arches across my forehead from running into some barbed wire at age nine. I sometimes tell people it's from fencing, which is not a lie. My upper lip curls like I'm sneering, which looks like I'm doing on purpose, but is actually from putting a tooth through it falling out of my highchair when I was five, maybe six. My chin has a dimple which is just a dimple. I'm missing only one tooth which doesn't show unless I yawn, which I do because I'm thinking about it. I wink large at the image looking back at me, and I get caught in another big yawn.

My morning begins with a lurch toward the door that bangs the nightstand up against the wall, knocking my big jar of coins to the floor.

"Too much noise," Hedwig howls from the kitchen below.

Criminy, I say, This sucks, and I get down on my hands and knees to scoop up the loose change and shards of glass. I pile the poor little pennies along with the nickels, dimes, and proud quarters in the middle of my sagging bed, dropping pieces of glass into the wastebasket as I go along. Looking around for a container, I find nothing and figure that I can leave the change on the bed until I scavenge an empty can or something.

I head out, skipping down the stairs, out the front door. I head for Sam's because that's where I go when I really need coffee, like this morning. It's getting colder, and there's a trace of snow on the lawns, on the windshields of parked cars.

Marie waves as I enter and make my way to the back booth. My heart does jumping jacks again like it does every time I come in. Oh, Marie! Sam glances up from the grill and looks back to his work without any recognition. Marie slides into the booth across from me and flips through the pages of her order pad. She leans over on one elbow, as always, looking beat like she's already worked a double or two.

"Coffee to start?" she asks.

You got beer? I ask.

Marie rolls her eyes like she does every day when I ask, and slides slowly out. "You're an idiot," she says, and I can't argue with her about that, not today.

I order a bacon and fried egg on a hard roll. When it comes, Marie slides in again, the other booths empty, for the moment at least.

"You get Veteran's Day off?" she asks, rolling her eyes, knowing the answer.

Yeah, actually, I say. You?

"Yeah, right," she says. "Other peoples' days off are my worst goddam nightmares around here."

Well, you let me know when you do get one, I say, I'll teach you how to ski.

"I need to ski like I need another tit," she says, and I

wonder where it would go and whether I might get a chance to peek at it some day. The front of her shirt puckers between the buttons, but it faces away from me today, toward the window. No help.

When is Veteran's Day, anyway? I ask, trying to keep her here in the booth a bit longer.

"Tomorrow," she says, "All day." She rubs her eyes with both fists and slides out.

I finish my breakfast and leave a real nice tip, like I always do when Marie is involved. I get a carton of coffee to go from Sam at the counter and wave it at Marie as I leave. As I open the door, I notice the calendar on the wall to its left.

What's today's date? I yell over to Sam.

"The 10th," Marie responds, "That's November, remember? Day before Veteran's Day?" Sam continues scraping the grill.

Holy shit! 'Scuse my French, I yell, banging hard against the doorframe in my haste to get out. I hear Sam ask Marie, "So, what's wrong with him?" But Marie doesn't know, and I certainly don't have time to tell her at the moment.

WITH THE BROCHURE IN FRONT of me on the bed, I first sort the coins into piles, then begin to count them. All my paper money lies off to the side of the pile on the bed: $152.00, much of it in singles. Every cent I have is here in front of me: my foreseeable future laid out on a sagging, lumpy mattress in a little room with cowboy-and-Indian wallpaper. I'm not sure how I got to this point, but I'm sure that this is where I want to be. Right here, right now.

I count the change beginning with the pile of quarters. Twenty-one dollars and seventy-five cents. I count out another twelve dollars and thirty cents in dimes. I count fifty-three nickels, and check by counting again. A flush of excitement rolls over me and I count out thirty pennies, leaving a dozen or so on the mattress. I'm so excited that I can hardly breathe!

As I spin down Main Street, the pockets of my pants bulging and my signature trench coat swinging back and forth with the jingling weight, I think about all the coming winter will bring. A fine snow continues to fall. I turn at the bridge to the tinkling percussion of coins a-jingling, watching my breath come out in little puffs as I part the cold air on my way up the hill to the lodge.

"YOU'RE KIDDING," SAYS MRS. KISTLER, eyeing the pile I have laid before her.

Count it, I say, It's exact, I don't need any change.

"Jesus Christ," she mutters as she counts first the bills, then the coins starting with the quarters. She writes the totals in a column on a piece of paper, then adds them up, penciling in the remains, or whatever they call them, at the top of each column.

"One-hundred eighty-nine dollars," she says, finally. "I've never seen anything like this before."

It's money, I say, Good as anybody else's.

She shakes her head and shoves a pass application and a pencil across the table. I fill it out quickly and shove it back well before she has the money sorted and into her coin box.

"Buck?" she asks, looking at my application.

I think we've been through this before, I say, That's my name. Don't wear it out.

"We need your given name for the pass, same as on your license or social security card," she continues, looking at me as if I'm a criminal or something.

My name is Buck, I say, Want me to spell it?

Mrs. Kistler rolls her eyes and leans forward on the table, her forearms perfectly parallel around my application between us.

"May I see your license, please?," she asks.

41

No, I say, without elaboration.

"Well," she says, "And, why not?"

Don't have one, I reply smugly, Don't need one to drive what I drive.

"Do you own a wallet, Mr. Avery?" she asks, beginning to get on my nerves.

I do, I say.

"Well then," she continues, "The only way you get a pass is to show me some identification."

I'm getting aggravated, but I need to hold it together until I have the pass in hand, my ticket to a winter of unspeakable bliss. So I reach slowly toward my back pocket, never taking my eyes off hers for an instant, without changing my expression, wondering if she might be thinking I'm maybe reaching for a gun or something. I gently fold my fingers over the wallet and slip it carefully out of my pocket, my eyes focused, silently and with as little movement as possible. With my eyes still glued to hers, I move slowly, ever so slowly, and then I just whip my hand around and slap the wallet loudly on the table between us. She jumps as if I've stuck her in the ass with a hatpin. Her chair slides back as she sits up real straight, her eyes get all big and she holds onto the edg... *Jesus, Ave, you really need to think these thi*...is oughta do it, I say, opening the wallet and extracting a dog-eared social security card.

"Averell H. Avery," she reads, "Okay, now we're getting somewhere."

Buck, I say, feeling like my face might be going a little red, and I'd also appreciate it if you could type in The Kneissl Kid below my picture on the pass.

"The what?" she asks, shaking her head.

The Kneissl Kid, you haven't heard of me? I ask.

"Well, no," she says, shuffling her papers and the application into a pile. "The best I can do is give you a pass in the same name as your social security card. Do you still want it?"

Do Popes shit in the Vatican? 'scuse my French, I ask, figuring that they probably still do.

"Please, Mr. Avery." she says.

She walks away from the table, motioning for me to follow. She stands me up next to a trail map on the wall and lines me up in the viewfinder of a huge Polaroid camera. She snaps the shutter and walks back into the office with the camera. I see blue dots until she returns with the photo.

"This okay?" she asks.

Well, no, I say, I seem to look a little disheveled. I run my fingers through my hair and scratch my beard out a little fuller. Can you try again?

She says something I can't hear, then lines me up again and quite a while later returns with a card, inlaid in plastic, with a little lanyard attached. I look it over, pleased that my large wink was perfectly timed with the flash on this one. Great! I say.

"Read the back," she says, "And make sure you understand the rules."

I grab it out of her hand, look at the picture of myself, all shit-eating grin and one eye closed, and I slip the lanyard around my neck.

Thanks, I say, I'll read it cover to cover when I get home.

I FINISH COUNTING, BUT I know that it really isn't necessary. I have a Huntington pass and something like a dollar and thirty-one cents, nearly all of it in pennies. I have five more days before another week's rent is due, and I'm already getting a little hungry smelling the cabbage cooking. I sit on the bed leaning against the wall, wondering what comes next, and just when that might be.

NOVEMBER 16TH

"**TOO MUCH NOISE**," Hedwig yells from the kitchen. Five minutes ago I informed her that I may not be able to pay the following week's rent for a day or two, and she told me that I can bring my things back and move back in on that particular day. "Mr. Pbrofonski's long-standing policy," she says. So, I'm taking my stuff off the dresser and nightstand, from the pegs along the wall, from the chair and off the floor, and packing them back into my duffel. I haul the duffel down the stairs and drop it off the front of the porch. I go back up, two at a time, my season's pass swinging back and forth at the end of the lanyard around my neck. No problem, I'm thinking, I have a pass. The rest is easy.

I grab my poles, hang my boots around my neck, and shoulder my skis. I turn toward the door, banging ski tips into the wall, removing a cowboy's eye, trailing a curtain from the lone window.

"Too much noise," Hedwig yells.

I take my last load down the stairs where Hedwig informs me at the landing that she may not have a room later that week after all. That's okay, I'm thinking, because I definitely won't have any money.

So we bid goodbye. The wrinkled hand that I kissed so elegantly last week now holds a large wooden spoon at the end of an arm akimbo at her side. Her other hand snatches the curtain from my ski tip and returns to the other hip, balancing the menace before me. "You are lucky Mr. Pbrofonski is not here!" she mutters as she turns and closes the door.

I shoulder the duffel, carefully arrange my skis and poles under opposite arms, and straddle the uni. I kick off and I'm free again, totally free and ready for the next day of the rest of my life. I head back down Main Street for the bridge, stashing everything except the uni back underneath before turning around toward Sam's.

Marie slides into the booth, as usual, flipping pages on her order pad in case Sam's looking, but I don't tell her that I'm homeless. What good would that do. She's already been sneaking me food for the last couple of days and pretending I've been paying for my coffee. But it's not like we've got the type of chemistry yet that would make her take me in, or anything. Besides, I'll have a place again real soon, as long as I find a job.

Sam ever hire anybody around here? I ask, I may decide to take a position someday, you know.

"Not till the season gets up and running, anyway," she says. "What do you do?"

Now, this stops me cold. I can do a lot of things, but most do not lend themselves to regular paychecks. Mrs. Kiss-ass up the hill apparently won't pay me to teach what I do best, and there aren't any other sure bets except the circus, riding the uni. I may be the best there ever was, and I could definitely get a clown job or something by just pedaling on in, but who wants that? What do I do? Well, let's see...I get fired a lot. I ski. I watch people. I drink beer.

Most anything needs to get done, I say. Cooking, painting, advertising, financial management.

"Coffee to start?" she asks, rolling her eyes.

Sure, I answer, And ask Sam to step over when he's got a minute.

Marie slides out, brushing down the back of her short

waitress skirt as she walks quickly toward the kitchen. I am again struck by the way she walks, the swing of her hips below the abrupt indentation of her waist, the tightness of her blouse across the bra strap dividing her receding back. Oh, Marie!

But today it is Sam who walks back bringing my coffee. I am struck by all he has that Marie does not possess: the pigeon-toed waddle, the belly that precedes his presence, the sweat beading up on top of his balding forehead. He slides in without grace.

"Marie says you want to see me?" he announces, without expression.

Yeah, I say, You need a good man around here?

"Got one," he says, poking himself in the chest with his thumb.

I mean someone else so you can, like, relax once in a while, I say, Someone like me. I poke myself in the chest with my own thumb.

Sam smiles and tries to hide it with the back of his hand, turning it into an artificial yawn. I know he's doing this because it's a trick I used to use all the time in high school, like every time I made fake fanny-burp noises when Mr. McKenzie was writing formulas on the board. C'mon, Sam, be a little more subtle if you're going to do things like that.

"Well, now," Sam says, "I could do with a little more help these cold mornings. You have any objection to bartering?"

I'm thinking that this started out with the need for immediate cash, but I can be flexible. Might as well see what he has in mind. What do you have in mind? I ask.

"You come in every morning at six, six-thirty to do the cleaning and set-up before we open. You work for an hour or so and I cook you anything you want for breakfast, within reason anyway," he says, looking me over, probably thinking I'll turn him down flat. But with my belly rumbling like thunder and my wool shirt hanging looser and looser on my shoulders, pride just has to take a back seat to survival in the car I'm driving.

Well, Sam...can I call you Sam? I say, I'd be pleased to work for you.

"Good, good," he says, "but call me Jimmy. Sam died four years ago, right after he sold the place to me."

Well, Jesum, I'm thinking. Just change the name. You have to use a dead man's name to bring in business? That's really sick. Just change it. If I owned a pl...*Ave...Ave? Is this what you really need now? You'd be better of...*figure I should just say okay and find out when he wants me to start.

Okay, I say, When do I start?

Jimmy straightens up in the booth and starts his slide to the right. "How about tomorrow morning?" he asks.

Six a.m. sharp! I blurt out, Do I get my own set of keys?

"I'll meet you here in the morning to show you what gets done. We'll talk about that later," he says, bending forward to get some extra inertia for his next attempt to get upright again. He releases a little fanny-burp with the effort and doesn't seem to notice. I wave my menu around behind his back and wink at Marie as he waddles off.

I LEAVE SAM'S AND LOOK up at the mountain over the roof of the building. I hear the snowguns doing their best to lay down enough cover for the area to open. The distant roar of the guns is reassuring, even if the weather report still calls for dry weather through the end of the month.

I decide to check on my stuff before looking around for more work. I vault the guardrail, stumble a little, and slide under just as a Huntington truck pulls up. I peek around and see two maintenance guys get out. I duck back under as one spits a gooey string of tobacco juice over the guardrail right in my direction. I hear a ladder scaping out of the bed of the truck. In another circumstance I might come out from under the bridge to give him holy heck for such bad manners, but I don't particularly want to get discovered down here before I get a new place to live. And who knows when that will be.

I hear them prop the ladder up on the post holding the big Huntington sign next to the bridge. One asks, "Ray, you wanna hold this thing so's I don't fall off, add another crack to my ass?"

Ray responds, "Fuck you, Jack. I'm the letter man," and spits my way again.

Jack goes up one, two steps, then wiggles the ladder left and right to test it. "You don't wanna hold it, don't hold it," he says, "Just hand me up the right letters for a change."

"Hope you know how to spell," says Ray, spitting again, "'Cause I don't."

There are now close to a dozen phlegmy, brown oysters next to the bridge where I have to climb back up. I am getting really aggravated, but I hold my temper.

"Okay, now," says Jack, "I need a 'O', a 'P', an 'E', a..."

"Slow down, slow down," says Ray, hawking another huge one almost into the creek, "You're getting paid by the hour, what's the goddam rush?"

"We'd be here all day if you were in charge," says Jack, "But I'd still be the one to catch the shit from Barnacre for your stupid-ass spelling."

They grouse back and forth as letters are passed up, some back down. "Just give me the capital letters, you know, the big ones?" says Jack, "Can't even see them little shits from the road."

"Yeah, well, they'll be turning in here tomorrow anyway," says Ray, leaning out and hawking a very runny one right next to my leg. Right next to my leg. This is the last straw. I scrabble out from under the bridge and up the gravelly embankment, carefully avoiding the worst of the disgusting spittle. Jack and Ray watch in astonishment as I tumble headlong over the guardrail, breathing like a she-bear and cursing out French words I didn't even think I knew. Jack slides down all the way from the top of the ladder using only the side rails, anticipating trouble.

What the hell you doing? I ask neither in particular, until I see the lump in Ray's cheek and turn his way. Why you have to spit that foul, fucking shit, 'scuse my French, down at me like that?

Well, they both look like they've just seen a ghost. They must think I'm some kind of troll or something and start backing up toward the truck, leaving the ladder up against the sign.

"Hey, cool off, man," suggests Ray, "Sorry if I got any on you or anything." He turns and spits to his left, over the other railing this time. "Okay, Billy, you done?"

"Yeah," he says, moving slowly to retrieve the ladder, "Close enough." I guess his name must be Billy. They back into the truck and drive off with Ray craning around to look at me.

I look up at the sign and see what they were putting up:

OPENING TOMORROW FOr ThE SEaSON!

Whooo hooo! I hoot, jumping up and down, lurching in circles, my pass flinging this way and that at the end of its lanyard, Whooo hooo!

But now I figure I've been discovered and I'd better do something quick about a new place to live. I don't need Barnacre coming down to take all my stuff, and I sure don't need to talk to Dudley Dooright about it. So I slide back down and quick fill up my duffel with my four blankets and my clothing. I toss my skis and poles out toward the guardrail and grab my boots and the uni. I pull everything up to road level, lean the skis against the guardrail and throw the duffel strap over my shoulder. I retie my inner bootlaces together and hang them around my neck and I pick up my poles. I get positioned behind the uni and get aboard, missing my skis as I try to pick them up. I balance on the uni and then do a circle to approach the skis again. On my second try I scoop them up under my arm without falling and pedal off toward Main Street. I think for a second that I might try stashing my stuff at Andrea's for a day or two. But then I think of the potential consequences and decide to figure this out on my own.

There's nothing in the world quite like riding a unicycle down a street in a little ski town carrying all your earthly belongings with nowhere to go. I would bet my pass and every penny in my pocket that this has never been done before, by anyone, anywhere, ever. Anyway, no one can do it as well as I do because I am maybe the best there ever was. I can pedal, I can balance, I can wink large at the cars, but I just can't figure out what to do next. And I really don't want Dudley Dooright running up on me again right now. So I turn down the first street I come to - Treman Street - and pedal three blocks before it dead-ends at the creek.

I stop at the little cul-de-sac and dismount, Buck-style, after dropping my skis carefully onto the grass. I am as alone as I have ever been, except maybe while I was at Marcy State the day before my roommate moved in. If I had a cigarette, I'd be smoking it now. If I had a beer I'd be drinking it now. If I had a home, I wouldn't even be here. One sorry-ass cowboy I am feeling at the moment.

But like everything else in my priceless life, this slips into the past and I set my sights on the important priorities, like the future. I look around the quiet street and notice that the third house from the end has a very convenient-looking shed nestled into the trees at the edge of the back lawn. Too small to live in, but just right for my stuff until I come up with something better. But first, I knock on the front door of the house to be sure nobody is home. My plan is to act real nonchalant and make like an obnoxious religious zealot if someone answers the door. I figure that talking about Jesum and his twelve disciplines - the precious promise of salivation and all - always seems to put most people off and get their minds distracted from what it is I really intend to do. But no one answers and there's nobody else around on this glorious Friday before opening day. So I gather up my bristling load and trot back to the shed.

The little shed shelters a lawn mower, various garden tools, a charcoal grill, two bicycles, three folding aluminum chairs, and a plastic pail full of children's' beach paraphernalia. This says a lot about the family living here, I'm thinking. Most everything is here for winter storage, so I figure that it's a safe bet my stuff won't get discovered any time soon. I begin hiding things here and there until I realize that anyone just walking in would see them anyway. So I leave them in the back corner and head around the front of the house. I scope out the neighborhood, noting that the shed can be reached by scrambling up from the creek if I need to get back in without crossing the lawn, without leaving tracks in the deep snow that's sure to come. It's too small to sleep in, but I don't really have that in mind anyway.

It's heavily overcast with a light breeze that feels twice as strong as it really is. I button my trench to the collar and hunch my shoulders as I spin back over to Main to make my rounds of the town's soda and cigarette machines.

SHE SITS DOWN NEXT TO me on the stool without seeing anything but my back. She orders a whiskey sour and I recognize the voice immediately. I am in the Troubadour - where the more upscale local residents seem to flock - with its quiet barstools, comfortable lighting, and a bartender wearing a necktie.

So how's Mrs. Kistler? I ask, turning her way. Have you finally come down off the mountain to offer me a job?

Mrs. Kistler looks over at me, then down at her name tag, which she begins to unpin from her sweater. She smiles.

"It's Miss Kistler," she says, pocketing the name tag,

"Mr. Barnacre insists on the Mrs. so that I don't give men the wrong impression, or so he says."

What kind of impression would that be? I ask, remembering the impression she left me with.

"Oh, that I'm available or something like that," she says, "It's like covering your face over there in Saudi Arabia, or something. He doesn't want young sluts out front in his organization. Making me wear the name tag kind of makes me wonder if he thinks I'm a young slut. I almost forgot to take it off in here. He'd fire me in a heartbeat if he saw me in here with it on."

What's his problem? I ask.

"Born again...and probably again and again after that," she answers. "He thinks he's God's soldier sent to keep this town wrapped up nice and tight with the ribbon of eternal promise."

Oh, I know all about salivation, I say. Live and let live, so long as he doesn't close the bars.

"Would if he could," she says, "Except that he's in the ski business and knows better."

Well, I can tell you that up north in the real mountains, at McCauley and Big Tupper where I came up, they all say the ski industry runs on electricity and alcohol, I say, tipping my glass her way in a toast. And I've done my share.

"What," she asks, "the electricity?"

Very, very funny, I say.

You know, you really ought to do something about your bedside manner at work up there, I continue, nodding my head in the general direction of the mountain. Keep putting off people like me and one day, mark my words, one day your business is going right down the toilet.

"Not my business," she replies, sipping her whiskey sour, "I listen to Barnacre, I do the hiring, firing, and front office work. I get paid enough to come in here every once in a while for a quick one while he's not around. Then I go home. Then I go back up there. That's as far as that goes."

Huh, I say, I'd give my left ball to work there teaching.

"Well," she says, "You'd have to give up a lot more than that, like about five inches of hair off your head and face, for example."

Well, that's not happening anytime soon, I say, I got two balls, 'scuse my French, only one head.

Mrs. Kistler upends the rest of her whiskey sour and turns the stool toward the door. "Time to head on home," she says, yawning. She gets up off the stool and walks across the bar, her stretch pants doing the job, her pumps elevating her heels three-four inches off the floor.

Hey, I yell as she opens the door, Nice shoes. See you tomorrow.

I decide that staying here for the time being is better than being out in the cold, but it costs money every time I come in. I count out another dollar and a quarter of my precious change and signal the bartender. He brings me another Utica Club which I intend to nurse for at least another hour and a quarter.

This is a real nice place, I'm thinking; full of decent furniture for a bar, nothing broken, nice lighting, basketry hanging on the walls - basketry always makes a place look homey and comfortable. And, by Criminy, I'm feeling more homey and comfortable by the minute. I spin the stool around and lean back against the mahogany, surveying the sparse crowd. There are things I definitely need to remember about this place, so I turn back around and reach across the bar for a couple of napkins. I spin back to face the room and pull my girlie pen from my shirt pocket.

Five burly-looking guys come in, attracting immediate attention from the bartender who walks around to the table they have taken next to the jukebox. I can't hear what he's saying, because one of them has wasted a good quarter on some really stupid, loud song about a ribbon tied around some tree in front of somebody's hou...*Simmer down, Ave, remember what they say about minding your own busi...*never listen to crap like that. And the five guys look like they're arguing with him. Finally he starts walking back, then turns around toward the table, raising a finger. "Just one," is all I hear him say. Jesum, turn it down, I'm thinking.

I ask the bartender what's up over there once he's back and pouring beers. "They're snowmakers going on their night shift at 7:00, want to get ready early, I guess," he says. "I threw them out two weeks ago, banned them, but, as you can see, they're back. Told them one beer is all they get today. See how they behave, maybe they can earn their way back in."

Why bother, I say. All they have to do is walk down street to the Klondike. They'll serve anybody in that shit-hole, 'scuse my French.

"Lot of people prefer the atmosphere - and the language - in here," he says, picking up the tray with five beers.

I take some notes on the napkin and fold it, put it back in my pocket. I shake my girlie pen and watch her titties spin around in the snow. Crack me up.

I am beginning to feel like I have just enough research and field notes done to begin my story. I pat the wad of napkins in my pants pocket and decide that now is the time. Right here, right now. The only way to ever get anything done is to just get it done, as Mom says. My only question is where, maybe how. I stretch and walk to the Men's Room, which is identified by a little top hat. The door next to it has a little bonnet. I know, just like everybody else, that I do some of my best thinking on the can. It's always a good place to sit and figure things out quietly and without pressure. So I go in and pick the stall next to the far wall.

Man, I'm thinking, so this is how it starts. My mind's eye flashes forward to a vision of myself sitting in front of a typewriter, at a desk, in front of an open fire, a pipe in my mouth, next to a window with a view of the Yalps, in a beautifully appointed library. But enough of that. I sit where I sit - right here, right now - and today I begin my trip toward that glorious destination. It hits me that the future is about as real as Santy Claus, and the past - well, that's another story entirely. I suddenly see - with the clarity and focus that only a bathroom stall can provide - that all I really have is right here, right now. It's the only place in life where anything really happens, where you can actually do something, kind of sangwiched in between the things you'd rather forget about and the rest of things that just come out of nowhere. So I take out my girlie pen and begin.

The back of the stall door has only one small area of rather disgusting graffiti, over which I mark a bold "X". I begin above it, indenting the first paragraph of what is sure to become a most sought-after novel some day. "It was 1979, and the Kneissl Kid was hungry - oh, so very hungry - for an early win this season. The course was set and the run was fast: just what the Kid was looking for..."

"You all right in there?" I hear the bartender call through the door.

Oh, yeah, I say, I'm definitely all right in here. "Fucking pervert," I hear the bartender mutter, and I write for another five or so minutes before I decide to pocket the pen for awhile and go back out, let my heart slow down a little and finish my beer.

I hoist myself to standing and pull up my pants. I return to the bar where I find that my half-full beer is altogether missing. The bartender gestures toward the door with his eyes and chin.

What? I ask.

"Out," he says, "We generally go home for that kind of thing around here."

Huh? I say.

"Out," he repeats, and I decide not to create a scene, on this day at least. I'll have to come back, though. It's my job.

On the porch, I lean the uni against the wall and take out a clean napkin. With my girlie pen I write a "1" and "Troubadour, door 3", using the porch railing as a desk. This will be my Table of Contents. I smile, thinking that I'll need a bunch of napkins before I'm through with this particular project.

I am consumed with anticipation, but I have hours before I ski tomorrow. I smile and kiss the pass hanging around my neck, and I decide to check out Momma's to kill some time. I don't know why I haven't been in there yet, it being a bar and all. I walk up the porch steps and almost knock on the front door because it looks so much like a plain old house from the outside. But instead I push it open and find myself in a foyer just like the one at Hedwig's: kitchen down the hall, living room to the right, dining room to the left. Except the living room has a plywood bar set up against the far wall and three tables lined up against the other. There is an old man sitting at one of the stools, bent forward over something, the hunch of his back almost hiding the fact that he has a head. He is the only person in the room.

I leave the uni next to the umbrella stand in the foyer and sit down two stools away from the geezer. I spin around to take a gander. It still looks like someone's living room except for the tables. There are pictures of flowers and a couple of snowy landscapes thumb-tacked up on the walls. There is a portrait of an old man in a three-piece suit and beard, his eyes burning and looking straight at me no matter how I rock from side to side. Just to make sure, I get off the stool and walk across the room where he still stares at me. I walk around to the other corner and he follows me over here with his eyes. Weird. The man at the bar does not move and I wonder if he's dead. There's no mirror behind the bar, just a half-dozen bottles and a row of assorted glasses on a breakfront. There is an old-style refrigerator next to the bar which I figure holds the beer.

There's no bartender anywhere that I can see. I am thirsty and I still have a little change left, so I sit down facing the door and put two fingers in my mouth. My whistle startles the man at the bar, nearly knocking him off the stool. He faces me with a grimace, his eyes blazing, without a word. I look him over and decide that he looks almost exactly like the guy in the picture with his eyes going like that, only a little younger, maybe. I hear footsteps down the hall and, presently, an old lady walks in wiping her hands on her apron.

"Who's the asshole?" she growls, looking in, seeing only the two of us.

Don't know, haven't seen him lately, I reply, figuring she probably knows the geezer, may even be her husband, for all I know. Buck, Buck Avery, I say.

She walks around the end of the short bar and stands there looking at me with my hand out. Seems like that's what a lot of people do the first time they meet me. I take the initiative and ask for a beer. She walks over to the refrigerator and pulls out a Budweiser.

Got anything else? I ask.

"No," she says, "Want it or not?"

Sure, I say. It's not beer, but it's not bad.

"Two," she says, setting it in front of me.

No, thanks, I say, or at least I'll finish this one first. I smile at the quality of the joke she walked into on that one.

"Two dollars," she clarifies, holding out her hand, palm up.

I reach in my pocket and pull out a handful of change and the dollar bill I just won by showing a drunk snowmaker in the Troubadour parking lot that I can ride the uni with my eyes closed. He didn't want to pay up at first, but he was pretty impressed and I guess he decided it was more important to honor his commitment than to have somebody like me following him all over town. I slide out the larger coins first, working down toward the nickels, counting by fives. She moves to take the dollar, but I stop her in mid-reach, having counted far enough to realize I probably have enough change for the beer. I slide the pile of coins her way and pocket the bill. She huffs and corrals the coins, sliding the pile toward the edge of the bar. She opens a beat-up metal cash box and begins segregating the coins, shaking her head.

Hey, it's money, I say, taking a tug at the bottle of Bud, wincing. So, where's the jukebox? I ask.

"You want music, go down street to the Troubadour," she says, wiping the bar with a dishrag. The old man sits, hunched and speechless.

Been there, I say. Kind of sucks in there, 'scuse my French. You got a men's room?

She points to the hall with her dishrag. "Second door," she says, "Open the window, use the spray."

It's a cold bathroom, with nothing to identify it gender-wise. The window is already open, giving the feeling it stays that way all winter. The walls are papered in a geometric zigzag pattern that makes my vision flip back and forth uncomfortably. No place to write, I'm thinking. So I trickle, flush, fanny-burp, and follow up with the can of Glade just to see how well it works.

As I sit back at the little bar to nurse my watery beer, it hits me that everything I've done today, everywhere I've been, has been to avoid the fact that I have absolutely no place to sleep now that I've been evicted from under the bridge. It's getting dark and I need to deal with this aspect of my life sooner or later, the sooner the better. I also need to think about my dwindling finances and the fact that I will need more food than Sam's big breakfast once I start burning it off on the trails tomorrow morning.

I thank Momma for the beer and her hospitality. I salute the inert form two stools down the line and wave to the nosy guy in the picture. I grab my uni and head out the door and down the steps to the street. I straddle it and begin pedaling back toward Treman Street to sit down and figure things out. I see lights on in the house, so I ride to the cul-de-sac and take the path between two houses leading down to the creek. Carrying the uni makes it that much harder to walk along the creekbank, but I'm certainly not leaving it out by the street somewhere. I skirt the back of a well-kept yard and climb back up right behind the shed. It's tough scrambling up a steep bank like this, and I really must be a sight to behold in the dark, where I can't see what my feet are doing. But it's dark and no one can see me any better than I see myself, so I slip inside and close the door.

The smell of uninterrupted cold creeps up my nostrils while my eyes adjust to the dark. I decide, through process of elimination, that this looks more and more like a bedroom to me, for tonight at least. I rummage in the dark and locate my four blankets which I arrange on a selection of cardboard someone has conveniently left stacked against a side wall. I button my trench to the throat and use my rubber bands to cinch up the cuffs of my shirt and pants. I pull my watch cap down low and curl up under my blankets. I can't stretch out, but this "ain't the fucking Moulin Rouge", as Marie would say. With this thought I begin to get aroused, but I know that, under the circumstances, it's too cold to address that particular issue right here, right now.

NOVEMBER 17TH

I AM UP BEFORE dawn after a night of occasional sleep between fits of shivering. I am more than ready for work, as a dream of Sam's brightness and warmth lures me up and out of the shed well before first light. I hear the snowguns up on the northeast ridge and I see the big dipper still hanging in the sky as I look up at the mountain. Clear and cold.

Sam's is empty when I arrive, since it's only quarter to six. I wait patiently, though it may not look that way since I'm jumping up and down and slapping my sides to keep warm. An hour or so of gruntwork, a nice, big breakfast, then I'll be off to do what I do best. It won't take long to get noticed around here, I figure. I'll be wearing a yellow jacket with money in both pockets in no time.

Jimmy pulls up in his old Chrysler around 6:15 and nods to me as he unlocks the front door. The lights all come on at once, making me squint and cover my eyes for a moment. Jimmy puts on his apron as I hang up my trench and head for the back storeroom. The routine is becoming established in my head: I start the coffee, clean and scrape down the grill, turn on the deep fryer, check the OJ machine, drink coffee, sweep and mop the dining room, top off the ketchup bottles, straighten up the little clusters of paraphernalia on each table, and drink coffee. It's not beer, but it's not bad.

I may not get paid, but I get all the breakfast I want when

I'm done. Jimmy always rolls his eyes when I order up my third plate of pancakes, but he probably knows this is the only real food I eat all day. Mom always tells me that breakfast is the most important meal of the day, and I certainly can't argue with that, not today.

Marie rushes in just before 7:00 as I finish mopping up and start pulling chairs down off the tables. She mutters and hustles out of her coat, giving me a quick view of a nice curve through the fabric of her white shirt. She rattles hangers as she hangs it up and trots out into the kitchen, banging the swinging door open with a shoulder as she ties on her apron. Oh, Marie!

I sit at the counter these days to eat my breakfast, mostly so I don't have to tip Marie, but I can't tell her that. I prefer the old booth in back, but I feel funny about making her carry free food way over there without a tip. So I sit at the counter on a strategic stool that always forces Marie to pick the next one to my right. So that the rising sun and the buttons on her shirt face me for a change. I act real cool about it, and I'm pretty sure she doesn't notice. If I sit just right, leaning on my left elbow over my coffee, looking bored and nonchalant, I get a great peek every now and then.

Well, I'm full again and ready to go back out into the cold. Today, though, I'm going skiing! My pass flutters around my neck as I mount the uni and pedal back to my shed, buttoning my trench as I go. I'm tempted to just walk right around the house to the shed in my haste to get to the mountain, but I get control of myself and take the long route down the bank and along the creek. I leave the uni up by the street this time, hidden behind a hedge. This should only take me a minute or so.

I decide to leave my duffel and blankets in the shed for the time being, though I'm sure I'll be able to move in under a real roof later this afternoon. I skid down the bank dragging my load of skis, boots, poles, and an extra sweater. I follow the creek until I reach my little path back to the street. I struggle back up the path, stand the skis up against the hedge, and mount the uni with the rest of my stuff under my left arm and around my neck. I grab my skis as I pedal off, adjusting them over my shoulder as I go along.

The hill up to the lodge seems even steeper riding a loaded uni, but it sure beats walking. The last time up without my stuff, I thought it was pretty easy, though hills are always a lot tougher than they are on a bicycle. Cars honk as they pass me and children turn around to peer out back windows. Kids always seem to recognize the Kneissl Kid, I'm thinking. I rock forward and back as I pedal to build momentum for the top. And then I'm up and over. Whew!

I put my skis and poles up against the lodge and walk around looking for a safe spot to stash the uni. I settle for a bunch of brush at the east end of the parking lot, a pile that I can rearrange to hide it. I walk back, whistling nonchalantly, looking around carefully to make sure nobody saw me. It seems I'm always looking around after I do things.

I pick up my skis and make for the front of the lodge, a bustle of early season activity as skiers chat and head off across the bare ground for the bottom of the chairlift. Above the lodge I can see several swaths of white against the brown of mid-November. I give a haughty laugh as I pass the ticket booth, a place where I won't be stopping now that I'm a season passholder.

Inside, I pick a nice table near the front windows and pull my boots from their tether around my neck. I untie the laces and set them on the floor in front of me, my pass dangling on its lanyard. A kid stares at the large-winking face on my pass as I wiggle my foot in and pull up hard on the inner laces, something he has probably never seen in the ten years now since plastic buckle boots took over. I tie a careful double bow and tuck the loops in between the inner and outer boots. Okay, I'm thinking, there's the left one, all ready. I fling my pass around to the back to keep it out of my fingers and I repeat the steps of tightening and tying my right inner boot. The kid keeps staring and I start on the buckles of the outer boot, working my way from the top to the bottom, then reversing direction to get one more notch of tightness out of each buckle. Whew! Now I'm ready to start on the other boot.

The leather is all scuffed along the instep surfaces where my boots scrape up against each other, because I ski with my feet locked together, never apart like all the city scum who think they know what they're doing. They ski like hockey players, all hunched over their little short-shit skis, two feet apart and wobbling. Jesum, just give them a stick to carry instead of poles. I can't stand these conceited, uncoordinated jerks and how they think they're God's gift t...*Two deep breaths, Ave, two deep ones, now. Please, you really shouldn't get so worked up over noth...*ings look good, though, real good. I could polish them, but I don't. It's one of those little details that make me stand out as the Kneissl Kid.

The lodge is a big wooden building with a central bar and kitchen that lets me walk around the entire floor without stopping, round and round if I feel like it. Right now, though, I do feel like stopping - at the bar - but it's not open just yet. And I've got something like four dollars to last me the rest of my life or until they hire me as an instructor this afternoon, whichever comes first.

I decide to scout the lodge for valuables before taking my first run. I check all the pay phones and candy machines, coming up with another thirty-five cents in change. I take five ketchup packets and a handful of cellophane-wrapped saltines from the condiment bar. I stuff them in my trench pocket for lunch. I paw through the lost-and-found bin, where I find a new scarf and a mismatched pair of excellent ski gloves. One is brown with a big "R" on the back. The other is dark blue - and just a little tight – with a yellow Tweety Bird whose eyes always seem to be looking right up at me no matter how I hold my hand. Both are real warm, and now I'm ready.

I carry my skis and poles to the bottom of the lift where I begin by unwrapping the six feet of leather longthongs coiled around my skis. I take hold of the end of each strap and pull upward, both skis spinning and clattering to the ground as I hold their tethers up over my head. This always seems to get people's attention, and several skiers watch as I carefully position my leather boot in the binding and flip the lever on the turntable heel - a binding that probably hasn't been made for at least a dozen years. The other skiers just step into bindings that snap shut automatically, without runaway straps, without having to even bend over. I bend waaaaaay over and begin lacing the longthong around my ankle, back through the binding's steel rings and back up around my boot again. I pull the strap up as tight as I can, grunting with the effort, and pull the end through the buckle to make it fast. Then I loop the extra through the buckle again so it doesn't flip around.

I stand back up and stretch, rubbing the small of my back. Then I bend down and start the same process with my other ski.

Before I'm even done I notice that an entirely different group of spectators is watching me. The others have long since boarded the lift and are on their way to the summit. It takes a little longer, but it's worth it when you're the Kneissl Kid. I notice that the other skis in the lift line are just over half the length of my Kneissl Red Stars, all painted up with the weird-ass neon colors I see all around me at ski areas these days. What's wrong with them? I ask myself. I button my trench up to the throat and get on the lift with an older woman in a hot pink Obermeyer jumpsuit.

Hey, ho, I say, as we get settled and pull down the safety bar. She looks over and stares at me through the yellow pane of her goggles.

"Hello," she says, turning back to face forward.

Been up yet? I ask, breaking the ice.

"No, I haven't," she says, "First run of the season."

Me, too, I say, pulling my pass out to hang between the two top buttons of my trench. I guess I ought to keep this out, I say, so the lifties know who I am, that I'm not ripping them off or something.

She looks at me long and hard again, probably thinking that she's seen me before. She looks around fifty or sixty, but pretty good in the jumpsuit. That's the problem with skiwear these days, I'm thinking. Some old hag looks great in the cut and color, but take it off and suddenly sh...*even now, for some reason you still like to leer at the older women? Ave, I thought we had this discu...*shouldn't have to look like some jiggly bag of jello with stretch marks. I mean, for what they have to pay for it.

"Don't you get cold in that coat?" she asks.

Nah, I say, I just tape newspaper across my chest and arms under the coat to break the wind on the real cold days. It's an old bicycle racing trick, comes in real handy.

"Do you race?" she asks.

Not bikes, I say, with a beguiling laugh, Too many wheels. I wait for a second, letting the pause set in.

Just skis, I say, playfully leaning my shoulder into hers, Heard about it though. Tried it one day and amazed myself at how much warmer it made me feel.

I see her eyebrows come back down behind the yellow of her goggles, and she says, "That's a good idea." She looks down at my skis.

Like 'em? I ask, wiggling them up and down, Kneissl Red Stars, 210s, best ever made.

"Yes," she says, "I'm familiar with them." She looks at my gloves, then looks away quickly, without comment.

Ski much? I ask.

"I live here," she says, "I've skied here daily since we opened the area in 1968."

Well, I'll be dipped, I'm thinking. She must know who I am. How could she not? Anyone who's skied that long knows about the Kid. Why doesn't she just say so?

I used to ski here waaay back, I say, wondering if she's getting a little senile, or maybe clocks just get set a little different after age 60 or so, with me being half her age. But I mostly skied the Adirondacks when I was coming up. Now, that should tip her off.

"Coming up to what?" she asks, and I'm definitely beginning to think it's a question of senility at this point.

Well, I say, puffing up my chest and extending my legs out straight, I meant before they started calling me the Kneissl Kid.

I feel the chair lurch with the twitch this seems to set off in her, and I wonder if it's because she suddenly realizes who I am. Although it could be some kind of weird sexual reaction, I'm thinking. I do see some of that from time to time.

"Who?" she asks, turning my way, genuinely interested in me now.

You're looking at the Kneissl Kid, I say. Ask just about anybody who ever skied McCauley or Tupper up north, they'll know me. And over in Vermont, I hear I'm kind of a legend after I skied Stratton a couple years back. Jumped that big rock up on North American. Oh, man, I got my speed up, I got real low with my poles held loose, ready to fly, and went so hi…*Ayuh, we were there too that day, Ave, but I certainly don't remember it that wa*…aaay out past the rock. Landed a little hard but didn't break anything.

She laughs. It's not a tight laugh of derision, but an easy laugh of surprise and wonder, I'm thinking. A laugh that says, 'Oh, my gosh! It's him! It's him! I can't believe it's really him!' But she doesn't actually say anything, just turns back to face forward again, her shoulders jerking one last time as she checks her watch.

"I'm sorry," she says, "I shouldn't have laughed."

Why not, I'm thinking, it's not every day you...

"Whoever gave you, I mean, how did you happen to get that name?" she asks.

Well, I say, It's a long story.

"Well," she says, "I guess it's one that will just have to wait for another time." She lifts the safety bar as the chair approaches the exit ramp. "Have a nice run."

We ski down the ramp and split off in two directions. She approaches several other skiers who all look my way after a few words are exchanged. Maybe they know me too. Who knows? I'm here and I'm the Kid.

I push off and begin skating downhill to gain speed. I swoop and carve, hop and whoop, pick out a bump and do my famous spread-eagle jump with two thumbs up, my arms and legs way out to the side. Now they'll remember, I'm thinking. I land like a cat and begin a series of tight little wedeln turns down the face of the steep slope in front of me.

On skis, I'm back in perfect balance again. No watching my feet, no stretching to make my shoulders the same height when I walk, no glancing around, wondering if anybody is looking at me. When I ski, I know that everyone is looking at me because I'm maybe the best there ever was.

I nearly knock over a young lady, blowing her a kiss as I fly past her on the left. My brain is buzzing with excitement, full of guitar-crashing, bass-rumbling Steppenwolf:

Get your motor running,
Get out on the highway,
Looking for adventure,
And whatever comes...

Mom always tells me how it's important to hum when

you ski, except I'm thinking my songs aren't quite the same as her waltzes. I do a little series of chop-hops to the quickness of the beat, then go into a broad, sweeping turn across the whole face of the trail as my brain hits the chorus. Someday, I'm thinking, somebody's going to invent some kind of little radio you can ski with, something loud enough to hear outside your pocket.

Halfway down, I stop and realize that my legs are on fire, searing with the pain of two years away from the boards. No problem, I'm thinking, as the shaking slowly subsides. I've got all season to be the best there ever was, again. I stare out over a panorama of brown that hasn't yet seen a natural snowflake. Soon, everything from horizon to beautiful horizon will be all fluffy and white. And by then, I expect to be wearing yellow.

I decide to check out what the Yellowjackets are teaching these days so I can have a leg up when I show them who I am and what I can do. I continue to the bottom and unbuckle my longthong, unclamp my turntable, unwrap my longthong, re-wrap my longthong around my ski, and stand it up against a tree. Then I do the same with my other ski. Then I pick up my skis, throw them over my shoulder, and walk across two acres of bare ground to the beginner's area - a place I generally never see because I'm the best there ever was. But even the best have to be prepared for the worst, for change, for whatever comes at you.

I get to the bottom of the T-Bar lift where the snow starts again, courtesy of last week's cold weather, lots of electricity, and unlimited water from the creek. I see a Yellowjacket half-way up with a small group of bumbling novices, their poles out in all directions as they cross their tips to control their falls. I make sure my pass is still hanging out between the two top buttons of my trench and skate over to the lift after five-or-so minutes unwrapping my longthong, cleaning off my boot, clamping my turntable, wrapping my longthong, pulling it as tight as I can, and buckling it carefully - one foot, then the other.

Got a pass, I say proudly, stepping in front of the next bar coming around the bullwheel.

"So do I," says the liftie, rolling his eyes. He grabs the bar and hands it to me, shoving the crosspiece under my legs for the ride up the hill. I've always loved the T-Bar, I'm thinking. Simple, fast, and over the ground. Lean back and let it do all the work.

I get to the top and pull the bar out from under my legs, playing the idiot to the appreciative laughter of the liftie as I grab the bar in a bearhug, scream, wobble my skis, and then get pulled up in the air. Just like a kid back at McCauley.

Whoa, I yell, Close call! He salutes and calls me Captain Asshole, which is incorrect. But I can't argue with him at the moment. I've got work to do.

I ski down the gentle slope toward the instructor and his bandy-legged brood. I do several 360s, all the way around, just for the fun, fun, fun, of it. I stop across the trail from the Yellowjacket and lean on my poles, watching. Two women are on the ground trying to get back up. One man is slowly headed for the edge of the woods, looking like he can't stop until he drops into a pile of gyrating arms and legs just in time to miss a tree. Jesum, I'm thinking, if some guy can stop like that to keep from getting himself killed, he doesn't need lessons. He already has everything he needs. Why, they ought to study him, find out why he can do something like that when his life depends on it, when his whole worl...*ould have probably gone somewhere, Ave, really been something if you'd only had a little more common s...*sense than paying good money getting certified to teach him, if you ask me. The Yellowjacket looks bored, lacking that little 'Genesee qua' flair of American nonchalance –– not European, and definitely not French –– that I would bring to the job.

I decide that there's nothing this little yellow twerp can

teach me, so I yell over for him to watch as I take off toward the bottom of the lift. I swoop and shriek, making like a screech owl, and do a couple more 360s before rounding the curve in a big royal christie, hopping on my uphill leg. I reach the bottom and skate over to the T-Bar. The liftie nods without smiling and hands me the bar. I take it and yell back. Turn that frown around, mister!

At the top I release the bar and fake a fall down the exit ramp for the liftie. He laughs and walks over, knowing there is nobody else behind me. He tells me that he would pick me up if I had decent titties, but that since I don't I'll have to just figure it out for myself. Which I do, except that when I stand up the next bar hits me in the head and sends me down again, for real this time. The liftie is howling with laughter as he checks to see if I'm alive or not. He pulls me up and away from the lift as I relax every muscle in my body, acting like I'm really screwed up or something. I loll my tongue out of my mouth and slobber, Where have you been all my life? The liftie howls again and pulls me to standing.

Buck, Buck Avery, I say, sticking out my hand, winking large.

"Where'd you get that glove?" he asks, reaching out to shake my Tweety hand.

Lost and found, I say.

"What, you lose the other?" he asks, grinning.

Very, very funny, I say, wiping his sarcasm off my Tweety glove on my pants. Got any whiskey?

Now, I ask him this for a number of reasons. First, I have none and want some. Third, I have no money to speak of. Fourth, I hear that lifties sometimes keep a little on hand.

"For you, Buddy?" he asks - rhetorically, I'm thinking, "Why, sure I do."

Buck, I say, Buck Avery.

"Well, I'm just so pleased to finally meet you," he says, winking and walking back to the shack, reaching in.

"Hoot, Hoot Houghtaling," he says, reaching back out with a pint of something brown I've never seen before. He twists off the cap and looks around to make sure Barnacre isn't hiding behind a tree or something. He knows that thing about looking around before doing something shady, I guess. Satisfied, he takes a big tug and hands it over. "Just don't kick it," he says, "Aaaaahhh!"

I take a respectable little burble out of the bottle, then look around as the burn spreads. Yes, sir! I say.

Hoot looks me over, then asks, "What's with the equipment?"

Whaddaya mean? I ask, knowing exactly what he means.

"Little old, wouldn't you say?" he says, "Might even be a little dangerous, huh?"

Old is kind of relative, a little subjective, I say. Then, it hits me that this might sound a little haughty, maybe kind of conceited and lame - especially to a liftie named Hoot who's never laid eyes on me before - and I decide that I might have to distract him. So I continue, ...when you're the Kneissl Kid.

Silence, except for the tinny, country-western music coming from Hoot's little radio, the distant roar of the snowguns up on the ridge, the gentle clunk of the bullwheel. And just like I figured, it distracts him and gives me plenty of time, time to look him over: all boots and a matched set of dirty Carhartts with the head of a wrangly kid just visible inside the cave of his hood. He's got lines on his face already, at twenty, maybe. He appears to have short hair and no beard, but he looks like he probably needed a Brush Hog to get a job here at Huntington. Barber in this town must be a millionaire.

Hoot finally nods and upends the bottle again. He hands it to me just as his shoulders begin to shake. His eyes close and his face seems to curl up at the edges, making his ears seem to wiggle. He suddenly spews out a huge blurt of laughter, sneezing whiskey and snot all down his overalls. He's twitching all over, like somebody jump-started his battery before strapping him down. I roll my eyes around like I see other people do, and I kill the bottle whether he likes it or not.

"You're the...you're the who?" he asks, finally getting control of his voice again. "Whoa, baby! The minute I got up, I knew today was gonna be special! I just knew it!"

I'VE DECIDED TO MAKE THIS a regular stop, whether it's the beginner hill or not. Good whiskey is nothing to sneeze at, I'm thinking, even though Hoot apparently disagrees. But he seems like a real nice guy. I clean off my boot, step into my binding, throw the heel clamp, wrap carefully, pull up as hard as I can, and buckle six feet of coiled leather around my ankle. Then I start the same process with my right foot. It's not fast, but it's not bad.

Hoot watches and shakes his head the whole time. "Jesus, Buck," he says, "Any idiot can do that in five, maybe six seconds these days."

It's not about time, I say, taking the time to cinch up my right longthong to the breaking point, at which point it breaks, a foot-and-a-half from the end. Fuck, I say, 'Scuse my French.

Hoot is falling over laughing again, and misses a customer who has appeared at the top of the ramp. He lunges her way as she deftly extracts the bar from under her legs, letting it swing free over her head. He looks up at her sheepishly, then hustles to the top of the ramp to look down the liftline.

Lucky, I say, as he walks back down my way.

"Nah...lucky's when they fall down, 'specially when they got..." he says, winking, hands flexing open and closed in front of his chest, "And I don't mean the arthritis."

Oh, man, I say, green with envy. They pay you to do this?

"Yeah, just enough so I can still live in my parents' basement, eat the shit my mom cooks, and drink my dad's cheap-ass whiskey every night," he says.

Sounds like paradise to a man like me, I say.

"Then I think you're fucked," he says, "You may not know it yet."

Not yet, I say, winking large. But that's another of the things I've been working on around here.

I cinch up my longthong, now considerably shorter than the left, hoping it will still give the Kneissl Kid enough ankle support to get the job done. I flip the snake of useless leather off into the woods.

I ride the T-Bar up again before trudging back to the main mountain just because it's such a cool lift. As the liftie at the bottom hands me the bar, he grins as wide as Arizona and says, "How's this, sir?" I shove the bar under my butt and I'm off again. The liftie yells something once I'm settled onto the bar, and it sounds like the Captain is defintely around here somewhere. As I approach the top, Hoot yells, "Hey, it's the Kneissl Kid!"

Now, this is the first time I've heard this from someone else's mouth in two, maybe three, years now, and it's just music to my ears. I smile from ear to shining ear, just like the liftie at the bottom, as I slip the bar from under my legs and slide down the exit ramp. I salute Hoot with my Tweety glove and push off on the next run of the rest of my life.

I MAKE MY LAST TURN of the day in front of the lodge, spraying snow as I stop. I begin the long process of unclamping, unbuckling, unwinding, and rewinding while others around me just poke their bindings with a pole to get their short, little skis off. My pass hangs dangling in front of me, interfering, as always, while I bend and huff my way through the task. But I can't complain.

I make my rounds one last time before leaving the mountain. I check the candy and cigarette machines, pay phones and dollar bill changer to find almost a buck-fifty in change that I guess the rich, fat, stupid-ass, city slime don't need when they go skiing. They just throw their money away with both hands when they come up here, all dolled up in thei...*ere you go, Ave. You know you have to try and get along with people a little better than that. I just wish*...it don't stink, 'scuse my French, but it does, just like mine and everybody else's. Then I pocket a half-dozen packets of saltines and some relish at the condiment stand, and I walk around the bar to see if anyone has dropped a bill under a stool or anything. I see a couple of tips left on the bar and I have the passing thought that I could nonchalantly sweep them up if the bartender would just turn around for a second. But she doesn't, so I don't. I check the stalls in the men's room for a wallet or a dollar bill that might have dropped during the torso-twisting end-game of some guy's last dump of the day. Nothing.

But I do find a stall door that looks just right for my next chapter. So I hoist my trench and pull out my napkins and girlie pen to settle in for a rewarding half-hour of literature. I fanny-burp twice, and note the location as Chapter 2.

NOVEMBER 20TH

THIS HAS TO change, I'm thinking, as I fold my four blankets in the stoop-shouldered, belly-rumbling dark of a shed I had never planned to sleep in. I'm hungry as an April bear, but I have at least an hour or so of work before I get to eat my only real meal of the day. The floor of the shed is becoming littered with cellophane saltine wrappers that remind me of the things I used to find under the school bleachers back in Utica. Every step crackles as I move around, getting ready for the day. I bet it's around 15 degrees outside this morning. The guns have been going up on the ridge all night, the sound making it feel even colder. I shiver as I layer on both my sweaters over my two wool shirts.

I decide tearfully that I have to stash the uni here in the shed until I find a home. The streets and sidewalks are getting too slick to trust, even for me, maybe the best there ever was. I kiss it, salute it, snuffle, and set it behind some junk in the corner. Then I slide down to the creek to stumble along the bank, back to my little trail. I climb back up to the street and walk toward Sam's, slapping my sides and hopping for warmth.

Jimmy is already inside as I arrive, bustling about behind the counter. I hang my trench and head for the broom closet. Marie stalks in this morning, slow and slumped, not her usual nervous self. She pushes into the kitchen without comment and comes out tying her apron in back.

Hey, ho, I say, pulling the last of my chairs off the tables.

"I'd say go fuck yourself," says Marie, "But you got nothing to do with it, so I won't."

Well, I figure it's probably not just the cold out there bothering her today, but I can't figure her out on a good day. So I just take my seat at the counter and wait for Jimmy to bring me my second coffee of the day. It's not beer, but it's not bad. Marie takes an order from a couple of customers at the back table, then drops heavily onto the stool to my right. She leans forward with her eyes closed, head on her crossed arms, obscuring the line of her shirt buttons for the moment.

Want to talk about it? I ask.

"Fuck you know about it?" she asks, her eyes glaring as she raises her head from the counter, "My business is my business."

Sorry, I say. Jimmy brings me my first stack of pancakes and a side of sausage. Don't hate me just because I'm a jerk trying to help.

"You're not a jerk," she says, patting my back, opening a pucker between buttons three and four, "You're just a loveable little idiot who means well."

Well, I'm thinking, that's not so bad. I can't argue with that. She hears the bell from the kitchen and slumps her shoulders again, sliding listlessly off the stool. Oh, Marie!

I eat quickly and signal Jimmy that I need another plate of pancakes, more coffee. The place is beginning to fill with skiers fueling up for a day in the cold. They are all dressed in colorful nylon, with stretch pants or those new bib overalls everybody seems to be wearing these days. Some clomp in on their colorful plastic ski boots, others in fur-trimmed après ski boots, some in sneakers. Marie is too busy to sit down, with everybody trying to get her attention and all these jerks in such a big hurry, like they're so much bet...*Turn around, Ave, Ave? Let's just finish up with your coffee and your panc...* kings and queens with a little money in their pockets. Period. So I finish up, grab two of the free tourist newspapers from the rack, and head for the mountain.

I don't have to carry my ski stuff back and forth anymore because I've hidden it all in key locations around the lodge. My skis and poles are in the brush at the edge of the parking lot where I used to leave the uni. My boots are shoved in back of a water heater I found in an unlocked janitor closet downstairs in the basement. I feel just like the other season passholders who rent lockers so they don't have to hump their stuff around. Except for the money.

I pick up my skis and poles along the way and drop them off at the ski rack in front of the lodge. Boy, this place sure feels like home when you have a pass. As I head downstairs for my boots it hits me that everything here is so special. And I know one thing: that no matter what else happens in my life between now and April, no matter where I'm living or what I'm doing, no matter who cares or doesn't care one way or the other, I can ski - right here, right now - any time I feel like it. How many people know that much about themselves?

THIS ONE SHOULD DO, ESPECIALLY since it's the only table left in this crowded Saturday morning cafeteria. I pull off my trench and hang it on the back of the chair, the chair I pick because it's right in the middle of the table and I don't really want a lot of company this morning.

Man, there's a lot of people here today. Maybe that's why I try not to ski on Saturdays any more. Or any less, I guess. Anyway, I decided to do it and a man's got to stand by his decisions. So I reach into my trench pocket and gingerly take out my wallet, the one – only one, actually – that I usually take out of my back pants pocket. I open it and begin to take everything out, one-by-one, to lay out in rows and columns on the table before me. I unfold three cocktail napkins covered in what is now a rather bleary-looking script containing my observations collected from a barstool at the City of Sin Lounge in Utica, New York some years back. These are important observations that will someday become the basis for a great story about, well, about ladies in their underpants who dance around fire poles and ask you for dollars you don't have and probably wouldn't give them anyway. I lay them out carefully, script facing up, and move on.

Next, I take out my emergency dollar bill, one that I would never give away, the one that I keep for some future date when I might have to get out of a jam by fooling somebody. It consists of two different halves of two different dollars, taped together in the middle to look like one. If I ever have to give it to someone, I hope they don't look at it too carefully, at least not while I'm standing there before I start to run down the street. I place it at the bottom of my napkin column.

Next, I unfold a receipt for one used unicycle, purchased a number of years ago from Fred's Cycle House in Rome, New York. I keep it because I just know that someday someone, maybe Dudley Dooright, will ask me about the uni and I'll have to prove things about it. I can prove that I can ride it easily enough, but ownership might be another kettle or dish entirely. I start column two with it.

Next, I find the picture of Mom that I cut out of her high school yearbook. She looks young and pretty. I lay it carefully under the receipt in column two.

Next comes my driver's license, dog-eared and looking a lot less official than it did on June 14th, 1977 when it expired. I keep it because it proves I'm who I am and that I can buy drinks in bars and that I used to be able to drive things with motors.

Next, I lay down my Bookaholics Discount Card from the Little Book House in Albany, New York. I was only there once on a high school bus trip, but I keep it because it will someday give me fifteen dollars off the price of my next book, assuming I ever go back there about twelve times before it expires on October 23, 1974. I lay it down to complete column two.

Column three starts with two matchbooks which I open and set up like little pup tents. I know somehow that these matches will never save my life or anything, but I plan to keep them anyway. One is from the Quarter Deck in Skaneateles, New York where I once spent a very pleasant half-hour with a cold beer before they threw me out. I like it because it has a martini glass on the front, complete with a speared olive and little bubbles skittering out over the rim. The other is an advertisement for the John Nagy Learn-to-Draw School and Saturday Morning Television Show. The back has a very cute little puppy on it that I may have traced and sent in a couple years back.

Next, and I look around real carefully first, is a prescription form for some two-thousand codeine pills prescribed by a Dr. Phil Abbruze of York, Pennsylvania made out in typical doctor writing that looks very much like the bleary script on the napkins. I would never try to redeem it in Mr. Buck's Pharmacy, but maybe someday at the Mortar and Pestilence… hhhmmmmm?

Next, I lay out a small plastic magnifying glass and one key to nothing I own anymore. I am now well into column four and the careful grouping is looking pretty good. I pull out a foil condom wrapper with the right-hand edge ripped open to reveal nothing inside. This I decide needs to go back into the trench pocket.

Next, I very carefully position my other picture of Mom after the operation at the head of column five. She looks a lot older than her yearbook picture which I pick up to compare again, holding it just above and to the right. You can tell it's the same person, but she looks a little quizzical in the second picture, taken when I was probably six or seven. She's got that high turtleneck on that she wore ever since her voice box got taken out because of the cancer, the turtleneck that she wore to remind herself and everybody else what a good skier she was, even in the middle of summer.

Next I unfold an eyeglass prescription for a Mrs. Janet Everly of 228 Pine Haven Drive, Inlet, New York. I have no idea why I carry this, but I keep it anyway. Who knows, I may need glasses myself some day.

At this point, a brightly clad young man in his early twenties walks by slowly with his over-loaded cafeteria tray, looking at the one corner of my table that isn't covered with my wallet contents. He stops and asks, "May I?" Well...sure, I say, as long as all he wants to do is eat, not get all involved or anything. He carefully sets down his tray without disturbing my array and begins to butter his pancakes. He pours a lot of syrup on top of them, syrup that really shouldn't have drained out over his bacon like that, syrup that he should have drizzled sensibly around the edges instead of just emptying the whole bottle all...*right, now, Ave, remember what happened when your Uncle Bernie drank all that beer too fast and you yelled at him to take his ti*...ny bites work better when you're going out to ski and it could all get clumped up in your tummy.

He looks up between huge bites and asks me what all this stuff is doing laying all over the table. Well first, I say, it isn't just laying all over the table. It's carefully arranged into rows and columns for a reason. "And what might that be?", he asks with ropy strands of sarcasm dripping from his mouth just like the syrup all over his goddam bacon, 'scuse my French. So I tell him how I had to run downstairs real fast to the Men's Room this morning to do some business that just couldn't wait and how my wallet fell into the can and how I have to dry out my stuff so it doesn't all freeze up in my pocket on the lift once I go outside. This shouldn't take more than another half hour, I say.

Where'd he go? I wonder. Jesum, he could have left his

extra pancakes if he wasn't that hungry. It's like I always say, skiing isn't what it used to be, and some of these people think they're just made of money these days.

I make my rounds again before putting on my boots and find almost a half-dollar in change in the phones and candy machines. Then I almost faint when I see a five-dollar bill on the floor next to the cash register that Joannie just closed up until the lunch-time rush. What a day this is going to be! I go through the line for another cup of coffee and I pocket my saltines and relish for lunch. Later on, I may buy myself a beer at the bar to celebrate my good fortune. Before putting on my trench, I tape four layers of newspaper across my chest to break the wind. Everybody seems to be watching me for some reason. I hold my pass in my teeth as I do my taping to make sure I don't trap it under anything.

The snowmakers have sure been busy. I ski three new trails this morning just to say I did, not necessarily because they are any good. Two actually suck, but I'm going to ski every inch of ground on the mountain this year. Just because I can.

I decide to take a walk over to the beginner hill to join Hoot for lunch, hopefully for some whiskey. I wobble a bit as I walk over, but frozen ruts can do that to you. To me, anyway. But, once I put my skis back on at the T-Bar, I'm back to who I really am, and I skate gracefully over to the base of the lift. The liftie at the bottom, now a real happy fella, smiles like mad and asks, "And how are you this morning, sir?" I salute him with my Tweety glove and take the bar for the ride up.

"Asshole!" he yells, probably to get the Captain's attention, to tell him something or other, maybe about me being here. Funny I haven't seen him anywhere yet.

"Hey," yells Hoot, peering over the top of the ramp, "Here comes the Kneissl Kid." I get off and skate over to the shack.

Got any whiskey? I ask, eyes wide, eyebrows arched in anticipation.

"You know any other questions?" he asks.

Got any hash? I ask, as an alternative.

"Man, you got a one-track mind," Hoot says, as he leans into the shack. He brings out a whole quart this time.

Whoa, I say. How'd you ever hide that honker, get it up here?

"This one I keep up here," he says, "I can fill up the little ones from it to carry around."

Jesum Crow, I say. From what I see around here, I'd be worried about getting fired for that.

"Barnacre don't even look for this shit," he says, "He's way too concerned about hair. Long as I keep it above the ears I got nothing to worry about."

Hoot looks around in all directions, then hoists the bottle. He belches and passes it over to me. I take a couple of glugs and smile. Thank you, sir! I say, the burn making me swallow hard. I bend over, unclamp, unbuckle, unwrap, and take off my ski, which I stand up against the shack. Then I do the other. I pull out my crackers. Hoot watches as I open the cellophane and squeeze relish between two saltines.

"Fuck you doing?" he asks, squinting at my lunch.

Eating my lunch, I say, taking the saltine sangwich in a single bite.

"That's it?" he asks, already shaking his head.

All I can afford right now, I say. At least until I get me an instructor job.

"Yeah, right," says Hoot, still shaking his head, "You could be God and never get hired up here with hair like yours. Seems like you might have some kind of attitude that might be a problem, too."

Me? Attitude? I ask, chewing. More whiskey?

"See?" he says, looking around, passing the bottle. I glug

it twice and hand it back. Hoot cranes his head around, then drinks again.

"Buck," he says, "Your best bet's to just find some little bar job somewhere nights, ski on your pass. Don't worry about no piss-yellow jacket or nothing." He reaches back into the shack to hide the bottle again. "Besides," he says, "You're the Kid."

Yeah, I guess he's right, I'm thinking. Better being free to carry out my responsibilities than to have to cut my hair and kiss up to some flat-top, European ski school director, or worse. Hoot is the first person to recognize me as the Kid in a long time, but word is sure to get out. Gotta start somewhere, I'm thinking. And I suppose Hoot's as good a prophet as anybody else.

I stand here digesting my crackers and whiskey, looking at Hoot's shack, consumed with envy for his job. I'm thinking I could live in this place.

You know, I say, I could probably live in a place like this.

"You know," Hoot says, "I know you could, 'cause I did for a month last year when my Mom threw me out."

No shit? 'scuse my French, I say.

"Yeah, just had to black out the windows at night so nobody could see any light or nothing from the bottom. Snowmakers come over here sometimes, but never up this far. I'd come down in the morning and make like I just arrived in the parking lot."

No shit? I'm thinking, maybe saying. This might be a real opportunity here. It's twice the size of my shed, and there's a gas heater.

"Used to sleep underneath in the ski patrol toboggan," he continues, "Just amazing how warm it is inside one of them things."

You didn't get caught, or nothing? I ask.

"Nah, just moved back into the basement after my

Mom cooled off a little, I guess. She didn't ask me back or nothing."

No shit? 'scuse my French, I say, scratching my head and smiling.

"FIRST THING," HOOT SAYS, "YOU need a cafeteria tray. That's your car around here. It don't work on skis 'cause you'll get caught if you try to stay on the hill after they close. You just wave goodbye to the patrol guys on your last run and act like you're going home. Best thing is to bury your skis under the snow somewhere down by the lodge, somewhere you can remember where you left them. Nobody looks for buried skis."

It's dark and we are at the bottom of the T-Bar. The sky is blazing with stars I have never seen before. The Milky Way is a huge smudge of white against the blackness of space, so close I could probably touch it. Hoot takes a tug at his pint and passes it. I oblige. He gets down on his hands and knees and reaches under the lift shack and pulls two trays out.

"Saved you the trouble of stealing one, though," he says, "Keep a couple around, just in case. Now, you do like this."

Then Hoot shows me how to locate the button that starts the T-Bar by reaching through the window to the left of the locked door. He starts the lift and motions me over, waving his tray. He sets the tray in the middle of the loading area and sits down on it Indian-style. As a bar swings past overhead, he grabs it and gets hauled away up the hill.

"Just grab one," he yells, looking back over his shoulder.

I sit down and set up for the grab, missing the first bar that comes past. I catch the next one and get spun around sidewards twice before I figure out the position I need to hold to keep going. But I can't get my legs under me on the little tray, and my flailing feet send up a blizzard of snow in my face each time they bottom out. I somehow get to the top where Hoot is already standing, holding his tray, laughing.

"Just let go," he says.

I let go and spin twice on my way down to the bottom of the ramp, laughing and rolling, the bar swinging wildly over my head and around the bullwheel. Hoot laughs, then shows me how to stop the lift by hitting the red emergency button on the box next to the door of the shack.

"Just make sure you pull this back out again after the lift stops," says Hoot, "You can't tell from the bottom that it's even been turned on or anything."

We walk into the shack, which has ample headroom and width enough for two, unlike my shed. Hoot shows me how to tape the window if I want to read or something, and how to light the gas heater. I ask if they'll notice that he's using too much gas. Hoot says they don't make a big deal about anything except hair around here.

Just like home, I say, looking around.

"Better," says Hoot, "Least it is when your mom's riding your ass."

I certainly know what that's like, I say, wincing at the thought.

We turn off the stove, un-paper the window, and take a tug apiece at Hoot's little bottle.

"Just don't touch my big whiskey unless you're gonna replace it," he says, "Have your ass thrown out of here so fast it'll leave your dick behind. They'll pull your pass, too, you get caught."

Nobody's going to find me up here, I say. I'll see to that.

"Mess with my whiskey, you'll get found. Guarantee you that," he says, winking.

With that, Hoot shows me the ski patrol toboggan in its own little cubby under the shack and how to wrap up inside it. I snuggle in and wish I could just stay right here tonight. Right here, right now. With my four blankets I can be comfortable to well below zero up here. But we have to leave since all my stuff is still back in my shed. Hoot sits down on his tray and is immediately out of sight in the dark, yelling back at me to follow. I sit on my own tray, feeling like a kid again as I gain speed and bounce on the gentle slope toward the bottom and parking lot beyond. Faster, faster. Then, all of a sudden, I'm sitting in a little group of trees with Hoot rubbing snow on my face.

"I was trying to tell you," he says, pulling me back to standing. As I shake out the cobwebs he tells me something about making sure I'm out before 6:30 every morning - not a problem since I have to be at Sam's anyway - and leaving the tray back in the bottom shack exactly where I found it. At least I think that's what he says. This definitely hurts. He reminds me to make sure to pull the emergency stop back out each time I use it, otherwise he has to walk to the top in the morning. "First time that happens, you'll find all your shit on fire behind the shack and the ski patrol crawling up your ass with an ice axe," he says.

And he tells me again not to touch his whiskey unless I replace it. Yeah, I get the message, Hoot.

I rub my head and walk back out across the empty parking lot with Hoot, who has a car. I talk him into a beer at the Troubadour before dropping me off at Treman Street. After all, I didn't buy a beer at the lodge and I have a brand new five-dollar bill in my pocket for that very purpose. We sit at the bar and I buy two beers, leaving enough just for a paltry, insulting tip.

"So, what's with the unicycle?" Hoot asks.

You got a car, I got a uni. Just my form of transportation, is all, I say, sipping at my beer.

"Can't ride it around here much longer," he says, "Bust your ass in no time."

Snow's a problem, I say. It's already put up for the winter, but it's worth it for the rest of the year. It's my freedom.

Hoot looks at me funny and chugs the rest of his beer. He asks if I want another. Do Popes shit in the woods? 'Scuse my

French, I say. He motions to the bartender who seems a little nervous about two guys like us in such a nice establishment. If he only knew who I am, I'm thinking.

I go in the men's room to trickle and I remember that my first chapter is behind door number three. I check and find that it's still here, just the way I left it. I feel a flash of pride that my work can live on in this sort of upscale place. So I come back out and tell Hoot to go in and do his business, and right where to do it. He looks at me real funny and I prod him, C'mon, just do it. He shrugs and slides off the stool, slouching towards the door.

"You're fucked," he says, returning. "But one thing's for sure. You're not boring, at least not yet."

I smile and spin the stool all the way around, my pass dangling and swinging from my neck. Well, I sure hope not, I say, I got lots more where that came from.

Well, one thing leads to another and Hoot buys a couple of whiskeys after I promise, real hard, to pay him back just as soon as I get my instructor job nailed down. We get talking about balance, which is the key to skiing, hard drinking, and riding a uni. I tell him that I'm maybe the best there ever was, and Hoot says he can drink me under the table on my best day. I tell him I'm actually talking about the uni, maybe even skiing, but that he also might be wrong on the drinking. "Yeah, right," he says. "The way you wobble?" Oh yeah, Hoot? Oh, yeah?

Well, this other thing leads to yet another, and I find myself showing Hoot my famous sense of balance by standing up on the backrest of the barstool, one foot out, no hands. Everybody's looking and I'm up here on the very top of the stool, where I swing my shoulders to spin the stool through 360 degrees without falling, something I've done before. This particular time, however, the stupid glue holding the dowels in the back of the stool must have been defective, or something, because the entire backrest comes apart beneath me and I land - on my feet, of course - next to a table which skids three feet to the right as I careen into it. Glasses hit the floor and two skiers jump up, wiping at the front of their gaudy sweaters. I quickly find myself being hustled out the front door by the bartender, who locks my arm behind my back and whispers something in my ear.

Say again, I say, not really hearing what he told me.

Instead, he kicks my butt down the steps and I land on all fours on the sidewalk, where I notice it's starting to snow. Hoot finishes his whiskey, then mine, then follows me out. My trench lands halfway down the steps as I stand up at the bottom.

Something tells me I can't come back here anytime soon. And with my first chapter published here, that's going to be a problem. Oh, man! Hoot drops me off at the head of Treman Street and I walk my best to the end where my path leads down to the creek. One more cramped night in my shed and I move to paradise!

DECEMBER 2ND

I'S A GOOD thing I have a clock in my head, because I don't have anything else to wake me up. But I pull my pocket watch and find that it's 6:05, kind of late to be getting up this morning. I unwrap the canvas cover of the ski patrol toboggan and pull myself and my four blankets out into the cold morning air. I carefully reposition the toboggan cover so that no one will notice, just in case they have to use it for some stupid beginner with a twisted ankle or something like that. It had better be back here pronto if they do, I'm thinking, because this is my bed and I'm not about to start sleeping curled up on a floor again anytime soon.

I hide my stuff and tidy up the shack before taking my morning tray ride to the bottom. I stash the tray, exactly as I found it, and cross the parking lot down to the access road toward town. I arrive ten minutes late at Sam's, but he doesn't say anything. Marie is already here, early this morning, sitting at the counter with her coffee and a cigarette.

I rush around putting chairs on the tables so I can do my usual excellent job at sweeping up the crumbs and mopping off the dinner stains of the night before. I find several of the paper covers from Sam's individual butter patties, upside down and stuck to the floor. I have to get down on my hands and knees to peel them off. It suddenly occurs to me that butter would be an excellent food if I could keep the little patties from melting in the pocket of my trench. I decide to hold this thought, to maybe figure it out by the time I'm ready to leave this morning.

As bad luck would have it, Marie gets real busy about the time I finish up. I sit down at the counter for breakfast as she bustles about the tables. With the season kicking in at Huntington, Sam's has become a busy place in the morning. A young man who doesn't know any better sits down on the stool to my right and I have to glare at him across the rim of my coffee cup, holding the eye contact as I bite the end off a rasher of bacon with a grunt. I follow this up with a little fanny-burp that turns out to have a mind of its own, I guess. He leaves abruptly as Jimmy brings his coffee, and I have to explain that he had a nervous wife in the car blowing the horn to get him out before his kids were late for school, or something like that. At least now Marie's stool is empty again.

One of these days, as soon as I get my instructor job, I'd really like to ask her out on a date. Under normal circumstances, I'd probably treat her to drinks and a steak at a nice place like the Troubadour, but that's out of the question for awhile. I don't really know how she'd react; I don't even know if she's married with kids or not. She doesn't wear a ring, but a lot of married women don't. Who knows? All I know is she's nervous, she works hard, she's got bras in at least two different colors, she talks dirty, and she gets moody on a pretty regular basis around here. Oh, Marie!

She finally sits down and lights a cigarette - a sure sign that she might be ready to sit tight for at least a couple minutes or so. I take a quick peek and see nothing but buttons, no gap. She takes a long drag, holds it, and blows it up and out of the corner of her mouth, away from me.

"Buck," she says, closing her eyes, giving me a chance for a better peek, "Life really sucks."

I disagree with her, since my own life is so rich at the

moment, but I want her to have someone she can talk to about it.

You sure? I ask, unable to come up with anything better, figuring this is a good place to start.

"Well, yeah," she says, "Sucks, far as I can see."

Maybe that's the problem, I say, leaving a pause for emphasis. I count to five under my breath to make sure I wait long enough for this to sink in.

"Fuck you know about my problems?" she asks, sounding a little aggravated as I get to three. Well, I certainly had my share at one time, I'm thinking. But I worked my way up and out of them. All the way to where I am today. And that's saying something, if you ask me.

I've been there, Marie, I say, looking into her eyes with compassion and warmth. And I think I can help.

Well, sweet Cruller of Criminy, I'm thinking, as she erupts in laughter, and three tables full of skiers turn to see what's going on. Now normally, I'd be a little put off by a lady making fun of my heartfelt sympathy. But with these particular circumstances come a couple of great views through the Huntington Gap, as I've begun to call Marie's button puckers. She continues to quake and rock with laughter. Oh, Marie!

"Sorry, Buck," she says, wiping her nose with the back of her hand, "It wasn't you I was laughing at. It's just me and my shitty life, is all."

Don't worry, I say. I've got skin like an alligator. You can laugh at me all you want. I signal to Jimmy for a refill, thinking I may have just snuck into the land of opportunity.

If life sucks, I say, rubbing my chin, stroking my beard to show I'm really pondering this one. If life sucks, just stand up tall, and...and. And that's about as far as I get. I really ought to know better, too. I had it right in my head when I started, but I...something about how a vacuum cleaner sucks too, changing the bad to good, something about new beginn...

*Nincompoop, Ave. Is that what you want people to think? Like this has never happened before, huh, Ave? You really have to learn from experience and think these things through befo...*re-adjust myself on the stool and smile, rubbing my chin. Like a vacuum cleaner, or something, I say.

Silence. This seems to happen quite a bit when I get real serious. Seems like it takes a while for people to really get used to the deep stuff, kind of like it is with skiing. You do get used to it, though, with a little effort.

"Buck," she says, finally, "Buck..."

Then she's up off the stool, shaking her head and on her way into the kitchen. Funny, I didn't hear the bell or anything. But she'll be back. Oh, yeah, she'll be back.

But she isn't back before I'm ready to leave, so I saunter over to Table 2, real nonchalant and all, and I take a half-dozen patties of butter. I press down on each one in the bowl to find the hardest ones, the cold ones that will last longest in my trench. I do the same thing at Table 3, faking a look out the window in case Jimmy's watching, which he isn't. These'll be just great with my saltines. Hold the relish, I'm thinking, the joke bringing a smile to my face.

It's a little tough hiding a handful of butter while taking my trench off the hanger and trying to put it on. I'm thinking I should have probably snuck them into the pocket first. But I stuff my fist into the right sleeve and wiggle it around to get the job done before Jimmy notices anything.

EVERYTHING IS OPEN ON THE mountain now, with a dusting of natural snow on top of what the guns have blown out. I stand in front of the ski racks and stretch my shoulders before unwinding my longthongs and beginning the long process of getting my Red Stars on. I no longer have to hump my skis across bare ground to get to the lift. The Kneissl Kid should never have to do that kind of work anyway.

My legs are now like finely tuned tree trunks, though a

couple people have looked at me funny when I use this clever expression. I guess they've never skied up north. The muscles don't burn on the way down a long run anymore, and I can push them as hard as I want now. This morning I had the pleasure of pocketing thirty cents in change from the phone next to the ski shop. I also grabbed three bags of the new oyster crackers the management has thoughtfully added to the condiment bar. Looking around, I just can't understand why Marie's so despondent about life. Life is great right about now, far as I can see.

And my new apartment is lovely, simply lovely. I just have to wait until dark before I walk back over to the T-Bar and crank her up for the ride home. This time of year I don't have to wait long after the lifts close, either. It's so much fun riding up and down the hill on my tray that I have to remind myself not to laugh and howl quite so loud.

I SIT HERE IN FRONT of the heater marveling at how my evenings have become so rewarding; a rich combination of Hoot's whiskey - which I have actually replaced twice from a pint I bought after hitting my jackpot - and plenty of time for literature. I tape newspaper over the window, just like Hoot showed me, so I can read by candlelight and take notes for my novel on my napkins. My girlie pen is getting a real workout lately. Every time I shake it I'm thinking, you just gotta love snow!

When I get bored or lonely I just blow out the candle and slide on down to the bottom of the hill. A short walk gets me to several of the warm places that are still open late, places where I haven't been thrown out yet. I often sit in the laundromat reading, pretending I have a whole basket of clean underwear tumbling around in the empty washers and dryers. It was there, last week, that I hit the jackpot while checking the dollar-bill changer machine, usually a fat chance on my best day. But, that day, I found a clinking pile of quarters from the last bill that the harried mother of some half-dozen little butt-wipes had just changed. She was leaving with a big basket of diapers, with that screeching horde climbing up her legs, when I checked the machine and just happened to find her five quarters left in the hopper. I kept my mouth shut until she was gone, and, leave it to me, what happened next was pure genius.

I take one of my remaining dollar bills and stick it in the machine. Brrrrr, click, Bingo! Five quarters. So, you can imagine what happened to the rest of my dollar bills once I realized I could get a 25% return on my investment every ten seconds or so. Jimmy was a little funny about me coming in so late to change 40 quarters into ten one-dollar bills just before closing, but he shook his head and did it for me. Then I went back and fed the ten bucks back into the changer for another five quarters apiece. I went through this routine a whole bunch of times that night, redeeming quarters at the Klondike, Momma's, Sam's again, and Gus's Gas. I finally ended up with ninety-eight dollars and seventy-five cents, all in quarters, before I ran out of dollar bills again.

But, by then, all the public establishments had closed for the night and I found myself with quite a heavy load. I filled my pants pockets, then my trench pockets, then I found an empty detergent box in the trash. This 'Duz' the trick, I thought, and I howled at my joke as I humped that jingling load all the way back up Main Street to the bridge and up through the parking lot. I had to make three trips up the T-Bar that night. Jesum, what a day!

When I went back early the next morning on my way to Sam's, there were two guys in the laundromat with the front of the changer open. So I just walked on by, very nonchalant, whistling and all. On the way back to the mountain I tried the machine again, and only got four quarters for my dollar.

Well, Criminy, I'm thinking, if not for a quirk of bad timing, I could have had one pocket full of paper instead of a sore back in the morning. Anyway, I now have a real heavy box of perfectly good money hidden behind the toboggan in the little cubby under my apartment. Life is good.

I HAVEN'T SEEN ANDREA IN a couple of weeks now, maybe a good thing, far as I can see. I guess she still hangs out at the Troubadour, but I don't hold that against her. I've been thinking about her a lot lately, for some reason. I kind of worry about her, but I know I'm a lot better off without her grabbing at me, and all. Poor thing. It's gotta be tough getting old in a ski town. Makes me kind of wonder, if I had kids - and I don't, for sure - how I could ever leave them way back in some place like Montana. Never been there, but I can't imagine it's so bad you'd have to leave your kids there and get out. Must be something else going on. I kind of miss her, too.

Anyway, I just want to make sure she's still okay and all, so I decide to take a tray ride down and walk into town. One of my trench pockets hangs low, full of quarters so I can maybe buy her a drink or two. I've learned that I have to duct-tape the pocket shut for the tray ride down or I lose more money than I do in the bars. I walk down Main Street wishing I could still ride the uni; walking just seems way too slow and jerky after a day of skiing the way I do. I sometimes feel like a rototiller walking around town, compared with the graceful swoops and balance I'm famous for on the slopes. But I see my reflection in a store window and I realize that the weight of all those quarters in my right trench pocket makes my shoulders look level, so I don't even have to think about walking for a change.

They've got colored lights running across the street, strung up on that rope they make out of pine trees, and most of the businesses are all gussied up for that Christmas holiday coming up soon. I don't expect to get any presents from Santy Claus this year, but I'm definitely going to get something for Marie. Oh, Marie.

But tonight, I'm thinking, it's Andrea I have to attend to. I'll probably end up getting her some kind of present, too. But it won't be that thing she says she really wants, I hope. I feel like I'm a church lady checking on some shriveled-up, sunken-eyed biddie from the prayer group who can't get out any more. Andrea's not that far gone, though. I pass Brookhaven and wonder if she might be at home. My pocket watch, which looks like 9:30, says probably not. So I make for the Troubadour.

I know I can't get in, so I walk around looking in the windows until I get a good view of the bar where she usually sits. I don't see her, so I go from window to window to get a view of each table. I'm about to give up when I suddenly see her right at the bar where I first expected her to be. Just like magic! Either that, or she just came out after doing her business in the Ladies' Room, maybe. I bang on the window to get her attention, but I drop like a rock as I see the bartender crane around. I wait a minute, then peek again. She's still there and the bartender isn't. So I bang on the window and she turns to see me. So does the bartender, though, because he is now on the porch looking down at me. I back up with my hands in front of me, palms out like I'm talking to a mugger or a cop or something. Then I bang on the window again and motion for Andrea to come outside. The bartender advances and I retreat. Andrea comes out on the porch.

C'mon out, I say.

"C'mon in, Hon," she says, "Cold out here."

Yeah, I know, I say, backing up. She probably doesn't know about me getting thrown out of the place yet. I have the passing thought that I should tell her about Chapter One, but that would probably get her thrown out, too. And that big, bad-ass bartender probably doesn't need to know about my work either.

Andrea goes back inside and I bid adieu to the hulk stalking my way, but only after throwing a handful of quarters at him, telling him to buy the lady a drink. He lunges and I run. But I come back around the corner once he's gone so I can get my quarters back.

I'm down on my hands and knees picking my quarters up off the sidewalk and out of little holes in the snowbank when Andrea comes out again, this time with her coat on. She stands there looking down at me with a strange look on her face, a look I've seen before, though maybe not on her particular face.

Buck, Buck Avery, I say looking up at her.

"Yeah," she says, "I know."

So I get up, pocket my change, and we walk down the street toward Momma's, which is on the corner of her street. This time, however, I have no intention of making that particular turn, so we go up the steps into the tiny bar where there is now a cardboard Santy Claus and a Huntington Hardware Holiday Calendar hanging on the wall. We sit down on two of the four stools and I do my polite introductions.

Andrea, this is Momma, Momma, Andrea, I say.

"It's Mrs. Glasheen to you," Momma says to me, sticking out her hand to Andrea with a smirk that says they've probably met already. I ask Andrea what she wants and she orders a dry Manhattan.

"Up, please," she says to Mrs. Glasheen. I order a beer and wonder if I have enough quarters.

"Four seventy-five," says Mrs. Glasheen, and I start making stacks of quarters, four apiece, on the bar next to the pack of cigarettes that cost me another ten of them earlier this afternoon. Mrs. Glasheen huffs like a bear and sweeps them jingling off the edge of the bar into her apron. It certainly sounds a lot like Christmas around here!

"So," says Andrea, turning to me as Mrs. Glasheen stalks out into the kitchen, "You got that big dick with you?"

Well, I just go red as Santy's suit on that one. I probably should have expected it, though, I'm thinking. I'm not making a play for her, just trying to make sure she's still fogging a mirror, is all. She's pretty drunk right now, but no more than last time I saw her. I don't want to push her off that bridge of depression again, and, Jesum, is she ever hard to figure out.

Nah, left it home, I say, sipping my beer, acting nonchalant.

"Where's home?" she asks, "Might want to take a little walk over there with you sometime, help you find it."

I cringe at the thought, but then she punches me in the shoulder and tells me to lighten up, that she's just playing her games with me. So I start telling her about my new home.

"You're making all this up, aren't you?" she says in the middle of my story, and I tell her that reality is one thing, making up good stories is another. And that I'm pretty good at both. Then, I tell her about Chapter One and how Two and Three are already published, and where. She looks at me real funny this time.

"What's it about?" she asks. So I tell her about the Kneissl Kid and how all kinds of good things are happening to him over in Europe, in the Yalps, maybe France. I don't tell her that the story is part autobiography, though. I show her my napkins and girlie pen so she can see that I'm a pro, not just using my work as a pick-up line or something.

She guffaws and snorts like a racehorse, bringing Mrs. Glasheen back into the room. I kind of expect to hear her yell, "Too much noise". Instead, she looks around to see if our glasses are empty yet, and tells us she will be closing in a couple of minutes. Jesum, I'm thinking, it's only around quarter to eleven. But since I've only got around eleven quarters in my pocket, it's probably not such a bad idea.

"So how do you expect me to read your book," she asks, "when you got it in goddam men's rooms?

Well, I say, It's not like I've never been in a girls' room before. She looks at me funny again, then shakes it off.

"I won't ask, Hon," she says.

I tell her that I can give her the napkin and she can just follow my table of contents and slip into each stall real quick-like so nobody notices. She shakes her head again and points down.

"Yeah, like I'd be real manly with these babies on," she says, pointing at a pair of pumps with six-inch heels so thin you could probably drill teeth with them. I'm thinking that from the ankles down she'd look pretty good under a stall door. And how she'd probably have company in no time.

Wear boots, I say. And if you want, I can escort you, make sure nobody disturbs you. Except for Chapter One, anyway.

"Buck," she says, tousling my hair like Mom used to do before the arthritis took out her shoulders, "You are just the cutest thing I ever met." And I can't argue with her on that.

I go on to explain that I just want her to understand me a little better, read my work, get to know me as an artiste. I explain that I'm not ready for any entanglements, and she tells me there's only one thing at the moment she'd be interested in getting tangled up in, "so to speak", she says. I think I get it, and go bright red again. I pull out my pocket watch, but Mrs. Glasheen saves me the trouble of having to make excuses. We upend our drinks and leave.

At the corner Andrea decides - winking large, kind of like I do - to head home instead of back to the Troubadour. In the mottled light of the streetlamp and the festive Christmas bulbs, she looks younger, less hardened. I figure she might have something besides sleep in mind from the look in her other eye, and get the passing thought that maybe I could handle a little entanglement, maybe just a quick romp with an old bag with such nice tit...*Tease, Ave. That's all she is. You know better, think about what could happen here. Just take a look at her, Ave, just look. I'm sure you can see that she's nev...* everything okay?" she asks.

Yeah, I'm fine, I say, slouching a little. Jesum. I only came into town to make sure you were.

DECEMBER 16TH

"**Y**OU ALRIGHT IN there?" the voice asks from the other side of the stall door.

Oh, yeah, I reply, thinking immediately that I probably sound too perky, that he probably thinks I'm whacking off or something. But the boots go away along with the mop pail.

I have purchased a sharp-tipped, indelible marker at the Mortar and Pestilence, and I'm following my napkin Table of Contents from stall to stall, going over my work to make sure it lasts. I had a real shock earlier this week when my girlie pen skipped a little taking my notes. I don't want to run it out writing my chapters, and I've also noticed that several of them are getting smudged a little. And I had to completely re-write Chapter Four when I found that some dumb-ass who probably can't even read had erased it all by painting the back of the stall door at Gus's Gas. Some people! Criminy.

But, my story is coming along very nicely, with the Kneissl Kid now madly in love with a waitress at this upscale little fern bar down the road from the mountain. He drives over after his races every day to see her, to bring her a single red rose that he buys from the florist in the nearby village of Grenouille des Yalps. He drives the twisty lanes in his Porsche, often with the top down, even though it's winter. The story takes place in Europe, maybe France. The Kid wears a carefully tailored, expensive nylon ski jacket emblazoned with his name inside a big red Kneissl star stitched on the back. Everyone who follows him around knows exactly who he is. People sometimes talk behind his back when they see it, though.

My greatest fear has always been that my work, like so many other important novels, will just lie around until somebody finds it after I'm dead. What good is that? I don't have any kids to make money off it once I'm gone, and the value of my estate, so to speak, might not warrant a second look at this point. But I'm certainly not checking out anytime soon. And I'm making real sure my work isn't just lying around somewhere. It's going to stand straight up and get noticed while I'm still here.

I keep listening to other people when I'm in a public place, especially in a place where I'm published, waiting to hear some critical comments about my work. So far, nothing. Nothing. So I'm thinking that I need to provide a little more direction for the average reader who probably doesn't know where to find the next page. My work doesn't lend itself to just flipping through pages like you do with most everyday writers. My feeling is that you should have to work a little reading a good story, but there seems to be a limit for some readers. So, as I re-write my chapters, I've been adding a line at the bottom of each telling people where to go next.

I finish work and pull up my pants. My marker clicks reassuringly against my girlie pen in my jeans pocket as I buckle my belt and ready myself for what may be my most challenging day so far. Not that every day isn't a challenge for the Kneissl Kid, who is always expected to be that much better each day than the day before. But today is special.

Chapter One is my only remaining re-write, the only chapter without directions on how to find the next one. It's probably my best chapter. It has to be to catch and hold the reader's attention. But without directions, I worry that the reader will be left hanging, if you get my drift, in spite of it being maybe the best work in the story. So I head down the hill toward Main Street and the Troubadour, using the time to scrape a blob of congealed butter out of my right trench pocket.

I stop in at the laundromat on the way, since I have a buttery five in my pocket. It's always worth a try, I figure. I feed in the five and I hear the whir as it checks the bill, followed by the reassuring clinking of quarters as they fall down the chute into the hopper. I paw them out and lay the pile on the underwear folding table. This is just like Las Vegas, I'm thinking, but I soon find that I have only twenty pieces of silver, so to speak. Next time, for sure.

I walk right on past the first time because I'm just too nervous to be nonchalant at the moment, thank you. I feel the sweat under my arms and across the front of my chest. My feet seem to take smaller steps, as if they are trying to slow me down, trying to keep me from carrying out the mission that is beginning to consu...*My, my, Ave, Just go on in. Always afraid to ever make a decision on your own, just like a little gi...* grip on myself, all these things running through my head, knotting up details that should probably stay separate. I stop at the corner and take six deep breaths to calm myself. I close my eyes and visualize myself walking into the bar like anyone else, across the room, into the Men's Room. No commotion, no chase, no fear. No problem.

And now, I'm ready. I stride confidently up the front steps and open the front door. I pull my hat down low and adjust my scarf with the nonchalance that I am counting on to carry me through the next half-hour or so. I look around, the bar half-full and relatively quiet. The bartender's back is turned and I sense my opportunity. I swagger across the floor toward the Men's Room until I hear the bartender yell, "Hey, I thought I told..."

I don't even hear the rest of what he says because I am now in the middle of Alternate Plan B, which involves actual running and simulated vomiting. I figure that this should keep him away from me long enough to carry out my mission. I bang through the Men's Room door - shoulders heaving, hands at my mouth - and into the stall next to the sink. I quickly slide the barrel bolt home to lock myself in. I take three deep breaths and hear the bartender come inside looking for me. Then I begin making the most incredible sounds ever to come out of the mouth of man.

I squawk and rasp, flush the toilet, cough and gag, hawk and spit, gasp and gargle. I slam my back into the stall door for emphasis and begin anew, flushing again. When I hear the bartender swear like a drunken Frenchman and stomp his way back out the door, I stop and take my seat.

I have carefully formulated Alternate Plan B in four distinct phases - the first now completed - since I need to be organized to pull this off. I stick to my plan and begin by adding the most important information, directions from my Table of Contents, at the bottom of the chapter, just in case I get thrown out immediately. But I don't, so I continue with phase three by writing over my chapter with the indelible marker, making fake puking noises and flushing occasionally to keep the bartender out.

As I trace over my words I'm thinking that certain turns of phrase, certain metaphors could stand a little editing. But I don't have the time and my chosen method of publication doesn't really lend itself to revision. I work quickly but carefully. Then I'm done, I'm not dead yet, and I'm thinking that soon I may even be the best there ever was at this writing thing, too.

I stand in the stall taking deep breaths to ready myself for phase four: my flight. Fight or flight - no contest, far as I can see. I never was very good with my hands, if you get my drift, or my feet, for that matter. Balance has always been my strong suit. I slowly slide the barrel bolt open and tiptoe out of the stall. I stand in front of the mirror trying to visualize myself as an antelope, maybe a cheetah, the fastest of animals. I take another half-dozen deep breaths and commit to my next challenge.

The door bursts open as my shoulder hits it. I fly toward the middle of the room with my trench flapping around me, my pass flying this way and that on its lanyard to the syncopated tattoo of my frenzied footwork. I fake left around a table, then make for a gap between the bar and a coat rack that I guess I didn't notice as I came in. Or maybe the bartender moved it, I don't know. I don't exactly fit through, though, and the coat rack falls, catching my foot and sending me into the wait station where I knock two carafes of hot coffee to the floor. I scrabble my way between two tables on all fours until I can get upright again, my eyes peeled for the bartender. I make a break for the front door as the entire clientele comes to standing. I have the passing thought that the noise I hear is their cheering. Time slows to a crawl. My feet feel like they are barely moving as my entire being focuses on the handle of a door that seems like it's off somewhere in the next county. The cheering seems to come from a hundred miles away, fading slowly as I finally bang through the front door in slow motion. Then I run my lungs out to their limit as time slowly resumes its normal pace in the cold, dark silence of early-winter.

DECEMBER 21ST

IT'S A LITTLE tough finding a single red rose on the first day of winter in a small town without a florist when you don't have a car. There's pure magic in my choice of this gift for Marie, but I have absolutely no idea where I'm going to get one. Part of the magic flows out of my story which I now have in six chapters all over town. Also, today is the winter solstice, shortest day of the year. There's got to be a little magic in that, too.

I'm so intent on finding this present that I may not even ski today. I stare at Marie's back as she bends over Table 3 taking orders. I'm looking for inspiration, waiting for an answer. So far, the curve of her back tells me nothing. Neither do her sneakers, or the short, white socks peeking out of them. Oh, Marie!

The closer it gets to Christmas, the more nervous she seems to be getting. Could be she's worried about having enough money for her kids' presents. That is, if she's even got any. I really don't know. Could be she's got a boyfriend in the service, home for the holidays, but she's in love with me and she's worried about what's going to happen when she tells him. Could be she's got nothing whatsoever going on in her life, and the holidays always remind her of this. Or, could be she's got kids out in Montana or somewhere, like Andrea. Now, that's gotta be a real nerve jangler this time of year.

Anyway, I've got a mission to accomplish, no matter what her situation might be. It seems to me, I fit into most any of these situations one way or another, and I just might be her ticket out of here.

But right here, right now, it's time for eating. I finish my first plate of pancakes and signal Jimmy for a coffee refill and another order of bacon. I drum my fingers on the counter - just because I'm very nervous about finding the gift, not because I'm getting antsy waiting for my pancakes. But Jimmy doesn't know this, I can't tell him, and he's probably thinking I'm an ingrate or something. He brings the plate and drops it in front of me with a clatter. He just stands there for a moment, and, under the circumstances, I decide not to ask him for anything else today.

Marie finally comes over and plops onto the stool next to me. I take a careful peek, but there's just no view at all down Huntington Gap this morning. Oh, well. Marie picks up her coffee and asks me for a cigarette.

Sorry, I say. Don't have any today. Truth is, I'm thinking, I haven't had any for a while now. She slouches forward over the counter on her elbows and takes a sip or two.

"Probably better off without them," she says.

She shifts her elbows and the shirt begins to pucker. A little vista opens down the Gap, like a beautiful sunrise just breaking through a bank of fog. I hunker down on the counter myself, acting bored and nonchalant. We talk, I glance. She drinks, I peek. Just another morning at Sam's, except that I only have a couple of mornings left to find my present for Marie. I don't know where, but I'm definitely going to find it. I have to, and that's all there is to it. I could always get her something else, but I've got to go with the magic. Certain things are meant to be, and I just need to think this one through a little better, as Mom always says.

Marie crosses her arms in front of her, shivering, her face an etching of distress. Her hands rubbing opposite shoulders, and asks, "Cold in here? God, I feel like I need my fucking sweater."

I shiver too, but not from the cold. A sweater would drop like a fog bank over my inspiration this morning, and I'm certainly not going to be part of that.

I don't think so, I say, fingers crossed. Actually feels kind of warm to me. Might be the coffee, though. I raise my cup in a little toast and take a sip, winking large. Marie rolls her eyes, but gulps her own coffee instead of going for the sweater. Yippee yahoo!

One of these days I'm going to just ask her straight out what her situation is. But this morning is not that day, I guess. My best bet is to just figure out where to find that single red rose.

I get up and walk over to Table 2 to look out at the weather, to give me cover as I steal a half-dozen butter patties. I put on my trench, say goodbye to Jimmy and Marie, and set off on my mission.

I know exactly what I need and I have absolutely no idea where to find it. I stand in front of Sam's long enough that Jimmy comes out to ask me if anything is wrong. He wouldn't understand about the rose, and I certainly don't want to talk butter with him. Not here, not now. So I make up a nice story about standing here watching a huge bald eagle soaring like a kite up over the mountain. This interests him greatly, I guess, because he walks out into the street to get a better view. He cranes his neck in all directions and asks where I saw it. I point up toward the trails on the northeast ridge, and say that he must have just disappeared around the shoulder of the pass. Jimmy shakes his head, saying it might be the very first eagle to ever nest in this area, especially this time of year. I tell him how sorry I am that he didn't get to see it.

I decide to look inside every public establishment in town to see if anyone has roses this time of year. Some places are very unlikely to have any, like the laundromat, but who knows? I've got the time to check each one, and I fully intend to find that rose somewhere in town. And, just as I thought, there are no roses in the laundromat, except for two in a very nice picture above the underwear folding table. I keep this in the back of my mind, and I try a dollar bill in the changer. I only get four quarters, so I try again, twice more to be sure. But no dice.

I almost write off Gus' Gas, but I go in anyway and look around. The closest I get - and it really is quite an interesting coincidence - is a sleazy calendar on the back wall of the shop with a very beautiful, half-nude woman named Rosie holding an enormous, open-ended box wrench. Wow, I'm thinking, there's magic all over this town! I can't give her this, though.

I proceed further down the street and peek into the theater lobby to see if they maybe have any flowers out in a vase or anything. Nothing. I pass the Troubadour and pull my collar up so that I'm less likely to be recognized, but I'm not sure this really helps anymore. It's actually a pretty good prospect, being an upscale establishment and all, but I can't go in. That's for sure. I make a mental note to maybe come back here after they open this afternoon if nothing turns up anywhere else.

There is nothing in the laundromat or the Little Indian Ski Shop. I stop in the lobby of the Huntington Manor Motel, the Klondike, The Sitzmark, Treadwell's Grocery, The Mortar and Pestilence, Gus' Gas where I find this picture of a girl named Ro...*See, Ave? You've already been here, haven't you? I think you'd bett*...turn up the street to Vinnie's Trattoria Italiano. Nothing.

I'm wondering where to go next as I pass the cemetery, and the thought hits me that there may be some plastic flowers on graves that the dead people don't need to look at anymore. I hate to settle for a plastic rose, but I'm thinking I'd probably take one as a last resort, from the last resort. I snicker at my joke as I walk up the driveway and through the first section of markers to my left. Somewhere half-way up the hill, it hits me that this is such a beautiful setting to be dead in. Even though nobody really knows what it's like to be dead, I'm thinking that this is where I'd like to spend eternity, assuming that I'd be aware of my surroundings. Just beautiful.

What do they see? Do they still hear the birdies when the sun comes up? Do they feel people walking over the top of them? Do they smell the flowers that their families leave on top of them? If they do, this is right where I want to be forever, that's for sure. Right here, just not right now.

I walk down every other row, figuring this lets me see more with less walking. The snow isn't that deep yet, just an inch or two, and I move quickly. This takes me further and further up the hill, and the view just gets better and better. This place just takes my breath away! But I still find nothing.

What if you really can't see anything when you're dead? What if you just go away into nothing? What if it doesn't make a bit of difference where they put you, way up here with a view or down by the creek? What if there's nothing you can do anymore to make anybody ever think about you again?

Yeah, right.

So I keep walking across rows and up toward the stone wall at the top of the hill. Nothing. Nearing the top, I turn into a row of identical little gravestones, with another row right above it. I'm suddenly feeling very lucky, the hair on my arms is all tingly, my eyes are wide open, and I'm about as awake as I've ever been in my priceless life. And I suddenly find myself running down the row, without effort, pulled hard by something or other beyond my understanding. And then I see it: a clump of color up ahead. I sprint the rest of the way up the hill like there's a fire in my shorts or maybe there's somebody else up here trying to steal my flower first. But when I get here I find that it's just part of a dumb flag left over from Veteran's Day. I finish my rounds and find nothing. Nothing.

I keep looking on my way back down the hill. Nothing. I stand in front of a stone and begin to wonder if I'll ever find my rose, if this whole idea is just some stupid-ass obsession or something. But I don't have time for doubts – not here, not now – and I do have to find that rose. Period.

I put my heels together in front of the stone, and I do a slow turn all the way around them, careful with my balance, looking at everything I can see for little inspiration. Start, marble, lots of marble, granite, wrought-iron, clean snow, pile of fresh dirt, maple tree, absolutely beautiful panorama, mountains cut by steep ravines, a stand of red pines, more snow, more marble. Stop.

I look back down at the stone I am now facing for the second time and I see: Vernon Fatzinger, Sr., born May 7, 1791, died January 12, 1844, Passengers as ye pass by, As ye are now so once was I, As I am now ye soon shall be, Prepare for Death and follow me, leaning a little to the left, just about half-way back down the hill, next to his wife, Henrietta.

I scratch my chin. C'mon, Vernon. I need some help. Hmmm, nothing. Hhhhmmmmmm, nothing but the best idea I've had in months, that is!

THE PHONE BOOK IN THE booth outside Gus' Gas tells me that Miller's Funeral Parlor is out past the end of Main Street where it turns back into Old State Route 28A headed for Schenevus. With no florist anywhere in town, could there be a better place to find flowers? I take off at a dead run down Main Street before I realize that I could end up going into Miller's feet-first at this pace. Criminy, I wish I had the uni under me, but I know that even a little patch of ice could take out the rest of my ski season and maybe even jeopardize my mission. I don't run very well on my best day, so I catch my breath, slow down, and start to hitchhike. This always seems to work for me.

But nobody seems to want to pick up the Kneissl Kid today. I begin to wonder if it isn't my Tweety glove, what with having to use the thumb on that hand and all. And, man, is it getting cold! I start to skip down the road to generate a little more warmth, and I find that it feels really good. It must be a balance thing, I'm thinking. I bounce up and down with my syncopated gait, the tails of my trench flapping behind me, reversing my lead foot every couple-hundred skips or so. I feel smooth and coordinated, fast and efficient. I don't worry about how I look, or feel like anybody's even looking at me. It feels a lot like being on the uni, but even more like skiing. I skip with grace and energy, dodging this way and that as imaginary moguls appear in front of my imaginary Red Stars. It feels like the Kneissl Kid is hardly touching the ground. I am flying.

God, I could keep this up for hours. But within another twenty minutes or so I see the funeral parlor up ahead and I slow back down to a walk.

Now, what? I'm here, but I need a better plan than just walking on in. I sift through some ideas that just pop into my head and finally pick the one that involves representing myself as a grieving relative who needs a hearse and a quick service. Just brilliant, I'm thinking. I stop myself from walking in long enough to come up with a series of answers that I might have to use if we have to get right down to the details: Dad, heart attack, last night, six-two, two-eighty-five (might need some big pallbearers), sixty-four, two kids, big money on Mom's side, heavy drinker, couple of rum blossoms that might need work, hates suits, never knew what hit him, thank God.

I walk in and quickly hide my Tweety glove in my trench pocket. My other pocket hangs low and jingles like crazy because I've brought plenty of money for this rose, just to be sure. There's nobody around, so I walk into the entry foyer and count the viewing rooms on both sides of the hallway. There are six areas I have to check before I leave. I walk into the first room on the right and find it empty as a burgled grave. Nothing. The room on the opposite side of the hallway has a casket set up on a gurney, either coming or going, I can't tell which. But no flowers. As I come out to check the third room, a man in a black suit, who I figure works here, comes down the stairs and seems pretty surprised to see me.

"May I help you?" he asks. And it hits me that there's nothing else this undertaker could possibly say at this moment. Nothing. I just know that these exact four words are the only ones that could possibly come out of his mouth right here, right now. I get this warm feeling that everything in the entire world is connected, everything written in stone, all planted in even rows and growing according to instructions on the packet, headed in one direction and lined up by somebody, maybe God.

God, I hope so, I say, wiping a fake tear from my eye. I certainly hope so.

So he sits me down for some preliminaries, but I start getting maybe a little overly distraught and nervous as far as his past experience with grieving relatives goes. I pace around and blather a bit using the information I have prepared; just enough so he knows a little about Dad and thinks we've got some real folding money in the family. I try not to jingle the left pocket of my trench taking it off for the man. One thing I've learned, you don't want to be jingling change when you want somebody to think you're holding Jacksons. I've learned that, alright.

Jesum, it's hot in here. I'm wearing my waffle-weave long-sleeve undershirt, a wool shirt, four pages of this week's <u>Huntington What's Up?</u>, another wool shirt, and a sweater which is just about right for being outside. But I guess the dead must like it hot, as Dad would say. I'm starting to sweat from armpit to asshole - as Dad would also say, or would have said - and I maybe divulge this to the undertaker as part of my story, I don't know. He just seems to be getting a little more concerned about me than for me at this point.

The pacing still seems to be my best bet, as it may allow me to move around and check out other rooms. But the undertaker is on his feet and moving with me now. I rant about the indignity of Dad's death, falling into the sink with that donut in his mouth, the hot water running over him and the shards of the carafe for hours after he hit the floor. I cry and moan how Mom, wealthy as she is, will never be able to stand the loss of her life-long soul-mate. I describe how they met in Chemistry class, and how they always talked about their electrons, so small you couldn't even see them, about that intense bond holding them together. I tell him he will definitely have to station one of his men next to the casket to keep her from climbing in at the wake.

Then he asks me where Dad and Mom live, as in street address. I guess this is one area where I haven't prepared as well as I might have, and it stops me cold for a moment. To give myself more time, I go into a little seizure and drop into one of the deeply cushioned chairs that line the room. I jerk my head and roll my eyes up under my lids a couple of times and ask for water. The undertaker trots out to get it, but I'm thinking he might also be headed for the telephone.

As soon as he's out of the room, I'm on my feet sprinting for the hallway where I check out two more rooms as quietly as I can. Nothing. Then I hit paydirt. There's a casket set up for viewing in the fourth room on the left, with a semi-circle of floral arrangements around it. But I hear the undertaker coming back so I make for the chair again. I drop into it sweating like a mausoleum in the middle of July.

"Here," he says, handing me a small glass of water, "Are you okay"

I splash the water on my face and down the front of my

shirt as I drink in great gasping gulps. I hand it back and ask for more. He leaves again and I sprint for the viewing room. I quickly move from arrangement to arrangement, looking for roses. As I paw through the fourth one, I see the undertaker in the doorway.

I begin to cry again, blubbering about the beauty, the metaphoric stillness of flowers at a time of such intense sorrow. He smiles politely and asks me to please sit down and drink the water. I gulp this one down and ask for another, but I can see that he isn't about to leave me alone again this time. So I ask him where the bathroom is located. He takes a deep breath and directs me down the hall and to the right. I walk quickly, holding my knees together to enhance the drama.

Inside the bathroom, I have some quiet time to plan my next move. This is a beautiful bathroom, like in a real house. It's got a claw-foot tub along one wall and a pedestal sink with brass faucets under a window looking out across the valley. There's a toilet in a little stall across from the sink. With the stall door open, you can see for miles. But I also note that there is a wonderful panel on the back of the stall door where I might want to place my next chapter. I drop my pants and pull out my napkins and girlie pen. I sit here thinking, shaking up some snow. Just cracks me up. But I decide that right here, right now is just not the time or the place. So I just note the location on the back of my Table of Contents, then I do my business. I've got more important things to do today, but I'll be back. I've got this feeling. I'll be back, alright.

"Are you alright?" the undertaker asks, knocking gently. I try my best and manage to fanny-burp quite audibly in support of my little story.

Yes, I snuffle. But it's hard, just so hard, wondering immediately if he might take this the wrong way, like some bartenders seem to do in this town.

"Just let me know if you need anything," he says, padding away on the thick carpet.

I quickly finish up some notes for Chapter 7, a scene where all the Kneissl Kid has to do is whistle in this tony ski bar to get more champagne for his sweetheart. They sure know who he is in this place! When the bottle arrives, the bartender sneaks him this single red rose that he puts in the flute in front of her and her eyes go all gooey. He peels off a Franklin from this big wad he always carries, winks large, and waves off the change.

Well, now I feel ready for the rest of my job here. I pocket my napkins and leave the bathroom, carefully closing the door. The undertaker is right there as I emerge all teary eyed from splashing some more water on my face at the sink.

Sir, I begin, there *is* one thing you could do that would make just a world of difference for Mom. Then I begin a story of how Dad gave Mom a single red rose the night she won the coveted Turner Trophy at the annual dinner of the East Utica Rolling Thunder Lanes back in 1961. And how a rose right now, today, might bring her around emotionally, let her send Dad off with a happier face, maybe without having to climb into the casket.

"Where's East Utica?" he asks.

Now I'm thinking this is one detail that maybe should have been a little more local. So I fall back into blubbering for a moment to think this through. He hands me a Kleenex.

As you may have guessed, I say, wiping my eyes again, Dad doesn't live here in Huntington. Then I break down into shoulder-heaving sobs again and hold up a finger that asks him to give me a moment to compose myself. Or anywhere else, anymore, I manage to get out between sobs, before pulling myself back together.

I wipe my eyes and tell him that Dad had always skied at Huntington and had always said he wanted to die here and have his ashes scattered all the way down Freefall on the east ridge. I tell him that we'd like to have the body trans...*Poor Ave! Is this what it's come to? This is just the most pathetic thing*

119

*I've ev…*urn after the cremation. I tell him that I can take care of the scattering, since I ski and I'm maybe the best there ever was, anywhere. Then I mention the rose again.

But the undertaker goes into his soft-spoken spiel about casket choices, several attractive package deals, and the details of picking up the deceased for transport to Huntington. I give him a false address in East Utica, along with excellent directions on how to get there, whom to call so that they can get Mom away from the body long enough to bag it, things like that. And I mention the rose again.

The undertaker says that he's sure I can get a rose – a dozen, even - in Plattekill, which is about an hour away in the wrong direction in a car that I don't have. So I explain that I'm headed straight back to East Utica, that I don't have time to fuck around, 'scuse my French, and that it would mean more than he would ever know to Mom if he could manage to find a single red rose right here, right now in Huntington. I motion toward the hallway and the viewing room beyond, saying that nobody would ever miss one rose, one little piece of a huge floral arrangement, if he could find it in him to remove just one for Mom.

Jesum, this guy is beginning to look bad. He's sweating almost as bad as I am, and he's twitching like a cat hung over a clothesline. He seems to be looking this way and that for help, I guess, and I'm thinking that it's time to wrap things up.

C'mon, just one? I whine, wiping my eyes. For a little old lady who just might not make it through this otherwise?

He shrugs his black-draped shoulders and walks me out of the room, down the hallway. He looks over several of the arrangements before he hears me yell over, Yeah, here's some! He rushes over and removes my hands from the arrangement, shaking his head and carefully extracting a single rose.

How about that one? I ask, pointing to a larger specimen, beautifully mottled in pink around the edges. He twitches again and carefully replaces his rose, extracting the one I promise will bring Mom the most heartwarming memory of Dad and his enduring love for her.

"This is highly irregular," he says as he hands me the prize. We quickly discuss payment, which I wave off as a detail to be dealt with as soon as they get the bag up here. I select the first casket he shows me and I sign a contract, careful to use somebody else's name, and certainly not the Kneissl Kid.

I can barely contain my joy! We walk to the foyer and he hands me my trench from the rack, the left pocket leaving a little divot in the carpet as he misjudges the weight and drops it. I have to cover my mouth with my hand to hide a huge grin just thinking about Marie and how she will gasp when I present her with this incredible rose. I bid adieu, or maybe adios, until tomorrow - as the door closes against my nose.

I carefully insert the rose through a buttonhole in my wool shirt. Then I button my trench over it and head for the road, skipping smoothly back toward downtown Huntington. I skip my fastest back toward town where I need to find a good place to hide the rose: one where it won't wilt or freeze, a place where nobody will find it.

I pass the bridge and the access road to the lodge, heading for Sam's; not to give Marie her present early or anything, but to sit and figure out a hiding place where a rose won't die in the next couple of days. I certainly can't bring it home. It would freeze up, wilt, turn black around the edges, and generally look like a curse instead of a thoughtful present.

I saunter in and wave to Jimmy, who is sticking a fork into a big, old corned beef that has its shoulders sticking out of his cookpot. Marie has left for the day, as she only works breakfast and lunch. I sit at the counter to plan and to drink coffee. It's not beer, but it's not bad.

Coffee? I say.

"Money?" Jimmy says, holding the carafe up and away

from my cup for the moment. "It's only free when you're working."

I reach into my trench pocket, still full of the quarters I no longer need for Marie's present, and drop a large jingling handful on the counter. Jimmy rolls his eyes and pours from two, two-and-a-half feet above the cup, spilling nothing.

"What's with you and loose change, anyway?" he asks, replacing the carafe on the warming plate, "You know, you kinda remind me of loose change."

That's for me to know and you to find out, I say, liltingly. But don't take a chance, sir, 'cause you'll never know the answer.

"That's exactly what I was thinking," he says, wiping his hands on his apron.

I pull up a pucker between two buttons of my trench and peek inside at the rose I have protected all the way from Miller's. Looks good, I'm thinking, maybe saying. Jimmy stares and shakes his head.

"You cold or something?" he asks, "Want to hang that up?"

Actually, I say, I feel pretty good right now. Just a little while ago I was sweating like a waterfall, but that's another story.

"Better left untold," says Jimmy, and I can't argue on that one.

You got a little piece of saran wrap I could borrow? I ask.

"What for?" he asks.

That's for me to..., I begin, but I stop as Jimmy turns and waves off the rest of the comment, working a length of the sticky plastic off the roll. He hands it to me and I begin flattening it out on the counter as Jimmy walks back into the kitchen shaking his head.

With Jimmy gone, the place is now empty and I make my move. I pull five napkins from the dispenser, lay them out on the saran wrap, and pull the rose out of my buttonhole. First, I look around left and right – just like Hoot does - then I lay the rose on the napkins and stop. Magic, I'm thinking, I have to go with the magic.

So I look left and right again, and hide the rose back inside my trench. I wad up the napkins and set them aside, then reach in my pocket for my own napkins. I remove my rubber bands and pull off a couple of cocktail napkins that I must have picked up at The Silver Chicken in Gloversville, covered with notes for chapters I have already published. I take five, which have already become some of the finest prose in any of the little reading rooms of Huntington, and I laugh right out loud thinking about Mom and how she always smacked me for using 'bathroom language'. Jesum, if she could only see me now. She always seemed to catch me doing the bad things, never anything good. Like seeing me when I told Richie Teetsel to go fuck himself, and marching me over to 'scuse my French in front of both him and his mother. I hardly speak any French at all, but she seemed to hear me every time. Or when she hid in my room that night, and caught me reading my letter in Gent magazine. If she could only see me now.

I lay my notes carefully on top of the saran wrap. I reach back into my trench for the rose, and I place it on top of the magic in my napkins. I kiss the rose, then roll up the whole package and head for the Men's Room. Buck's.

I stand here looking around. First I unwrap a corner of the saran and hold it under the faucet, to let the napkins soak up water, just like Mom taught me. I watch as my deepest thoughts, straight out of my girlie pen, fade and go fuzzy on the napkins. Ashes to ashes, rust to rust, I'm thinking, as I stretch the saran back in place and look around for my next idea. There's magic in these napkins, and Marie will see it soon enough.

I slip into the stall, that special stall that I have reserved for my last chapter, whenever that happens. For most people, a men's room stall is not the best place for coming up with ideas, but I'm not most people. So I use what I have found to be my best technique when I need ideas: I put my heels together and turn all the way around. I look at everything around me, which isn't a whole lot in this particular situation. But, as usual, it works like a charm, which it probably is, for me at least.

I remove the top of the toilet tank with care, so that Jimmy doesn't hear a lot of porcelain clanking, so I don't break it or anything. I look down into the dark reservoir, at the flusher contraption hooked up to a big, copper ball floating on top of the water. More magic, I'm thinking...a hiding place that freshens and waters my present. I can't wait to see the look on her face! Oh, Marie!

But I still have a few problems to solve, including how to fix the rose to the inside of the tank so it stays in one place.

Got any duct tape? I ask, the Men's Room door banging home behind me.

"Any what?" Jimmy says, "This is a restaurant, not a hardware store, Jesus."

There's always room for duct tape, I say, winking large, I know you've got some back there somewhere. Just need a little piece to fix my coat.

Jimmy shakes his head some more as he goes back out into the kitchen, returning a moment later with six inches dangling from his finger.

"Here," he says, "Need anything else while I'm up?"

Nope, I say, This'll do just fine. Thanks!

I rush back into the Men's Room with the tape as Jimmy stands there watching, arms akimbo, shaking his head.

I flush the toilet twice and watch the rise and fall of the water. Once I have my finger on the exact level, I flush again and tape the saran-wrapped rose to the inside of the tank next to my knuckle, while the tank refills. Bingo, I say, as the water comes to just over the bottom of the saran wrap. I carefully reposition the top of the tank and turn to leave. I look at the back of the stall door, thinking of how proud I will be when it's finally covered with my last chapter.

"You got something going in there?" Jimmy asks as I exit the Men's Room.

Huh? I say, acting dumb like there's nothing at all going on in there. Nothing.

DECEMBER 24TH

YOU OPEN TOMORROW? I ask, shoveling home fries into my mouth.

"What?" Jimmy says, cocking an ear in my direction and frowning.

You open tomorrow? I repeat, the words garbling their way around a mouthful of potato mush. Repeat, I'm thinking, really ought to mean 'eat again'. As in, every morning here at Sam's I repeat. It's the only meal I ever get to repeat these days. "...ristmas, for Christ's sake," he says, looking at me funny. "I'm sleeping late and drinking egg nog tomorrow. Skiers who don't want to celebrate the birth of the little Lord Jesus can eat at the lodge. Anybody else? Let 'em starve, for all I care."

Well, I'm thinking, I guess I'll be eating at the lodge tomorrow, maybe. I'm not starving in this town, not yet anyway. Marie breezes past my back with two plates of eggs for Table 4 and I swear I get a whiff of her musk right through the heavy smell of Jimmy's home-made sausage. Oh, Marie! She delivers her load and sits down next to me again. She asks me for a cigarette.

Don't smoke, I say.

"You're a lying sack of shit," she says, wrinkling up her brow in the most alluring way.

No, I mean you shouldn't smoke, I say. You'll live longer.

"Yeah, just what I fucking need," she says, "Somebody to remind me about what I shouldn't be doing so I can live a little longer. Now, do I have to ask again?"

I rummage in the right pocket of my trench and find only a crumpled, empty pack that once held my Luckies. I also find a slick of melted butter - courtesy of Mr. Miller's overworked furnace - and somewhere around two dozen quarters.

I'm out, I say, But I've got money in both pockets this morning. This, of course, is a lie. All my money is in one pocket and coated with butter this morning. I walk over to the cigarette machine and insert eight quarters. Several require the push of the next to get through the slot and down the chute. I pull the lever under the Luckies and nothing happens. I kick the machine twice and hear the last couple of sticky quarters fall into place. The Luckies drop into the hopper.

Light? I ask, holding the pack out to Marie with three, exactly three, sticking out like you see in the movies.

"I don't plan to sit here just holding the goddam thing, if that's what you're asking," she says, taking two. I almost tell her all about Andrea and how she never lights her cigarettes, but I figure I don't need her thinking there's another woman in my life, as if *that* were true. Not here, not now. So I rummage in my pants pocket and come up with my lighter. I'm glad it was in my pants because I worry that it might set itself on fire if it got covered with butter like my quarters.

"Thanks," she says, taking a long drag and setting the second cigarette on the counter, out of my reach. "What are you doing for Christmas?" she asks.

Skiing, I say, Like I do every day. What are you doing?

"Oh, I don't know," she says, "Probably watch Mom and Dad get drunk and throw shit around again, like last year."

Well, there you are, I'm thinking. Now we're getting

somewhere. I can probably rule out kids, here anyway, and it doesn't sound like there's a sailor coming into port for the holidays. It's time to make my move.

Well, I say, since I won't see you tomorrow, I've got a little something for you today. I get up and walk into the Men's Room, which puzzles Marie to no end, I bet.

I walk into the stall, carefully remove the top of the tank, and set it across the seat. I reach in for my rose and my hand hits nothing but water. Nothing. A wave of fear flushes over me as my hand frantically stirs up a sea of waves in the tank. I flush the toilet and lean over the tank, watching. And there it is, the duct tape stuck to the bottom of the ball valve, the saran-wrapped rose slowly rising with the water level. I reach under and pull it free.

My heart is beating wildly, skipping beats and throwing in extras, just in case. I peel away the saran wrap and napkins to find that the rose is pretty much as I left it, except for the color. It now has a distinct black tinge around the edges, thanks to the ink from my girlie pen. The little patches of pink that were so beautiful yesterday are now dark black against the red of the rest of the flower. Oh, man!

I toss the saran wrap and dripping napkins into the trash can and I hold the rose under the cold water faucet for a second to see if the black washes off. Nothing. So I shake it off and walk into the next minute of the rest of my life.

Here, I say. Merry Christmas. I go to give her a little kiss on the cheek. She recoils, and I miss, licking her collar.

"You okay?" she asks, eyes wide.

Yeah, I guess, I say, glancing down at the rose in my hand. This is for you.

"Huh," she says, squinting, "Weirdest color I ever saw on a rose. Where'd you get that?"

Well, sweet Crutch of Criminy, I'm thinking. I give her a thoughtful present and she doesn't even say thank you or nothing. Nothing. You'd think that someone would just be a little appreciative and mayb...*Be careful, Ave, let's just calm down a little bit an*...ank you," she says.

Well, that's better, I'm thinking, but I don't really want to tell her about it. So I make up a nice story about a florist guy over in Schoharie county who does this genetic thing on roses to turn them different colors for special occasions and all.

"No shit," she says, squinting at the rose, "Why the black around the edges this time of year?"

So I continue with more of the same, about how they used to have all-black roses way back in the time of the Druids and all, that they used to give them to each other to celebrate the winter solstice, darkest day of the year.

That's all Christmas really is, I say. Just another name for some old winter holiday from waaaaay back.

"No shit," she says, still squinting, "How'd they ever keep them from freezing back then."

Well, here I am unprepared again. To give myself a little thinking time, I fake a coughing fit that sends a half-mouthful of coffee across the counter, onto the stainless steel soda fountain taps in front of me. I cough and sputter, gag and gasp, patting at my chest. Marie reaches behind me, patting my back with the hand holding her cigarette. This clever ruse gives me the time I need, along with a quick peek. Oh, Marie! I continue.

Oh, man, I say. Something went down the wrong pipe on that one. Anyway, they always grew them in these greenhouse-type caves they had where the sun came in through a special hole and hit this little patch of horse shit, 'scuse my French, that they grew them in. The manure kept everything warm and all.

"No shit," she says, still squinting.

Yes, shit! I say, rising on my stool in animation, eyes bulging. 'Scuse my French, but that's exactly how they did it!

I look around for a little help, knowing I have nothing to continue with if Marie doesn't buy my story. Nothing.

Refill? I yell in to Jimmy in the kitchen, hoping to break the story line before she catches on.

"Get it yourself," he yells back, "It's on me, Merry Christmas."

I look over at Marie. Hear that? I say. It's on me, he says. If he'd been in front of me a minute ago, it'd be on him for sure. I laugh uproariously at my excellent joke, hoping it distracts Marie from my tall tale. It does.

"You douchebag," she says, turning to face the counter, taking the last of her first cigarette, reaching for the second. I feel kind of insignificant and alone all of a sudden, but this changes fast when I get a great view down Huntington Gap as she turns toward me for a light. Oh, Marie!

She sits there quietly turning the black-tinged rose around and around in her hand, staring and smoking.

"Just like my life," she says, "All black around the edges."

The place is suddenly real quiet. I find myself very intent on Marie, listening with both ears for her next words, concentrating in the silence until Jimmy bounces a 12-quart pot off the kitchen floor, startling me into knocking over my cup of coffee.

"Fuck you doing?" asks Marie, bounding from her stool and brushing a spreading slick of brown away from her own cup on the counter.

Jimmy's fault, I say, trying to contain the spill, to keep it from rushing over the linoleum cliff onto my stool and the floor below. I wad up a half-dozen napkins and blot like crazy. I toss the brown wad at the trash can, where it hits the wall and separates into six smaller wads, some dropping to the floor, two popping and sizzling on the grilltop. I walk quickly around and pick them up, burning my finger. I walk back around with my middle finger in my mouth up to the second knuckle. Our eyes meet.

"Jesus," says Marie, shaking her head.

Somehow, the reality of the Christmas season, especially for Marie, is not living up to the magic of my expectations. My own life is a bubble of magic that gets bigger every time I look around. She always seems so down and nervous, scary sometimes. The way she talks dirty all the time is probably one of those defense mechanisms that psychology teacher was always talking about back at Marcy State, but that's another story. I guess I just have to try harder to understand her.

I gather up my remaining quarters from the counter and I give Marie the rest of my cigarettes. She needs them more than I do, I guess. I stand, patting Marie on the back. She cringes.

Well, I say, I hope you have a nice holiday tomorrow. I won't see you so, you know, have fun and all.

I lean over to give her a little peck on the cheek, and this time it lands more or less where I aim it, just a little down and off the jawline. Merry Christmas, I say.

"Yeah, you too," Marie says, "Thanks for the flower, I guess."

I head for the door and Marie slumps at the counter, smoking above her coffee, turning the rose in her other hand.

"Jesus," she says.

DECEMBER 25ᵀᴴ

LIKE I ALWAYS say, Christmas is the best day of the year to ski. Nobody around, no noise, nobody to bother you. Just another day in paradise, far as I'm concerned.

Jingle bells, Batman smells, Rob..., I sing as I ski, swooping turns all the way across an empty trail as wide as three superhighways. I stop halfway down and look around. Nothing. Nobody in any direction. Nothing but the silence of nature in the winter, except for a clunking noise from the chairs going over the sheaves on Tower 12 behind a little stand of spruce.

It's so beautiful here. If I had any whiskey I'd be drinking it right now. If I had a sangwich I'd probably pull it out and eat it right here, right now. If I had a girlfriend, one who could ski anyway, I'd probably have her with me. It's just so perfect. How could life be any better?

It seems like things are really happening for me, that today is another turning point in my life. Christmas, God's very own birthday, the next day of the rest of my life. And life is good. Right here, right now.

I haven't gotten any presents yet, and I don't really expect any. I already took care of the one present I planned to give anybody. But life's a present, far as I'm concerned. Every day since I arrived here I've been getting presents. One after the other, hand over fist.

Today I will probably be hungry, so I've decided to make it a fasting day, like some of the other whacked-out religions do. I didn't get my breakfast at Sam's today, but I have some left-over butter I can scrape out of my trench pocket. And I have a half-dozen crackers from today's condiment bar. That would take the edge off, but I'm thinking I might just go all day without anything but water.

It's not like I'm religious or anything. I couldn't tell you much about Jesum at all, like his middle name or that kind of stuff. To me, he's just another God, like Buddha or Mohammed Ali, something like that. I like him and all, but I don't bow down in front of him or anything.

I wonder if Andrea called her kids this morning. It's what, two, three hours different out there? Maybe she has a set time she calls them on holidays like this. Or maybe she doesn't call them at all, I don't know. Must be tough having kids. I know I don't have any. But that's another story and I'm not talking.

"HOLY SHIT, IT'S THE KNEISSL Kid," yells Hoot as I approach the top of the T-Bar, my apartment. He does this little hootchy-kootchy dance as I hit the top of the ramp and pull the bar out from under my legs. I hold the long bar out in front of me for a second with two hands, with my eyes all bulged out and all, pretending again like I can't let go or something. Hoot laughs like he's never going to stop.

"Merry Christmas," Hoot yells once he stops laughing, "How was church this morning?"

I don't know, I say. Took too long opening my presents, never got there.

"Here," says Hoot, reaching into the shack, "I got one last night." He cranes his neck in all directions, then pulls out the biggest bottle of whiskey I ever saw, anywhere. It's got to be a gallon, I'm thinking.

How'd you get that one up here? I ask.

"It's Christmas," he says, "Nobody gives a shit today." He uncaps the bottle, lays it into the crook of his elbow, and raises it for a couple of glugs. "Aaaahhh," he says, handing it to me.

I imitate Hoot's elbow-cradling technique and hoist the huge bottle to my mouth. It glugs way faster than I expect and I end up coughing half of it back up my windpipe.

"Oh, man," Hoot moans, "You don't wanna waste bad whiskey like that."

Sorry, I say, finally mastering the method and taking four big glugs, barely changing the level in the bottle. I hand it back to Hoot, with two hands.

"So, what's the Kneissl Kid got on tap for today?" asks Hoot, raising an eyebrow, "Prime rib up at the Horizon House, a little lobster down at the Troubadour?"

Nah, I'm still kicked out, I say. Besides, I'm fasting today, you know, for religious reasons.

Well, I thought Hoot was laughing pretty hard when I made like I couldn't get off the T-Bar, but that was nothing. Now he's on the ground on his back like a flipped turtle, laughing his butt off, his arms and legs flailing in the air. Man, this guy knows how to have fun, I'm thinking. Then again, maybe this wasn't his first whiskey of the day, either. Merry Christmas, Hoot.

ANDREA STANDS THERE LOOKING DOWN at me, her coat still buttoned to the throat. "First you wake me up before noon, you make me wait in the laundromat while you get quarters out of some stupid machine, then you make me walk up to the ski lodge for some kind of surprise on Christmas day," she says, "Now you want to make me go inside the goddam men's room? I ain't going in there if you got something kinky in mind. What do you need quarters for in there, anyway?"

No, just take my word, I say, pulling off my left boot on the bench next to the door. Just sit down and put these on.

"You want to do it barefoot in the men's room with me wearing your boots? You don't think that's kinky?" she says. "Never done anything like that before, ever."

All I'm going to do is watch, I say.

"I ain't doing anything kinky for you to watch, either. Not in there, not on Christmas day, no way," she says.

Don't worry, I say. All you're going to do is some reading.

So I pull off her pumps and I shove her little feet into my size 12s. I look around first, like Hoot does, then I pull Andrea into the men's room, my finger in front of my lips to keep her quiet. I shove her into the first stall and tell her to sit down, shut up, and read.

I stand here in my stocking feet, soaking up God knows what, watching for intruders. But being Christmas, there are few people on the mountain and even fewer needing a seat in a men's room stall this afternoon. I see my big boots under the stall door with pink stretch pants coming out of them.

After a good ten minutes, Andrea asks if I might have anything else for her. I laugh and say no, not here and now, but there's more where that came from.

Don't forget to flush, I tell her, smirking at my joke.

"I would if I could get it off the door," she says, "No offense."

So, what do you think? I ask, once we are back outside on the bench, trading shoes again.

"I'm really not sure what to say," she says, pulling a heel back into the tightness of her pump. "Either you're nuts and it's a piece of shit, or you're some kind of genius and it's that avant garde crap. I don't understand that new stuff, anyway. Give me a good Danielle Steele, something easy with at least one good fuck every couple of pages."

I guess I haven't gotten that far yet, I say. The Kneissl Kid is a virgin, you know, and needs a real special girl for doing something like that.

"A what?" she blurts out, eyes wide and growing wider.

A virgin? I say, wondering if this is what she's wondering about.

"Whoa," she says. "Holy shit."

What? I ask.

"First you bring me up to a ski lodge on Christmas day, then you take me in the men's room to read some kind of graffiti, then you tell me you're a virgin? Is this my present?" she asks, eyes ablaze.

It's not the writer, it's just a character, I say. But I'm not sure you're ready for the rest of it today. When I'm done you can read the whole story.

"I am not going in the rest of the men's rooms all over town to read some story," she says, huffing. "How about we go back over to my place and you can tell me the whole thing, all night long, take as long as you want."

I shudder and look away.

"What?" she says, "Did I insult the artiste or are you just scared of getting your silver polished?"

My what? I ask.

"Never mind," she says, "Can you buy me a drink, at least?"

We walk upstairs to the bar where one of the four customers leers at Andrea through bloodshot eyes, winking at me with one of them. I wink back and we sit down. Andrea says hello, calling him Eddie. He winks at me again and makes some kind of signal or something with his hand. I shrug my shoulders at him since I have no idea what he means by it.

Anyway, Andrea has a Manhattan and I have a Utica Club. Now, that's a beer! She nurses her hard stuff, I chug my beer and signal for another. Now, there's a hand signal I can understand. I haul out a pile of quarters and line them up in stacks of four in front of me. The bartender takes five-and-a-half stacks and rolls his eyes.

"I kind of thought you had asked me up here to give me a present, you know, being Christmas and all," she says, sipping, looking away.

Huh, I say. I'm kind of on a bad roll with presents right at this point. Sorry.

"That's okay," she says, patting me on the back of the head. "You probably still don't want to give me the only present I'm looking for anyway. And I guess I don't blame you for that."

Right now, I haven't got a whole lot of things, especially things I can give away, I say. Once I'm dead, that'll change, though.

"Huh?" she says, cocking her head my way.

Well, it's like Van Gogh and these guys who throw together great masterpieces that go nowhere, that nobody understands, I say. At least, not until they're dead and gone.

"You're not thinking about..."

Nah," I say, "I'm going nowhere fast, and I just love what life is throwing my way these days. It's just that someday when I do end up dead with nothing but butter in my trench coat pockets, I'll want to have something more. Something that I can keep on giving people, like talking back from beyond the grave, you know.

"Yeah, so?" she says, sipping at the Manhattan.

So, I gave you something, a present, a little glimpse of what I'll have for real some day, I say, beaming.

"What, graffiti?" she asks.

You only saw Chapter Three, I say. You need to see the whole arc of the story before you say things like that.

"So you got animals coming in next?" she asks.

Very, very funny, I say. Merry Christmas anyway. I chug my beer and get ready to go, to go nowhere.

"You don't need to write on bathroom walls to talk to people from under the dirt," she says, "My Daddy talks to me all the time, tells me I'm a whore."

Andrea, you know you're not a whore, I say, throwing my arm around her shoulders, squeezing.

"Yeah? Well, I can prove you wrong in less time than it takes to…*Oooh, Ave, What, are you blind? Just look at her, Can't you see what she's af*…turn you over like a hot pancake," she says, "Christmas or no Christmas."

Well, I say. You'll never prove it to me.

"Yeah, I know," she says, turning to the bar, leaning in on her elbows again.

I just need to make sure there's something out there, I say. Something I can say is mine, before I disappear. But I don't plan on that anytime soon, don't worry.

"Well, I guess there's nothing scarier than thinking nobody's gonna remember you when you're dead," she says. "At least my Daddy has somebody who remembers, who still listens to him every day."

I know just what you mean, I say, rolling my eyes.

God, I'm thinking, it must be awful to have your Daddy calling you names after he's dead. I won't be doing that when I'm dead. Not me. Not with a story that speaks for itself, I won't. And especially without any kids.

You want to read the rest? I ask. I have seven chapters done and another ready to go.

"I'll pass," she says, "At least until I can read it without pulling my pants down."

DECEMBER 31ˢᵀ

TONIGHT THE WEST side of the mountain is open for night skiing and I have to be extra careful about getting caught coming and going from my apartment. New Year's Eve, new beginnings, new opportunities. Even though my life is richer than it's ever been, I know that even better things will be happening for me. As long as I don't get caught tonight, that is.

Hoot has been real nice about his whiskey. He doesn't seem to care if I drink it as long as I let him know and I get him some more before too long. Great guy, that Hoot. Says he might take me home some night for a meal if I can stand his Mom's cooking. He says it sucks, but I can't imagine it's worse than crackers and ketchup. But maybe. But for now, I just take a couple good tugs on the whiskey before my tray ride to the bottom, into town to maybe spend the rest of my quarters.

New Year's Eve is a busy time in the Huntington bars. I figure I'll just hit a few, spend all my money, maybe have a little drink with Andrea. I know she'll be out tonight, somewhere. If it gets real crowded and crazy I might even be able to slip back into the Troubadour. If I get really lucky - I mean really, really lucky - I might even run into Marie out here somewhere. Oh, Marie!

I wish I could ride my uni around barhopping tonight. This particular night always feels like a unicycle night for some reason. Too dangerous, though, even for me. It feels like I'm barely making any progress sometimes when I walk into town. Riding is faster and a lot cooler.

I've untaped this week's *Huntington What's Up?* from around my torso for the trip into town. It's definitely not as warm, but I won't get those funny looks when I take off my trench in the Klondike. What's the big deal, anyway? Nylon or newsprint? They both work and you just have to make that choice, is all. And when that choice involves twenty bucks or so, don't even ask.

You'd never believe the Klondike is the same place I walked in that first night here in Huntington. It is filled to the walls with people in every kind of clothing you could imagine. I mean, my newsprint probably wouldn't stand out at all. The place is full of skiers, ski patrol, snowmakers, Yellowjackets, just-plain townies, guys in suits, one woman in shorts, tight dresses, short dresses, long gowns, Carhartts, granny dresses, party hats, streamers, crepe paper, and one guy in Groucho glasses. It's wild, and I fit right in.

The noise is so bad I can't seem to get the bartender's attention. I wave, whistle, jump up and down, sway sideways, yell, swing my hat around, and wonder why. Maybe he remembers me from the first time I came in. I guess I might have been a little impolite or something, I don't know. Finally, I get his attention when he brings a beer to the guy standing next to me. I grab his sleeve as he sets the beer down and he stops instantly. I mean, every muscle in his body stops moving as he slowly looks up to my eyes and then back down to the sleeve in my hand. When he looks back up, I ask him for a beer - a real beer, not that flat piss from Milwaukee. He still doesn't move, so I let go so he can get me my beer.

Is it too much to ask for? All I want is a beer? I ask, some ten minutes later.

"Oh, yeah," he says, "You're the guy that likes to grab hold of my arm when I'm working. The guy who likes to ride that wheelie thing around my bar, knocking over chairs. But I suppose I can find you a beer somewhere around here."

Criminy, I'm thinking, this guy's a real cut-up. I stand here for another five minutes or so getting jostled by drunk snowmakers before he shows up again after getting drinks for most everybody else in the bar.

"Here," he says, "Two bucks."

This is a Bud, I say. I thought I ordered a beer, a UC.

"Two bucks," he says, holding out his hand, "And don't touch the sleeve this time."

Well, I figure it's too noisy to argue with him and he's probably too busy to discuss it anyway. Some people. I just can't understand sometimes. I was always taught that bartenders have to be good listeners. This guy? Oh, man! I probably should have ordered a half-dozen. Might never get another around here.

I back up carefully so as not to spill my beer, and I slop a couple of other people's beers all over my back. Either that or they maybe poured them on me, I don't know. It's crowded and anything can happen, I guess. I shoulder my way through the crowd looking for anyone I know, and I see a number of people I recognize, people who seem to recognize me, but nobody I can say that I know. But I'm not going anywhere until I know that Marie is definitely not here. I look all around, thinking about what to do if she's with a husband or some other guy. I guess I'd just stand there and put the love stare on her, see what she does. I can't just pull her away from a table if she's got a date or anything, but I bet there's something I could do to get her attention. But I guess I don't have to because she's just not in here.

I'm also looking for Andrea, kind of as a consolation prize, but I'm not sure I need the kind of consolation she seems to prize. She's pretty hot for her age, I guess, but I can't get past her age when it comes to getting hot. She's like a big sister now, and I don't need any of that going on.

Two Yellowjackets are sitting at the table next to the cigarette machine with three babes just hanging all over them. I figure the third one is probably waiting for her own personal Yellowjacket who is late getting here. The Jacks are both European, maybe French. Barnacre's got this thing for European instructors, I guess. And they have this thing for porking as many American babes as humanly possible while they're over here teaching on their green cards. It's really disgusting, if you ask me. I mean, all Hoot does is help them up by the titties when they fall down, which is actually a pretty nice thing to do. These guys stare into their eyes and make all these stupid promises in their garbled, half-English European, just trying to get into their pants, leave them with a screaming, little bastard in dirty-ass diapers and just fly on back to Eu...*you're doing it again, Ave. This is just the type of thing that gets you in trouble, remember? Every time you get all worked up about some little thing like this, you start acti*...ingle one of them, I would.

But instead, I decide to join them.

Buck, Buck Avery, I say, extending my hand out to the closest Jack, the one with the crew cut. But then I realize they both have crew cuts, which doesn't surprise me, I guess. Mind if I join you?

Well, the one Jack says something in European to the other and they both laugh, then he looks up at me and pulls out the empty chair, furiously wiping off some invisible dust with the back of his hand. That's so nice, I'm thinking, maybe I've got these guys figured wrong. I sit down and we introduce ourselves all the way around the table: Hansi, Crystal, Tawny, Karl, and Destiny. And, man, are these girls ever pretty!

So, I ask, looking at Destiny in particular, How have you been doing on the slopes this weekend?

This sets off a series of guffaws among the women and Hansi, who whispers something to Karl, who then laughs as well. Well, I'm thinking, maybe she's not doing so well. She certainly isn't wearing her ski boots, that's for sure.

"Never tried it and never will," she says, winking at Hansi, "Break one of these legs, I go totally broke in no time."

So I look down at her legs, which is what pretty much anybody would do under the circumstances, and I see that they are long, lean, covered in fishnet, and quite muscular. Just right for skiing, I'm thinking.

Don't sell yourself short, I say. Those legs were custom-made for skiing, if you ask me. The other two girls laugh like chipmunks. I wave at the waitress and hold up my empty beer, or at least what they call beer in this place. Utica Club this time, I yell. Three of them, if you please. I pull out a handful of quarters and line them up in stacks of four.

I turn to Karl and ask if he is teaching the other two to ski. He looks puzzled until Hansi whispers something and makes him laugh just like the girls.

"He says he wants to teach them a few things, but plans to learn a lot from them, too," says Hansi, winking at Destiny.

The waitress brings my beers, squeezing her way through the crowd next to the table. Karl grabs her around the waist, pretending to bite her in the butt. Hansi howls with laughter and makes a gesture over the table that looks like he wants to buy a round for all of us. Then Karl makes this other gesture and the waitress smacks him in the side of the crew cut. He makes this google-eyed face and I laugh just like the rest of them. Hansi waves a ten-dollar bill at her as she sashays her way toward the bar with my handful of quarters.

"What do you do?" asks Tawny, looking at me and taking a drag on her cigarette.

I ski. I say, And I write.

Hansi whispers something to Karl who laughs even harder than before. He looks over at me real intently, then looks back at Hansi again, his shoulders kind of shaking.

"Are you the Kneissl Kid?" asks Hansi.

"The who?" asks Tawny.

You're looking at him, I say, beaming with pride that a European, maybe from France, actually recognizes me.

They're all looking at me now, and, man, do I feel important! I wonder how the word got all the way over to Europe, maybe France, and whether it has anything to do with my novel. Maybe he's been inside Gus's Gas, who knows?

Hansi whispers something to Karl who looks at me again and turns away with some kind of coughing fit, I guess. I know how that is, so I pat him on the back. The others laugh again and my beers get to sloshing around as their knees bounce up and down underneath the table. It's starting to get pretty raucous here on the last night of the decade. It certainly looks like I picked a great place to party this year!

"So, you ski Kneissls?" Hansi asks, "My father, he ski on them many, many years ago."

Oh, yeah. I say, And if there's an extra yellow jacket hanging around anywhere, I'm the man to fill it.

Hansi whispers something in European to Karl, who now looks over at me with a sneer on his face. He says something else in European and Hansi pats him on the back, laughing and saying something I can't understand. But it gives me an idea and I pull out my napkins to take some notes on where I go next with my novel.

"Let me see that," says Crystal, grabbing at my girlie pen. I hold it out in front of her and shake it. The whole table erupts into laughter as the snow falls and the little titties spin around. I laugh right along with them.

"Where did you ever find that?" Tawny asks, still laughing, wiping tears off her face.

I got it in a little store right next door to Mr. Buck's Pharmacy in Utica, I say. This is the only thing I would ever buy in that kind of place, though.

"I used to work in Utica," says Tawny, "You from up there?"

Oh, yeah, I say. Can't you tell?

"Actually, yeah, I can see that," she says.

Where did you work? I ask, thinking retail, waitressing, maybe secretarial work somewhere.

"I used to dance at The Glass Slipper," she says, closing her eyes, shimmying her shoulders to the beat of something unrecognizable coming through the jukebox across the room.

"Me, too," says Destiny, "For a while, at least. I used to do the club circuit from Buffalo around to Albany, and down the river to Newburgh."

No shit? I say. 'Scuse my French, but this is like old home week all of a sudden.

Hansi whispers something to Karl, who laughs and does a little hootchie-kootchie in his chair and throws Destiny a little kiss across the table. I figure she must be his girlfriend and Hansi is sweet on Crystal. Now, that leaves Tawny for me, far as I can see. So I scooch my chair over a little closer and throw my arm around her. I ask her if she's a professional dancer too.

"Hell, no," she says, "I started right out in the business, never needed anything like that. Not with these puppies." She makes that little gesture with both hands in front of her, like Hoot telling me about the arthritis.

You take anything for that? I ask. Aspirin works pretty good.

"For what?" she asks, looking pretty confused, "Can't get high on that, can you?"

Well, now I'm the one who's confused. I scribble a couple of quick notes to keep things fresh in my mind as the others at the table stare at me with funny looks on their faces. I'm thinking that pretty soon I'd better let them in on what I'm doing here.

Well, anyway, I say, my job is skiing and writing stories, and I don't need to take anything anymore. Used to, though, but I'm not talking.

Everyone seems to be leaning in listening to me now. It's pretty cool being the center of attention every once in awhile. I sit here with a grin on my face that I probably couldn't wipe off if one of them died in front of me. So I decide to reel them in.

You know, I've got a piece of my novel right here, if you're interested. Hansi whispers something to Karl and the girls are giggling again. They're looking at me like I've got a briefcase full of paper or something. That's funny, since the only paper I have with me is my napkins.

"Let me see that pen again," says Tawny, reaching across the table.

Look with your eyes, not with your hands, I say in sing-song fashion, shaking up some snow for her. Crack me up. If you want, I can prove that it works. I can show two of you, at least. Right here, right now.

I look back and forth between Hansi and Karl, the only two at the table who are qualified to read my work at the moment. Turns out that only Hansi is really qualified, since Karl seems to have a little problem with his English. But he does seem to understand a little sign language, so I just stand up and motion for the two of them to follow.

C'mon, guys, I say. I've got something to show you.

Well, Karl looks puzzled and Hansi looks like he thinks I'm bluffing or something. So I motion again and start squeezing my way through the crowd toward the men's room. They follow, with Hansi now yelling something in Karl's ear because of the noise.

Karl is shaking his head as I open the men's room door and beckon them in. He and Hansi have a pretty animated discussion in European as I motion again. They follow, shaking their heads. I head for the stall next to the sink and motion for them to follow.

Well, this seems to really get Karl going, talking a mile-a-minute and making that hand gesture thing he was doing back at the table. Hansi laughs and starts pulling him in behind me. We squeeze into the booth, with Karl getting pushed in between the toilet and the partition so I can finally get the door closed. He is definitely not a happy pappy right at the moment.

Ta daaaah! I say, swinging my arm around as best I can toward the writing on the back of the door. Hansi cranes his head around my shoulder and I duck a little so he has room to read. I see his lips moving as he looks at my work so I know he's into it. I just stand here, all squished up against Karl and the toilet tank, smiling like the Mona Lisa.

Well, Karl starts barking something loud, and a little impolite from what I can gather, but Hansi keeps reading and waves a hand behind his back to shut him up. When he's done, he sort of pushes my head down and to the side so that Karl can get a better look, talking away in European. Then they both start laughing so hard that none of us can move out of each other's way.

"Kneissl Kid!" yells Hansi, "Kneissl Kid!"

"Kuh-nice-ll Keed!" yells Karl, his back slumping down against the partition, tears running down his face.

"Everything all right in there?" someone asks, feet visible below the stall door.

Oh, yeah, I say. Oh, yeah!

Back at the table, the girls are arguing with a couple of country-looking boys who want to sit down in our seats, I guess. Hansi tells them to get lost and Karl does this hand signal thing with a thumb gesturing back over his left shoulder. They leave when Karl starts screaming away in European and Hansi grabs him from behind, holding his arms to his side.

"So," says Tawny, "Did you all have fun in there?

"Oh, yeah," says Hansi, "*Oh*, yeah!".

"Kuh-nice-ll Keed," Karl yells, trying to get me up standing on my chair to be recognized by the crowd, "Kuh-nice-ll Keed! You funny man, funny man."

It's just great to hear this after being away from the boards for over a year. I think about how I could have probably gotten to right here, right now, that much earlier if I hadn't given Marcy State a shot. With Mom all over me about it, I hardly had a choice. But, when you try and something just doesn't work out, you just leave, right? Why keep doing something that doesn't move you forward. Just move on. I don't need any more of that to do what I do.

The guys both stand up at this point and put on their yellow jackets. The girls put their heads together and whisper something before getting up after them. I ask, So, where are we going next?

"We," says Hansi, winking large and pointing to everybody, one after the other, except me, "We are going home to dance."

Well, Jesum Crow, I'm thinking, I can dance with the best of them. Why, back in Utica, they called me King of the Jerk because, man, could I ever swing it! I could twist and shimmy with the be...*tter than that, Ave, you've just got to do a little better than that. Why, these people, Ave? Why? I don't understand why you always have to pick out the...*best there ever was, anywhere. Where? Where'd they go? Oh, shit, 'scuse my French.

So, I pull out my pocket watch and check the time. Eleven thirty-one. I've got to get hold of Andrea, I've got to get hold of Andrea, I say, to no one in particular, especially now that there's nobody left at the table to listen anymore. I'm definitely drunk by now and I really don't have to ring in the New Year, not with it ringing pretty loud inside my head already. I stagger a little more than usual as I head for the door, but I do just fine, just fine. It's good that I have my uni stashed away, because I know I'd try to ride it home. Riding drunk on a uni isn't a good idea, though, even when you are the best there ever was.

I walk down Main Street toward the Huntington access road singing Old Lang's Sign at the top of my lungs. It's about quarter-to-twelve and I'll be home by midnight. I'll have a little snack, tug on Hoot's whiskey a couple times, then maybe a couple more, and go to bed early. I can see Andrea some other day.

THERE SEEMS TO BE A whole lot of activity just down the creek when I cross the bridge, and I need to make sure nobody sees me coming up toward the T-Bar. I take the short cut along the edge of the parking lot, skirting the treeline to stay out of sight. There are flashing lights and a bunch of cars at the end of the lot where the creek runs past it. Looks like there might have been a fire or something. I'll be really pissed off if something happened to the T-Bar and I have to climb all the way home tonight.

So I make my way as close as I can without getting recognized and sit just inside the treeline on an old oil drum. I sit and watch but I can't really make anything out. I could just saunter up and ask what's going on, but somebody might ask what I'm doing up here at the crack of the new year. I mean it might be some kind of burglary and they might want to give me the old third degree on it. Since I haven't done anything, I'd be fine with that, but I don't want to give them any reason to snoop around and maybe find my stuff hidden up in Hoot's lift shack.

So I sit and wait. After a pretty long while - and I know it's after midnight because I've already heard a bunch of screaming and firecrackers from down in town somewhere - the last two cars leave and everything is quiet again. I wait another ten minutes to make sure nobody's still here, then I skirt the parking lot to the bottom of the T-Bar.

Everything looks normal. Nobody around, no burnt-down lift shack, everything just quiet and peaceful. I reach in through the window, hit the start button, and the bullwheel starts turning, sending T-Bars around and up the hill like any other night. So I reach under the shack until I feel my tray stashed behind the cinderblock, same as always. I set up and grab a bar. Next thing I know I'm halfway up the liftline in the dark with T-Bars swinging over my head, pawing around in the dark for my tray. I find it after awhile and try standing on the tray since I have to stretch a bit to catch a bar way up over my head. This is a bad idea and I fall again. I've never had this problem before. So I hold the tray against my butt with one hand and jump to grab a bar with the other. I guess this works better because next thing I know I'm home with the lift turned off again. All my stuff is right where I left it and nobody has touched Hoot's whiskey. Home again, home again, jiggedy-jig, I'm thinking, as I tug three times on the huge bottle. Happy New Year, Buck!

PART TWO

JANUARY 1ˢᵀ

REALLY DON'T THINK I was all that drunk last night, but this tray ride is maybe the worst I've had since moving into my apartment. Whoa! The bumps were never this big. I lose my stomach on each one, just like when Dad used to drive fast over the railroad tracks on the way to the zoo. Oh, man! I'll make it to Sam's on time as long as I don't have to, as long as, whoa, whoa, have to pu...*You be careful, Ave. You've got to wear those clothes to work, and you know you should have changed out of them before going to bed last ni...*I guess that's over. I can just rub some snow on this spot on my trench, maybe my pant leg. Rub hard, and the snow will dry right away once I'm in Sam's. Get most of it out and it shouldn't smell a bit.

The walk never seemed this long before. The hill seems steeper and slipperier today for some reason. I see the bridge at the bottom, but it doesn't seem to be getting any closer. And, man, am I ever hungry! My head is banging and I may just have to take the day off and not ski today. I have to work though, if I want to eat. And I really need to eat something this morning. Especially now.

Well, would you look at that. There's Officer Cotterly drinking coffee and working on his first dozen in the cruiser already. If I remember right, he was up at the mountain pretty late last night with whatever it was he had going on.

Either being a country cop is a fun job or he takes it way too seriously. I mean, he probably got less sleep than I did and I'm pretty green after only four hours myself. He might not have been quite as drunk, though, driving the cruiser and all. All I know is, I certainly need more than donuts today.

I'm only fifteen minutes late, which I consider to be a real accomplishment this morning. Jimmy usually makes a big deal about responsibility and all when I'm late, but he's cool about it this morning. Maybe he's too hung over to care, I don't know.

It feels like it takes me twice as long to stack my chairs and mop my floor this morning, and maybe it does. I put my third cup of coffee on the end of the counter and take gulps every time I get near it. It's not beer, but it's not bad, especially this morning. I finish mopping and look back over my work, which must have been pretty sloppy from the looks of the puddles and streaks under the tables. I figure Jimmy won't see a thing as soon as I get these chairs back down. Now, as long as nobody slips and falls, I'll be eating in no time.

Marie barges in looking pretty good after the night on the town that I'm not even sure she had last night. I didn't see her out anywhere, but I figure any woman without a man and without kids just has to be out on New Year's Eve. Then again, I have no idea about the man or the kids, when you get right down to it. Someday I'll just have to ask her.

She slinks her way out of her coat, stretching her blouse over her curves real nicely this morning. As soon as I see her take down the apron from the shelf I sprint around toward the kitchen door with my broom where I can line her up with the window. I'm pretty sure she won't notice, but I sure will. My next move, like every morning, will be to take my special seat at the counter and put something like a wet dishrag on the stool to my left. Man, it's tough being in love!

Jimmy, I yell. How about a dozen or so of those pancakes you make back there?

"How about I just pour the batter on your plate and give you a spoon," he says.

I don't know, I say. Might work better in a big glass with a straw.

"Your call," he says, bringing out a large plastic pitcher with streaks of white down the sides.

I think I'd prefer them cooked this morning, I say, my stomach doing squat thrusts and jumping jacks under my belt.

"Fine," says Jimmy, "But don't look for a dozen of them."

All you can eat, I say. Remember?

"Today, we got butter on the menu," he says, "All you want."

Got any take-out? I ask, suddenly thinking I should have looked around first before this one.

"You tell me," Jimmy says, staring.

Well, I'm thinking maybe he's started counting the patties. I'll just have to be a little more nonchalant about it from now on. How about coffee? I ask. I'll take some of that with me.

But first I've got to see if there's anything happening down Huntington Gap this morning. I sit hunched and waiting as Marie lights her cigarette and shakes out the match. She takes a drag and holds it between two fingers of the hand cradling her head as she leans on the counter. I'd be worried about lighting up my hair, if I were her. Then I see my opportunity.

Please pass the sugar, I say, watching for the pucker as she leans to reach the dispenser. She stretches and the glorious vista opens up between buttons two and three: a glimpse of white lace with a slight roll of belly going taut as she pulls the dispenser toward me.

"Since when do you use sugar?" she asks.

I don't know, I say. It's good to try new things every once

in a while, don't you think? You know, with the new year, and all.

Since I've never used sugar, I'm not real good at the routine, especially with a touch of the hangover, I guess. But I've watched others do it, and it seems like I can do just about anything I try these days. So I hold my spoon out over the cup and pour the sugar into it and over it just like I've seen the other skiers do. I do it twice, then twice more, because that's what they all seem to do. I lean on my elbow and stir the cup nonchalantly, like I see other people do, hoping for another peek down the Gap. Then I lift the cup and chug most of it at once, Buck-style.

Well, this may not have been such a good idea, I'm thinking. It's another of those situations where I probably should have looked around first, like Hoot does, instead of afterwards - like now. I look right and left as my first swallow gets stuck about halfway down my throat, my mouth still bulging with the rest of the syrupy mix. I can't breathe, I feel something warm crawling in the back of my nose, and I wish I could go back in time a few seconds to before I asked Marie for the sugar.

But time stands still, just like they say it does in these situations. And everything goes into slow motion. Marie just sits there looking into her cup, which is certainly better than having her looking at me right now. I see the second hand on Jimmy's clock stuck on the 5 for way too long before clicking real slowly toward the bottom of the dial. I don't actually see my life passing before my eyes or anything, but I do see myself rolling off a cafeteria tray in a blur of snow, grabbing myself around the belly with both arms.

Time is flowing like a glacier, and I see that there are lots of alternatives. But most of them involve doing a few things differently before taking the whole cup at once. I could have just poured in the cream and not been so intent on Marie's... *So, what's next, Ave? A little impulsive again, don't you think?*

Was there really any reason to put on such a perfor... Man, this tastes bad!.

Anyway, it's time to deal with this, so I slowly slide off the stool and saunter - careful not to run or stumble into anything - toward the men's room door, easy to find because my name's on it. I scratch my head, and normally I would yawn at this point to look even more nonchalant. But my mouth is full and my throat has this bulge of sickening sweetness going up and down, up and down like that fake bird Dad used to perch on the rim of his beer glass; the one that just kept on bobbing and drinking, bobbing and...each step feels like I'm in some dream where I've got a lion or something chasing me and my feet are glued to the floor, my legs rooted like finely-tuned tree trunks. I reach for the door handle and watch my hand inch its way through the distance. The hinges sound like a muffled elephant call as they squeak open.

Then I'm in the stall releasing my mouthful, and time returns to normal, or as close as it gets for me, I guess. Three more heaves and I'm ready for some real coffee this time. As I turn around and reach for the barrel bolt on the stall door, I can't help noticing again that this will be one great page for the last chapter of my story, whenever that is.

Marie looks at me funny when I walk back to my seat at the counter, normal-speed this time. "Why'd you run in there so fast," she asks.

I had a little tickle in my throat, I say, instead of telling her how my little ruse to get a quick look at her tittie had backfired so badly. But I'm back now. What did you do last night?

"Watched Dick Clark's bad hair on TV," she says, sipping her coffee like a civilized person.

Watch the ball drop? I ask, just for conversation.

"No balls to drop or do anything else with in my house," she says, and I wonder if she's talking French or sports. Though a lot of times, the two are pretty much intertwined, especially in bars. That was my big problem, one of them anyway, when I bartended in Utica. These guys would come in all fired up about the Oilers, Giants, or the Saints, and all I could do was agree with them. How about them Yanks? Fuckin A, 'scuse my French. I couldn't tell you what sport most of these guys even play. It's all about television and the big companies that own people, treat them just like sla…*Ave, quite an interesting little sidetrack this time, Ave. You've really got to start thinking about how…*ours and hours at a time, might as well just shit or go blind," she says, and I have pretty much no idea what she's been talking about.

Yeah, I guess, I say.

"Huh?" she says, arching her eyebrows and turning to look right at me. But Jimmy is coming through the kitchen door with a big pot of soup for the day, and it gives me the opportunity to get out of this one with a little nonchalance.

What's cooking, Boss? I ask, leaning over the counter as he brings the steaming cauldron to the grilltop.

"New Year's Stew," he says, "Full of stupid resolutions that last a couple days before going bad. Want some?"

I got my own resolutions, I say, glancing over at Marie in spite of myself. Got a little project to finish up here and there.

"You got a project?" Marie asks. "You're going to actually do something?"

Well, this is a real stinger, coming from Marie, but it's maybe like those double-sided swords they talk about. On the one side, she sounds like she's criticizing me, my lack of plans, my way of doing things. On the other side, though, I'm thinking she might be challenging me to pick her up or something. But since I still don't know if there's a big husband or crazy boyfriend involved in all this, I'm not stepping in that just yet. I'll just up and ask her someday. Someday.

Marie gets up and walks into the kitchen, maybe because I've stopped talking. I didn't hear the bell or anything. But she'll be back. Oh, yeah. She'll be back.

160

JANUARY 3RD

CUP FOR THE road? I ask, eyeing the carafe across the counter. "Suit yourself," says Jimmy, motioning for me to take care of myself as he barges through the kitchen door with a tub of dirty glasses.

It's below zero this morning for the first time since I've been here. I about froze last night in the toboggan, even though I was wrapped in my four blankets, two wool shirts, long johns, all my dirty socks, and two sweaters. Criminy, I had to come back upstairs around 2:00 and light the heater. I had the passing thought that I'd just stay there dozing in the shack, but I kept thinking about getting caught and the fact that it's just so much warmer in Sam's this time of day. Days like this, I'd definitely rather work than sleep, sick as that may sound. But anyway, some fresh snow blew in with the cold air, and the trails should be just spectacular this morning. I grab two copies of the *Huntington What's Up?* as I leave.

The snow on the sidewalk is the fluffiest and driest I have ever seen. It swirls out of my way in front of me even before my feet touch the ground. The wind is gone, and the sun should be up in no time. Today, I'm thinking, I'll do some speed practice for the Huntington Cup race coming up next month.

The race is an annual event that draws skiers from all over the northeast. It's a giant slalom that starts on Upper

Darbyshire and runs all the way to the base lodge. Last time I was here, the racers nearly all had on those funny skin-tight suits they wear on TV for the agony of defeat.

Me, I'll be wearing my trench this year. I've never run a real race before, but I'm maybe the best there ever was. One of the fastest, too. And when I win the cup this year, they'll have to let me back into the Troubadour where I figure I'll just drink my beer right out of the trophy. Everybody will be buying beer for the Kneissl Kid on that day! Just pour it in, I'll say, go ahead, pour it in. Last year, some kid from Catskill named Kevin won it from out of nowhere. Cocky little bastard, 'scuse my French, but it beats seeing a European win it, thank you. But the Kneissl Kid will give him one kick-ass run for his money - that is, if he has any. I'll just close my eyes, concentrate on the Kid's last win at Grenouille des Yalpes, and become myself - that is, if I'm not already.

I walk to the lodge and get my buried skis and poles from over by the compressor building. I always leave a little length of longthong sticking out of the snow so I can find them easily. I get my boots from behind the water heater and take them upstairs to my table in front of the big window. I sit down and begin the long process of lacing and buckling, then re-buckling from the bottom up to get them on as tight as dimeslots.

I take my three copies of the *Huntington What's Up?* and begin taping four layers across my chest today. Cold as a witch's tit out there today, as Dad would say, but I've got the secret. I pull off a double sheet and tape it across my chest and stomach. Then I button up my second wool shirt and tape on another double layer. Then I start making the tubes for my upper arms, but I stop dead – with four inches of duct tape hanging from my finger - as I read the headline on page one:

Woman Dies After Falling Into Creek

I drop into the chair and begin reading about the incident that I must have witnessed the other night. I get only a paragraph into it when my fingers start to shake and my eyes blur over. I blink twice and see that my life is about to change forever.

> Andrea Collins, age 43, of 131 Brookhaven Drive, was found lying face down in the shallow waters of Huntington Creek at 11:31 p.m. on December 31, 1979 after apparently slipping on the bridge and tumbling into the creekbed. Collins was pronounced dead at the scene by County Coroner Henry J. Miller and transported to the Plattekill Medical Center for autopsy to determine the time and exact cause of death. Constable Edward Y. Cotterly has tentatively ruled out foul play, noting that Collins appeared to have been quite inebriated. Toxicology results are pending.

Huntington Hootowls Win Sectionals!

An hour or so later, Janet asks me to move my feet so she can sweep under the table, but I just sit here, like I've been sitting for the past hour or so. She asks again and I tell her to go fuck herself. She politely leaves to take care of that, I guess, and I lean back, my chest and arms still covered in newsprint, my trench in a heap on the chair next to me, four inches of duct tape still on my finger. People seem to be watching me more than usual today, as if I could really give a shit. My boots are still on my feet, though I may have to take them off again soon to get some circulation back in my toes. But, then again, I may not bother.

Barnacre and two of his maintenance men stop across the

room from me and whisper back and forth. I just know they are talking about me. I just know it. And I'm right, because one of them comes over to ask me if I'm okay.

Fine, I say. I've got a dead girlfriend, no feeling in my toes, and the *What's Up* taped all over my body. He doesn't know what to say next, I guess, because he doesn't say a thing and just backs away, watching me as he goes. I know he's watching because I'm staring him right in the eyes as he backs off.

Well, I decide to take off my boots before somebody else does. And that's actually happened once before, so I know what comes next. I really don't feel much like skiing right now, and it looks like even more people are starting to whisper.

I'm numb and I don't know what to do or where to go next. I'd like to climb into my toboggan and sleep for the next twenty-five years, like Rip Van Winkler, but Hoot would kick me out before I tucked in my third blanket. I might as well go over and drink his whiskey, though, I'm thinking. Good idea, since I must have forgotten my plan to take my boots off. I loosen them up a bit to get some feeling back in my toes, and I slowly get out of my chair. I pull on my trench and button it to the neck against the cold that I'm sure will hit me as soon as I get outside.

I don't bother with my longthongs; I just flip the clamps on my turntables and throw the straps up around my neck to keep them out of my way. I shuffle off to the T-Bar crying like a baby, tears freezing to my trench as they drop from my cheeks.

"WELL, FUCK A DUCK," YELLS Hoot, "It's the Kneissl Kid." He has a big grin on his face as I approach the exit ramp and pull the bar out from under myself and just let it go for a change. He looks all around and reaches into the shack as I slowly sidestep his way.

"Have a little tug, buddy," he says, handing me his big bottle. I raise it in the crook of my elbow without speaking, letting it glug as many times as it wants. "Whoa," says Hoot, grabbing at my arm, "You're gonna die, keep that up."

Sounds good to me, I say, as the bottle is ripped away. Mind if I turn in a little early today?

"Well, yeah," says Hoot. "It's 10:30 in the morning."

It's okay to drink at 10:30, but I can't sleep? I ask.

"It's your call, buddy," he says, looking at a little me funny now, "You're not exactly invisible under there. And if somebody gets hurt, they'll be looking for that sled. You'll scare the living shit out of them."

Let them shit, 'scuse my French, if they want, I say, reaching for the whiskey that Hoot is again pulling away.

"So, what the hell is wrong with you?" asks Hoot.

My best friend just died, I say.

Hoot gets this real funny look on his face and starts patting himself all over. "Whoa," he says, "Still feels like I'm in one piece. Do I look different?"

Well, this makes me grin a little, I guess. With a best friend like you, I say, A guy wouldn't need, wouldn't need... But I can't finish the witty line because I'm blank, just completely blank inside. I don't have any words anymore. I just stare at Hoot thinking about what to say, thinking about Andrea's last couple of minutes, thinking about why she was down next to the creek by the T-Bar in the first place. And I wonder whether I'm really empty inside, or just so full of stuff I can't control that I can't talk straight. And I break down into huge, snuffling, shoulder-shaking, belly-wrenching sobs. Right here, right now, standing up with my skis on.

Hoot slips and falls as he rushes over. He scrabbles up off the ice and throws his arm around my quaking shoulders. He tries to steer me out of the off-ramp and up to the shack, but I still have my skis on, my longthongs now in coils at my feet. I point down between sobs and Hoot leans over to unclamp my turntables, a binding he has never touched before in his life. I step out of my skis and Hoot kicks them out of the way as we head for the bench in front of the shack, his arm around my shoulder. Hoot glances down the lift line, then sits me down.

"Easy, buddy," he says, "You'll be okay in a minute."

Buck, I sob, Buck Avery.

"Yeah, I know," he says, looking around for a roll of toilet paper. He finds one just inside the door and rips off an arm's length. "Here," he says.

I wad it up and rub under my eyes, under my nose, and just drop it at my feet. I sit here hunched forward, elbows on my knees, waiting for more words to come out. I think again about Andrea's last moments and how words didn't do her any good, whether she got any out or not. I wonder about her last words, whether my name was one of them, whether she maybe called out for help as she fell, all alone. Whether she was on her way to find me.

It's not you, I say, finally. You're not dead, Hoot.

"Well, I'm sure glad to hear that," he says, wiping his brow with the back of his hand. "You scared the shit out of me."

So I tell Hoot the story, as far as I know it. I tell him how I pulled my watch out for no reason exactly when the paper says they found her, that I said I had to get hold of her at probably the exact second she fell. I even unbutton my trench and pull off a couple layers of newsprint to find that I have the actual column from the first copy of the *What's Up* I taped to my chest. I read it out to Hoot, stopping several times to regain my composure. But by now I'm pretty much calmed down and not blubbering any more.

"So, who is she?" he asks, "Forty-three, Crissake, she's old enough to be your mother."

All I know is she seemed to want my unmentionables,

'scuse my French, real bad, and I got kind of scared the first time we got drunk together.

"Whoa, you were getting some?" Hoot asks.

Never touched her, except to hold her while she was crying, I say, beginning to cry again myself. I don't really know what it's all about, but we had some, some kind of connection going. I just don't know.

"Forty-three," he says, "Jesus, how'd you meet her?"

Troubadour, I say, snuffling back a wad of snot and tears, I don't meet a lot of people in church, you know.

"I hear you," says Hoot, "I hear you on that one." He looks around and reaches in again for the bottle.

I take another two tugs and hand it back. I'm feeling better already, I say, wiping my mouth with my Tweety glove. But I still don't feel like skiing.

"Well, I don't think you ought to be sleeping underneath right now," says Hoot. "You can hang out here if you want, but you've got to leave before we close, come back afterwards."

I know, I know, I say, shaking my head. More whiskey?

"You go ahead, kick it if you want," Hoot says, handing me the bottle, "I gotta stay a little bit sober for awhile yet."

I'll buy you one, soon, I say, taking another good tug.

So I sit here on Hoot's bench drinking away the afternoon. Hoot keeps me talking while he makes sure nobody falls and blocks his exit ramp. Twice he winks and shows me his technique for helping up young ladies with the nice figures, as Mom says. He winks each time he gets up off the bench, and he yips and howls like a coyote once they are up and on their way. Hoot has picked up both of those from me - the wink and the howling, anyway - and it makes me feel a little proud, even now, that someone copies what I do. I'm drunk enough by now to even forget about Andrea a couple of times, and to think I'd really like this job of his.

Hoot, I say. Why did I pull my watch out the second she died?

"Huh?" says Hoot, who doesn't even own a watch and was probably thinking about titties while I was quietly turning this over and over and over in my mind.

You know, why would I say her name and look at my watch when she was falling into the creek and dying like that?

"Who you think I am, God?" he asks, shoulders hunched somewhere deep inside his Carhartts. A skinny face, sunburned and scraped raw by a razor, sticking out of a frayed hood drawn in tight against the cold. "Do I look like God?"

Nope, I say, reaching a hand out for the bottle.

"I don't know why *I* do most things, let alone you. Here." Hoot hands me the bottle, which appears to be heading fast toward empty. I know why *I* drink, especially today, but I guess I can't say why Hoot does.

At 4:00 Hoot rouses me from a torpor that is fast becoming a stupor and says I have to ski down and wait for the lifties to go before I come back home. Usually I ski down and go into town for a while, but today I just feel like staying here.

"Patrol has to sweep the whole area, and you're done living here if they find you," he says, watching me sway back and forth in front of him. "You can come back up after 5:00 or so." He turns off the radio and stows it inside the shack.

Well, I figure I have to leave now, drunk or not. I don't worry about making it down because I'm still maybe the best there ever was. Things like that don't change just because you're drunk. I stumble badly getting my skis on and I maybe don't tighten up my longthongs to my usual high standard. I wave to Hoot and push off toward the bottom. I point my skis down and head all the way to the bottom of the lift without turning. I skid to a stop as I careen into a ski rack, knocking several pair to the ground, several children skittering out of my way. I fall and begin to cry again.

I wave off the patrollers standing around at the bottom

waiting for sweep, get up a little awkwardly, and shuffle over toward the main lodge. My balance seems to be a little off this afternoon, even on skis. But, under the circumstances, it's understandable. I take off my skis and tie the longthongs to the ski rack, cowboy-style again. I lumber into the bar and pull a handful of quarters out of my trench pocket.

A beer, please, I say. And not that flat piss from Milwaukee, 'scuse my French.

The bartender, a really sweet, young thing on a good day, scowls and rolls her eyes at either me or the pile of quarters, I'm not really sure which. She brings two bottles and slams them both down on the bar in front of me, startling me a little bit.

"You got a choice, Bud," she says, "We got Genesee or Utica Club."

Buck, Buck Avery, I say. Anything but Bud is okay.

She rolls her eyes again and walks off with the Genny, which is exactly what I hoped she might do. I ignore the little glass and tip the bottle up, draining it before it touches the bar again.

Aaaahhh, I say. Got another where that came from? Then I realize that the bartender is back in the kitchen somewhere and can't hear me. So I bang the empty bottle on the bar, hard, three times, rattling my little pile of quarters. This brings out another bartender, maybe even the manager, I don't know. He stands there right in front of me without speaking. This always gets my goat, if you get my drift, because it's just common courtesy to introduce yourself and act like a civilized human being in situa...*Ave, this isn't a good day and you really need to keep a lid on it. Remember what happened that day you got fired over at Buck's for throwing all those d...* on't put up with any of that around here." he says, and I'm not really sure what he's been talking about.

Put up with what? I ask, weaving just a little on the stool.

"Alright," he says, "You're done here for the day. Did you pay her for the beer?"

Well, normally I tell the truth because I'm just that sort of guy. But here and now I feel like I'm being a little mistreated and misunderstood. Period! So I just tell The Incredible Hulk that I paid Little Miss Muffet already and that he should just go check it out if he doesn't believe me. When he leaves for the kitchen I quickly rake my quarters into my trench pocket and sprint toward the door.

Outside, the cold air hits me like a bus from New Jersey. I stagger to the ski rack, step into my bindings, throw the clamps, and fall over when I get to the end of my longthongs, which I've forgotten to untie from the hitching post. I scrabble up off the snow and fiddle with the big knots until they loosen up and fall apart. I step out of the bindings and drag the skis by the long leather straps over to the side of the maintenance building where I do my best to bury them in the snow. Then I look around to make sure nobody saw me and I start walking into town.

But when I get to the bridge, I break down into huge sobs again, holding onto the railing to keep from slumping into a pile next to the road. I hang over the railing, shake like jello, and shriek into the gathering darkness as children in passing cars crane around to watch, to frost back windows with their tired breath.

JANUARY 4TH

"**OH, MAN,**" **SAYS** Hoot, shaking me by the shoulders, "You gotta get out of there right now. Fuck you trying to do, get caught up here?"

I cover my eyes against a scorch of daylight wrapped up in 10-degree air. But I feel nice and comfy wrapped up in the toboggan with my four blankets and Hoot's empty bottle. I have a hole in my stomach where my breakfast was supposed to be by this time, so I guess I forgot to go to work this morning.

"C'mon, out!" Hoot yells. He is banging me on the head with my tray which I guess I must have left outside on the exit ramp last night. "Asshole," he yells, "You left the fucking lift on all night. I should throw all your shit right out of here, right now."

Huh? I say, trying to pull all of this together in my muddled brain, opening one eye to look for the Captain. Hoot is pulling the canvas cover off me and yanking at my right arm, and I feel, maybe dream, something like a beautiful butterfly wriggling out of a cocoon, into a new world, a world where, a world wher...Then I think I recognize where I am, but can't be sure until I open my other eye.

"Get up, goddam it." Hoot yells, pulling the toboggan out of its cubby under the shack. "Get me fired, I'll kill you. I swear to God." He rocks the sled sideways and I fall half out of it, the snow all over my face beginning to bring me around.

I look around at a panorama of brilliant sunshine bouncing off pure-white snow and I can't see a thing. I rub my eyes with the hand that Hoot isn't pulling on and try again to open them. My Tweety glove comes off and Hoot throws it down next to me.

"Asshole," he yells, walking back to the exit ramp, and I look around again, hoping that I get my eyes working in time to finally get to see him this morning.

Hoot doesn't even want to talk any more once I tidy up the toboggan and stagger up to his bench. He's polite and talkative with the skiers, but he seems to be ignoring me. So I stand up and get right in front of him where he can't hide from me.

Hoot, I fucked up, 'scuse my French, I say. And I'm very, very sorry.

"I don't know how sorry you are," he says, "But I know for shit-sure you screwed up bad last night. This is my job and my lift. You leave this thing running and I'm the one who gets fired, not you."

I been fired before, I say, almost immediately wondering why I added this. And I'm very, very sorry about the whiskey.

"Whiskey don't mean shit. I'm looking at getting fired," he says, turning to grab a bar from underneath a struggling novice, "I get fired, your ass'll be in a half-dozen pieces going downhill on two trays tonight."

Well, I certainly don't want to see that happen, I say. I'm just very, very, sorry, and I know it won't happen again.

"Yeah, well you just get out of my face for the rest of the day and I might not give Barnacre a call just yet."

Yes, sir! I say, saluting with my Tweety glove. I'm already gone. I rush down the ramp to where my skis are lying, one upside down, both in a jumble of leather strapping. Since I'm

172

not sure I'll ever see this place again, I reach back into my toboggan cubby and scoop out as many quarters as I can fit into my right trench pocket and both pockets of my jeans. I wobble badly getting my first ski on, and I fall down working on the second. I wave at Hoot from the ground, picking up quarters, letting him know I'm fine.

I take off straight down the hill without turning or slowing my speed before I realize that I really am already gone and I don't need to do this anymore. By the time I stop at the bottom I also remember why I got so drunk last night, and I begin to cry again.

I snuffle most of the way to Sam's, where I hope Jimmy will understand and at least give me a cup of coffee. It's not beer, but it...oh, man, am I ev...but, I buoy up a little by telling myself that it's probably the hangover and not a deep and devastating depression. But I have a hard time arguing with my mind's eye which apparently sees me heading downhill fast. And not on skis, either. The pain in my head scares me, reminds me of what happened last time when it hurt like this. I feel like banging it against a wall just to make it stop. But it didn't work the last time I tried, and it won't now, far as I can see.

Marie looks up as I walk in. Jimmy is in back cooking something with lots of cloves in it, from the smell. The cloves bring my stomach up to somewhere around my adam's apple for a second or two, but I swallow it back into place.

"I did your fucking job this morning," says Marie, "You owe me big time."

Sorry, I say. I had a very bad day yesterday.

"Yeah, well, we all have them," she says, "Some of us come in to work anyway."

"He pays for anything he orders," Jimmy yells out to Marie, who shrugs and raises her eyebrows.

"Whaddaya want?" she asks.

To go back five days, I say.

"Excuse me?" she says, having no reason to understand this at all, "I'd kind of like to go back five years."

Five years would put me in a worse place, I say, wincing at the thought. I don't know.

"I guess I'm supposed to ask what you're dealing with now, huh?" she asks.

Well, it's a long story, I say, using one of my standard openings, one that sometimes sends people off on errands. This time Marie can't leave because she doesn't get off until 2:00. I've just lost a very close friend.

So I proceed to tell Marie all about Andrea: about her troubled marriage and years of spousal abuse in Montana; how she placed her kids in foster care out there to keep them away from a manic-depressive father with a very valuable and functional gun collection; how she was here working in the east as a dance instructor to put together a college fund for them; how she asked me to take her back to Montana next month to bring her kids back east; how she fell to her death calling my name.

"I think I read about this, some of it anyway," says Marie, lighting a cigarette and dropping the match into her saucer. "You never said anything about her."

You never asked, I say, thinking again that someday I have to ask Marie some questions.

"Where did she work," asks Marie, "I grew up here and never knew there were any professional dance schools around. I might have gone myself as a kid."

Well, at this point I have to come up with some detail that escapes me for the moment. So I use another old favorite of mine that always seems to change the subject when I find myself in a bind like this.

You dance? I ask, leaning in closer, arching my eyebrows.

"Well, I used to do that step-dancing - Irish, I think it was - in gym class back in junior high school. We had this teacher who thought we might keep our juices a little more under control if we burned off our excess energy dancing. I loved it. All that bouncing up and down, clicking our feet around, the kicks."

Tell me more, I say, leaning her way on my elbow, watching her face light up with a memory of the past that might keep her from digging too deeply into the present. Tell me more.

"Not much to tell," she says, drawing deeply on the cigarette, "Hot, little adolescent girls bouncing away all their energy in gym class. Miss Crandall maybe figured she'd get lucky, that we'd all go dyke before the boys got to us. Nothing special."

Well, I say. I can see it didn't work.

"You can't see shit," she says, "How'd you know anything about that?"

Well, this opens up another whole element to my love quest. I may be all screwed up, not thinking my best at the moment, but I think I'm still in love. I think so. Could she be a lesbian? Could my speculation about a bed-shaking hubby be barking up the wrong tree? She is a little crude and mouthy when she gets uppity. She walks real fast and serious, like she'd knock you right over if you get in her way. Oh, man, this just makes things a lot more complicated all of a sudden, right when I'm all screwed up to begin with, right when I've got Hoot all bent out of shape over sleeping late in my apartment, right whe…*Any time you're serious about someone, Ave, you've got to be completely truthful, like we've been telling you for how long? You know that someday you have to stop all this si…*ince November? What, maybe two months you've been here?" Marie asks.

I look at her with absolutely no idea what I'm supposed to say next. She's practically glaring at me from maybe a foot or less away, close enough to knock my fanny right off the stool if she's as put off as she looks right now. Yeah, that's about right, I say, looking up like I'm calculating in my head. Let's see, got here around the first week of November, then I...

"Asshole," she says, turning to face forward, looking down in her coffee, and somehow I know he isn't here, either.

Seen him? I ask.

"Huh?" she says, looking at me again, then away, shaking her head.

Never mind, I say.

"Thank God," she says.

Huh? I say, then shrug it away, concentrating on my coffee again.

Where was I? I ask.

"That's the fucking problem," she says, "You just have no idea. If you'd listen to people sometimes, I don't know."

Oh, I hear things, I say. I hear what people are saying.

"I bet you do," she says, patting me on the back, back to her beautiful, sweet self again, "I bet you do."

So I tell her the rest of the story about Andrea. How we were so close, so very close over the years, like brother and sister. How we had this connection that didn't even need words at times. How I knew, just knew, she was dead at the very moment she died. About pulling out my pocket watch for no reason at all. How I heard her call my name from beyond the wall of death, and all that.

"Paper said she lived here," says Marie, "What, over on Brookhaven somewhere."

Well, yes, I say, sipping at my coffee to make the pause work better, to keep her attention. She had taken a room on Brookhaven for a week or so to visit me, to see if I'd take her back to Montana.

"So, where'd she work, where'd she live?" she asks, real attentive again. And again, I find that I have to come up with more detail.

Oh, not around here, I say. She teaches the dance back in Utica, little place, Mrs. Flannery's School of the Irish Spirit,

I think it's called. Every Tuesday and Thursday it's basic step for the little kids. You know, the five-year olds who don't know their left from right yet. Used to drive her crazy, she'd tell me, just crazy. Stepping on their own toes, on the other kids' toes, all the crying. Then Saturdays, she'd take the teen-agers, the real serious ones, on field trips to see the best of the Irish bands. She used to love that part, talked about it all the time.

"Sounds like she enjoyed her work," says Marie, "Not like this shit."

You should maybe think about that kind of work, I say. Especially since you have the training.

"All I got out of that was sweaty, tired out, and not knocked up," she says, "Sucked, actually."

Oh, well, I say, patting her on the back this time. There's got to be something else to do in a town like this.

"Like the job you found when you got here?" she asks, getting that sarcastic look again.

This is just temporary, I say, hoping that today hasn't made the job even more temporary. I still plan to be wearing yellow real soon.

"Better than wearing white, in a white room," she says, and I wince. Comments like this throw me quite a curve and I never really know how to deal with them, except by changing the subject.

I hate doing my own laundry, I say. Can't really see myself getting paid by some Chinaman to do it for other people.

"Huh?" she says.

Jimmy comes lumbering out sloshing a large pot full of stock for some kind of soup he's putting together for tomorrow, giving me another opportunity for distraction. I ask him what's in it.

"Well," says Jimmy, "It's a chicken stock made up from the bones of dead chickens with some chicken meat left on them. You paid for that, right?"

Not yet, I say, raising the cup to my lips. But I'm planning on it.

"You do that," he says.

Things are starting to spin around in my head again at this point, and I wonder if it's the coffee, the story, or maybe just the outside of my head beginning to spin around a bunch of things stranded here inside it. Hard to tell.

My one goal for the day is to replace Hoot's whiskey before he leaves his post, before he decides to throw my stuff out onto the exit ramp. He seemed just upset enough to do it, too. I brought lots of quarters with me, and I hope I have enough.

So I walk the eight blocks to the liquor store, which gives me time to clear my head a little, to slow things down a bit. I seem to be kind of pre-occupied lately. Andrea's death has thrown me for a loop, I guess, especially since I never got a chance to see her again, dead or alive. Nobody did, far as I can see. No viewing, no relatives, no friends, no money, no reason to make a big deal. Nothing. They just cremate people like that, I guess. Don't know what they did with her ashes, probably buried them in a little can somewhere out back of Miller's parlor, who knows? Everywhere I go, I think about it. All the time. She's here, she's gone. Alive one day, dead the next.

When I die, nobody's going to pull out a watch and know what time I check out, that's for sure. Hoot's probably - or was, at least - my closest buddy, but he doesn't even own a watch. How'd he ever know? It's got to be weird knowing you're dead and knowing that nobody else knows it. I know it's pretty weird when you do know exactly when somebody died without being there to see it, that's for sure.

This gets me snuffling again, but I buck up and keep going, because that's just who I am. The liquor store is empty except for the owner's wife, a nice lady in her mid-to-late-sixties, I figure. I walk in and give her the high sign, which seems to make her want to follow me around the little store for some reason. We walk over to the whiskey corner, as I call it, and she asks if she can help me.

Well, I say, I'm looking for a bottle of good whiskey about this big. I hold my hands around an imaginary bottle the size of Hoot's and show her how it's so big you have to flip it up into the crook of your elbow to drink from it. She seems to have a hard time following all this, what with the bottle being invisible and all. She shrugs and gestures toward the corner where I don't see anything at all like Hoot's bottle. Maybe they're all are invisible here. Then she says they do have a few bigger bottles on the bottom shelf under the imported wines. Now there's a really stupid place to keep whiskey, if you ask me. Who would look for it underneath wine, anyway? Winos never drink good whiskey. I mean, all they do is just try to get as drunk as they can as cheap as they can. T-Bird, Mad-Dog, bad port, stuff like that. I just don't understand why they have to put i...*it's getting hotter in here, isn't it, Ave? The room always seems to get hotter when you start to g...*over here, I think. Your bones are younger than mine, you lean down and see if it's under there," she says.

So I get down on my hands and knees and I see more whiskey in one place than I ever saw before in my life, a line of ten or so gallon bottles that look more like they're made for apple juice than whiskey. I feel like staying right here, right now, for about the rest of my life. I drag a bottle out onto the floor and hold it Indian-style between my legs for a bit, petting the dust off its shoulders. Then I make my way back up to standing, pulling its heaviness up with a grunt.

How much? I ask.

"A gallon, I think," she says, "Though I never drink it myself." Criminy, even old ladies want to get into the joke business.

How much does it cost? I clarify. Like in American dollars?

"Twenty-one dollars and seventy-nine cents," she says in a sarcastic voice that I've been hearing a lot of lately, "Plus tax."

I tell her I think I have enough and I head for the checkout counter, reaching into my heavy trench pocket. I pull out a handful of quarters, then another, then another. Then I pull the rest out of my jeans. She winces as they continue dropping onto the counter, rolling this way and that. She corrals two or three that want to jump off onto the floor then asks if I really want her to count all of them.

Would you? I ask.

"No," she says, looking straight at me.

So I begin stacking them by fours and lining up the stacks in rows of five in front of her. I make sure they are lined up just like well-trained soldiers: twenty-one dollars and seventy-five cents worth of them.

"Plus tax," she says, looking at a little tax table taped to the register, "You need another dollar and thirty-one cents."

So I count out four more quarters, then another, and I fish around in my jingly pocket for some smaller change which I dump on the counter as well. I make quick work of sorting this pile and proudly push the exact change her way.

She shakes her head and says she's never had this happen before. I tell her that I know it's unusual for people to buy such large bottles, that many prefer the smaller ones for some reason, but that I'm buying it as a gift.

She shakes her head and rakes quarters over the counter into her open hand, maybe eight, ten times. She reaches for a bag, but I tell her I don't need one because I have a trench coat. As I walk out with the bottle hanging from two fingers through the convenient handle, I know she wonders how a trench coat has anything to do with carrying the bottle. I guess she doesn't know about the hole in the bottom of my left pocket, the one I can't use for money anymore. So I put my hand in the pocket, stick two fingers through the hole, and pass the huge whiskey bottle under the coat with my other hand. Bingo, no bag, no problem with people knowing you're carrying enough whiskey to kill a half-dozen people, let alone yourself.

I walk back toward the mountain with my gift, looking like I have some kind of tumor growing on my leg. I have to be a little more careful about my walking with this much weight on one side, but my legs feel just fine. Just fine. It's my brain that's hurting like mad ever since Andrea died.

I get to the mountain and I dig up my skis next to the maintenance building. I stand here for a couple of minutes with the bottle in one hand and a ski in the other, wondering why it just doesn't feel right. Well, it doesn't feel right because I don't have my ski boots on yet and I certainly can't take a full gallon of whiskey into the lodge with me. Normally, I would have thought my way straight through this without having to stop. This worries me a little as I rebury my skis and find a little hidey hole for the huge bottle of whiskey.

Inside the lodge, I go downstairs and fetch my ski boots from behind the water heater. I carefully look both ways as I leave. I put them on in front of the big window and I don't know how long it takes. All I know is I see my mind's eye, the one that never winks, floating over the creek and watching Andrea, watching her walk right straight - actually kind of stumbly and crooked - toward the bridge. Five times I watch it, just like a TV show. I want to yell out to her, to watch out for that rock, can't you see it? It's been there in the same place the last four times, Jesum. I want to warn her, just let her kn...Andrea! I yell, I guess, and the room comes slowly back, all bustling with the activity of the morning, with my fingers holding tight nylon laces and several people looking over at me.

So I wink large at them and give them the thumbs-up, which would be far more effective in my Tweety glove, but a man's got to do what he's got to do. And I've got to get my boots on.

I run, as quickly as a hangover in ski boots can run, back to the maintenance building and find the tail of my longthong sticking out. I look this way and that, then change my mind and start digging out the whiskey first. I hit glass and mark the spot with a ski pole. Then I pull out my skis and begin the process of putting them on my feet. It's times like these that I think about just buying new boots and bindings for my beautiful Kneissls, which I will never, ever replace. But then I think about having no money, no chance of having any more money now that the slot machine in the laundromat's gone cold on me, and I remember that my last pocketful of cash just went for a gallon of bad whiskey. It's times like these that tell me I probably won't be making big changes anytime soon.

I have a pretty hard time hiding the whiskey with my skis on. It looks a little suspicious holding my hand in my pocket, with my poles in my other hand. So I take and loop my belt through the finger hole so that the bottle hangs down in front of me under my trench. With this, I can use both hands to pole my way to the bottom of the T-Bar.

The liftie is definitely suspicious. He looks at me with that way of his and shakes his head as he hands me the bar. I take the bar more carefully than ever before and ease my butt onto the crossbar ever so slowly. The bottle is riding comfortably in my lap, under my buttoned trench. The liftie laughs like a monkey throwing turds, and calls me Woody, yelling it over and over until I'm up and over the ridge. Some guys.

Hoot doesn't see me coming until my skis hit the ramp and I've shoved away the bar, supporting my bottle with both hands.

Got a little something for you, Hoot, I yell, pulling the neck of the bottle out between two buttons to show him.

"Aaaauuuuugggghhh," he yells back, covering his eyes, sort of peeking between two fingers.

It's a big one. Want some? I ask.

He yells for me to put 'that goddam thing' back in where it belongs, and I go all red when I realize he's probably not thinking what I'm thinking. I guess it kind of looks like I'm doing some dirty business with myself - and that I'm a pretty impressive guy, if you get my drift. So I act real nonchalant, like I knew all the time what he was thinking.

Ta daaaah! I say, pulling my knees apart, exposing the whole thing for Hoot, who peeks out again between two fingers.

"Buck," he says, "and I say this with all respect. You are a really nice guy for being such a fucking idiot."

It's for you, I say. I remember what you said, and I really, really don't want to get kicked out just yet.

Hoot skids over to me and looks all around before taking the bottle and hustling it into the shack, behind the cupboard under the window.

"I'd offer you some, but you still look kind of green and I'm still kind of pissed off."

Better than being pissed on, 'scuse my French, I say, pushing off with my poles. I'll be back after dark. Please don't throw me out, Hoot.

"Okay, okay," I hear him say, then something I don't quite hear. But I've heard enough for one day.

JANUARY 10TH

I'S COLD, AND it's dark out, but I'm just toasty here inside my apartment this evening. I have the *What's Up?* taped over my window and the gas stove is roaring. I have a candle lit and two more spares in Hoot's little cabinet. I've been reading *On the Road,* off and on, for the past two hours. I've been taking little tugs at Hoot's whiskey and I feel warmer than the stove at the moment. But I'm still upstairs here because I know what's going to happen once I go downstairs to the toboggan in my bedroom.

My nights, though comfortable and warm wrapped up in the toboggan, have become full of these little demons since Andrea's death. They talk and they talk and they take me places where I don't want to go. They start the moment I lie down, even before I've got my four blankets tucked and the cover pulled into place. I've seen them before. They've come and gone from time to time since way back when, but I'm not talking.

The Demons of the Horizontal – a philosopher or somebody at Marcy State who was supposed to know about this sort of thing told me about them once. I don't remember a lot about it except that she said they go after just about everybody from time to time when they lie down, when they get horizontal. Something about being ninety degrees out of whack from the earth's magnetic field when you lie down, she claimed. It's supposed to be better if you try to sleep with your head facing north, though. She said that humans started thinking straight and got the better of them only after they stood up. Seems to me you could get smarter just because you see more stuff when your head is up off the ground. When my head goes down lately, I don't get stupid or anything. I just get scared. And there isn't much I can do about my toboggan facing west down in the cubby. But I never did believe that part, anyway.

Tonight I may stay up here to keep the demons quiet. It's comfortable and warm, but the shack is too small to stretch out in. It's a typical lift shack, taller than it is long or wide. I can probably get some sleep slouched on the bench, leaning up against the cabinet, legs curled in under me. If I keep my head up it will definitely be quieter tonight. Everything's a trade-off one way or the other, I'm thinking. I may get more rest in the long run upright like this, but I know I'll be stiff and tired in the morning. Just have to try it, I guess. See what happens.

I wonder if it was the demons who told me to pull my watch, made me talk about Andrea when nobody else was there talking to me. Do they ever let you in on the real important things when you're standing up, or just ride your ass when you lie down? Who knows? I wasn't lying down when Andrea called me, but if I'd had a couple more UCs, I would have been, for sure. I don't think it was a demon telling me anything that night, though I may have been too drunk to hear him anyway. But the Klondike was pretty noisy that night.

Reading my Kerouac keeps my mind off where I am and what I'm doing. This is probably the best situation I've had in maybe five years, but I feel like something's started slipping, like the gears are wobbling in my head. Problem is I can't read forever. Maybe that's why I started writing in the first place,

I don't know. I just can't close my eyes and expect peace and quiet anymore. Not without being drunk, anyway.

Where is she? Where do you go when you're dead? Where did they even put her body after she died, I don't know. All I know is there's always something left over after the lights go out, and they have to do stuff with it. And I'm not talking souls, either.

Like the guy in the box when I found the rose for Marie. He got the full treatment, all dressed up in a suit and chock full of formaldehyde. Bet that cost his family a boatload. Andrea had nothing, no money that I know about. They must have driven her over to Miller's, far as I can see. Nowhere else to take a stiff in this town. I just wish I had been there to show a little respect. But I wasn't, I guess. I just wasn't.

SAM'S IS STILL CLOSED, BUT I'm not surprised since I'm here so early this morning. Might as well get up and out of the shack, since I stayed up and out of the toboggan all night. Sitting up all night does help, it really does. And the earlier I get up and out, the more beautiful it seems around here. The sky is all milky with stars, and there's no wind this morning. I hear owls over on the ridge behind me and coyotes across the road somewhere close. This beats hell out of the demons crawling around in my hair, no question about that. I'll try staying up again tonight for sure.

Jimmy pulls up in his New Yorker and acts surprised, like he does every time I get here before he does. He sleeps like a rock, is my guess. Some people can just ignore the demons, or never even hear them at all, and come to work all refreshed and invigorated, like I used to.

"Morning," says Jimmy, "Looking a little rough around the edges today."

I'm fine, I say. Ready for a new day, new way.

"You just do it the same way as usual and we all stay happy," he says. He unlocks the door and bows for me to enter first. I go straight to the hook where I hung up my apron yesterday and I tie it on behind my back. I turn around to the sound of Marie banging her way through the door, early today for a change.

Hey, ho, I say. Nice morning out there.

"Will be when the sun decides to come up," she says, leaning her hip into the counter as she ties her apron on, yawning.

I bustle about, hoisting chairs on top of tables, sweeping, mopping, cleaning out coffee carafes with ice cubes and salt. I glance at Marie from time to time as she sits hunched over her coffee, waiting for customers. Jimmy is throwing pots around the kitchen and swearing this morning for some reason.

As I finish replacing the chairs around the tables, I get an idea that might cheer up Marie, and maybe even myself, for a change. I slide a chair out into the middle of the floor and I climb up on the seat, then up on the back, balancing the chair on its two back legs.

Hey, Marie, I say. Look at this. She turns to see me drop the two front legs back on the floor, then she sees me carefully remove one foot from the back of the chair, balancing on the other with my arms out wide.

"Holy shit," she says, "You're going to break something doing that."

Been doing it all my life, I say. Never fell once. Well just once, maybe. I climb down off the chair back and jump from the seat to the floor, simulating one of my famous spread-eagle, thumbs-up skiing jumps.

"How did you ever learn to do that?" Marie asks, as Jimmy comes into the dining room with the soup of the day.

"Learn what?" Jimmy asks, "Didn't know he knew how to learn things."

Very, very funny, I say, and I give him the finger as he turns around to put the soup on.

Never had to learn it, I say. I've had perfect balance as long as I can remember. You know how some people have perfect pitch?

"I don't follow sports," she says.

Ha, I say. Good one.

"Huh?" she says.

Anyway, it's time for breakfast and I need to fuel up for the day, especially today. I order doubles on pancakes and sausage, and I reach over to get my own coffee as Jimmy goes back to do the cooking. Marie is on the wrong side today and I feel kind of put off by it. She really ought to know better, I'm thinking. She's on my stool and there's nothing on the other side. I always sit there and she knows it, for Crissake. How hard would it have been to just sit on her own stool this morning. I mean, she got here early, there's nobody around today, just no reason at all to do that to me. I should just tell her to b...*Balance, Ave, just balance. You have to keep it steady and not think about anything el...*lined up for today?" Marie asks.

I guess I didn't quite hear what she was saying, but I usually get the drift from the words around the ones I miss, from the words I do hear, I guess. That's exactly what I do: I guess.

I guess I'll just ski all day for free, I say, wagging my pass at the end of its lanyard. I got a pass!

"Big fucking deal," she says, "Most people in this town have one. Except for me."

I keep telling you, I say. I can teach you everything you need to know in no time at all.

"Well, that's great," she says, "Because time's what I've got none of right now in my life."

Well, that's depressing, I'm thinking. If she's got no time, she must have other stuff going on in her life, like a family, maybe, or a second job somewhere. It just seems like all the women I have in my life are either leaving it in the past or getting further and further away from whatever it is I have coming at me in the future. Oh, Marie!

I slump over my coffee, my shoulders rounded in depression with the exact same curve as Marie's. Why did I come here in the first place? Why am I still here now? How long will I stay here? Then I see my pass dangling down into my coffee and all these questions get answered without another word being spoken.

But I have work to do and I can't afford to get any more depressed than I am right now. I put on my trench and I bid adieu to Marie who probably doesn't know what it means. But, then again, I'm not certain either, since it's just some European expression I picked up somewhere for my story. But it sounds a lot like adios, which I know means 'see you tomorrow' in Indian talk.

I LEAVE SAM'S INTO THE glare of the rising sun coming up through the crack of the valley in front of me. I have to go back down that road headed east, so I'd better get used to squinting. My sunglasses are still in two pieces in my apartment, and I have no plans to fix them soon. Actually, I don't have many plans at all right now. I flip a quarter and it comes up heads, so I head straight down the road for Miller's.

The walk is pretty long, and I remember the last time I was here. So I start skipping to save energy and smooth out my gait. If it was summer and I had my uni right now it would be an entirely different story. I wouldn't need this trench, either. I'm thinking that this may be the last season for this old trench, my trademark as the Kneissl Kid. I've worn it through so many winters I can't count them anymore. Now, with a big hole in the left pocket and a rip starting under my right armpit, I'm just hoping it takes me through the rest of the winter. I really don't know what I'd do without it. But I can't think about that right now, can I?

I get to Miller's a half-hour later, all warmed up and a

whole lot less depressed. Then I remember why I've come here and my spirits drop like rain. I knock on the door several times without an answer. The door is locked and there's nobody home, so I walk around the building looking for another entrance. I find a loading dock in back with a hearse parked next to it, and still nobody answers when I knock. I try the door and find it unlocked.

I walk in on tiptoes, but decide that the best approach is probably to be right out in the open with my request.

Hey, ho, Mr. Undertaker, I yell. Anybody home?

The thought crosses my mind that this would be one strange place to call home, but I understand that many undertaking families do live in the same house with the stiffs.

I call out a couple more times before a little smile comes across my face. I can't see it, but I can feel the old familiar muscles starting to move, right through the depression. Nobody home. I begin by going from room to room, looking for records, ledger books, anything that might tell me what they did with Andrea. I have to think that this is where they brought her. I look inside all the caskets I find, in case they still have her inside one for some reason. Nothing.

I look in a really scary room with two adjustable tables, a couple of sinks, and several glass-fronted cabinets. It looks like a busy place, but I find nothing.

I tiptoe halfway upstairs before realizing that the two inches of carpeting would probably muffle the sound of a bulldozer. I try several rooms before I find what looks like the main office. I paw through a couple of ledgers. Nothing.

I turn to go, but decide to check out a loose-leaf notebook on a chair in the corner. It seems to have more recent dates and names like Callaghan, Edmonds, Birdwhistle, Smith, Burns, Pbrfonski, Kagan, Ernst, Malchovich, Collins, Turner, Katz, Jurgen...wait a minute. I feel a shudder and the sweat starts to flow like the Huntington Creek, even though I'm not even wearing the *What's Up* this time. Collins - January 1, 1980. Bingo. My breath starts going in and out like a fat dog in July, and I have to wipe some tears with my Tweety glove.

The notebook says she was cremated without a viewing and that the county's going to get billed for "indigent service" or something like that. That means she must still be here somewhere, I'm thinking. With renewed vigor I begin a search that takes me through every room and closet in the old Victorian house. Nothing.

I'm getting kind of depressed again after the major high of seeing her name in the notebook. They can't just toss her out back somewhere, can they? They wouldn't, couldn't. Criminy, you can't even do that with pets anymore. The last door I try has a staircase leading down to the basement. I figure I might as well check there, too.

This time I do have to tiptoe because the boards are creaky and there is an echo that scares me a little. It's dark and creepy down here, that's for sure. I grope around in my pockets until I find my duct-tape lighter, which I'm not entirely sure I want to flick down here. It seems more dungeon than basement and I'm very edgy right at the moment. But the lighter does its job and I see that it's not quite as creepy as I had thought. It's actually kind of typical - full of odd junk, books, broken chairs, tools, jars full of things I don't even want to think about that actually turn out to be little nails and screws, an old dog collar, some ragged blankets, some zippered bags that I definitely don't want to think about, and a row of metal tins. Nothing.

I'm about to leave when two things happen at once: I see that there are labels on some of the metal tins, and I hear a door open upstairs. The door closes and I hear somebody whistling The Happy Wanderer. My lighter flicks again and I see that there are names on the labels. My heart flutters out of my chest and circles a foot over my head. The Happy Wanderer slams the bathroom door and fanny-burps obscenely, three times, before taking up the tune again. I flick my lighter. Collins - 1/1/80. Bingo.

I slump in a heap on the floor and try to catch my breath, which is coming in and out with silent, little sobs at this point. Tears are running down my face like melting icicles, and I hug Andrea to my chest, rocking back and forth in the dark.

"Valereeeeeeee, Valeraaaaaaaaaaaah, Valereeeeeeeeeeeeee, Valerah-ha-ha-ha-ha-ha-Valereeeeee..."

JANUARY 14ᵀᴴ

ACTUALLY, GETTING OUT of the funeral parlor was the easiest part, I say. I waited down there quietly until I heard the undertaker flush – and I'm not real good at waiting - then I heard the door squeak open and him walking down the hall until he hit the rug and his footsteps went silent on me. Then I just made myself invisible so that he wouldn't see me leave. I just walked up the stairs and out the door with Andrea under my trench.

"Invisible?" says Hoot, leaning in close, really interested in me – and a little pissed off - since he found Andrea in his cabinet this morning. "How do you know you're invisible?"

Well, I'm not now, I say. But I knew I was invisible then, and the place was just crawling with people. People in boxes, people paying their respects, people taking care of them, handing them Kleenex. I just walked up the stairs, down the hall, and out the back door. You didn't see me sitting there with Andrea when you pulled her out this morning, did you?

Hoot rolls his eyes around and scratches at something down inside his Carhartts. He shakes his head, slowly.

I'm just pulling your leg, I say, even laughing a little. I wasn't really there.

I am definitely feeling a little better since rescuing

Andrea from the basement. And it always feels good to catch somebody in one of my jokes.

I just walked across the back yard and sat by the road for awhile to make sure I was still invisible. When nobody stopped, nothing happened, and I started getting real cold, I just skipped back into town. I kept Andrea with me until the mountain closed and I could get back home. End of story.

"Beginning of problem," says Hoot, looking around, reaching inside for his whiskey.

So, where is she? I ask.

"It's safe," says Hoot, his face cold and unforgiving, "That's all you need to know." He takes a tug at the whiskey as my face starts to go red and I feel my fist balling up inside my Tweety glove. He swallows hard and looks straight at me, like he's ready for a fight. He slowly screws the cap back on the whiskey bottle. We stare.

Then Hoot's face explodes into laughter, all lines and happy wrinkles. He holds up his wagging finger to slow me down from punching him or something while he gets his voice back. I try breathing a little slower while I'm waiting.

"I'm just playin with you, Buck! Just playin. Whoooo!" He reaches inside and pulls Andrea out from behind the door, still laughing, "But don't even think about keeping it up here in the shack," he says.

Her, I say, reaching out to take her from him, my face still hot, You're not going to tell, are you?

Well, everything seems to amuse Hoot this afternoon, and it's another minute or two before he can talk again. "No way, Buddy," he says, "You get more and more interesting by the day."

Buck, I say, Buck Avery.

Hoot's done laughing again, and now I have to find a good place for Andrea. I can't blame him for not wanting her upstairs; he didn't know her or anything, and I guess some people might think it's strange. But, Jesum, I only left her in the cabinet. Why should that bother anybody? It's not like I spilled her all over his precious bench or anything, I mean why can't he ju...*Stay calm, Ave, Ave? Isn't this one of those things that can get out of contr*...all get along, just lighten up a little. I don't think I really need to keep her warm and all that, but it's hard to think of myself being comfortable if she's out in the cold somewhere. No place to hide her at Sam's, far as I can see. She won't fit in the toilet tank, the only place I've ever hidden anything, and I'm not about to subject her that indignity anyway. And the rose didn't work out exactly the way I expected, either. I wouldn't want Jimmy finding anything he doesn't need to know about. He'd probably just toss her in the dumpster out back.

The only other warm hidey hole I have is where I stash my ski boots behind the water heater. So I set Andrea on the snow and start putting on my skis. This will actually be the first time we've skied together, since the tray ride up here doesn't count. I hold her squeezed between my knees under the trench, push off, and make like I'm a skiing, bow-legged idiot for the Yellowjackets and their students. All the way down.

Now, it's been a week since I really skied, three days since I did anything more than hang out and sleep sitting upright in the Laundromat. This feels pretty good, I'm thinking. It almost feels like I've been skiing with her all my life. If Andrea could talk, I know she'd be screaming like a banshee. But you just have to love skiing. I swoop left and lean hard so she dips low to the rushing snow. Then I arc a right turn followed by a quick left again. I can almost hear her screaming now. We turn across the whole width of the slope and I have to re-assure Andrea that she has nothing to worry about, remind her that I'm maybe the best there ever was. I smile at the thought - and at the mere fact that a such beautiful thought is back in my head again - and I instinctively hop off a nice bump doing my famous spread-eagle, thumbs up jump for everyone to watch.

Well, that was a mistake. Andrea is now bouncing and sliding all over the beginner area. And it's me doing all the screaming now.

Andrea, Andrea, I yell, I'm here, Andrea.

I pick up speed to catch her, see my one opportunity, and aim for a little bump out ahead of the hurtling tin, throwing myself into the single most important turn of my entire life, the turn that probably began with my first day on skis at age four-and-a-half, the turn that I've been practicing all through high school and ever since, without even knowing why. But today I know why. I throw myself to my right, digging with my edges, launching at the last moment, going horizontal with my outstretched arms in front. As my body hits the snow I close my eyes, grab Andrea, and bring her to my chest. I slide and tumble twice, all the while holding tight and whispering reassurances. But since this is the beginner area, I probably come to a stop in no time at all, even though time has again slowed to a crawl.

There are maybe two dozen people staring as I boost myself back to my feet and stuff Andrea up under my trench again. I wave and set off on the rest of my run to the bottom, telling Andrea all the while how sorry, how incredibly sorry, I am.

I SKATE OVER TO THE lodge with Andrea under my arm. I set her down gently next to the ski rack and begin unbuckling, unwinding, and unclamping my skis from my boots. I lean my Kneissls up against the rack and tie the longthongs to the crossbar, cowboy-style - which is fast becoming Buck-style since getting kicked out of Hedwig's. I stretch out some kinks from skiing in such a strange position, and I pick up Andrea and take her into the lodge.

On my way to the stairs I generally take to the basement,

I walk past the bar and feel the need for a drink. It's only 11:30, but that's pretty close to 12:00 on my clock. You know what they say, it's always 12:00 somew...*e've discussed this, haven't we, Ave? You know that all this – and I'm not just talking about the drinking - is not what you need at this point in your...*ight down on an empty stool and I place Andrea on the stool to my right. I pull out a handful of quarters and spill them out in a pile in front of me.

Two beers, please, I say. And not that watery Milwaukee piss, either, 'scuse my French.

This bartender knows me pretty well by now, but he still shakes his head most times I do business with him. Today is no exception, I guess. I organize my quarters into piles of four as he pours my Utica Clubs. He brings me my beers and rakes four piles off his side of the bar into his other hand. He drops them one-by-one into the cash register drawer from two feet above it, shaking his head, just like Jimmy.

Andrea would just love sitting here drinking a beer with me, except that she would probably have a Manhattan, a drink I would never touch. I can almost see her here on the stool, legs crossed, her stiletto pump rocking back and forth, that unlit cigarette in her mouth. This image does the trick and I'm starting to cry again. I dab my eyes with a napkin and I try my best to stop. I pick up Andrea and set her on my lap for support and slowly stop shuddering. When I look up, the bartender and several customers look down.

I finish my first beer and pick up the second, tinking it up against the tin in a silent toast to Andrea, her life, her kids out in Montana somewhere. She had so much to live for, I'm thinking. So young, so much ahead of her. Well, maybe not so young. But she had the nicest figure I've ever seen, and I check them all out, believe me, I do. Well, this image does the trick too, and I'm a little embarrassed that I may have to order another beer before I stand up. I quick move Andrea off my lap so she doesn't get all excited like the first time we met, but I guess she doesn't notice these things anymore.

DON'T WORRY, I SAY, CARRYING her down the stairs now. It'll be warm and I won't be far away. I walk down the basement hallway to the maintenance room door, look both ways like Superman outside his phone booth - like Hoot outside his lift shack - and slip inside.

I'll be back around 5:00, I say. Then we can take a tray ride back home. With this I gently push Andrea in back of the water heater and I slump down next to it myself.

"I'm scared, don't leave me here."

The adrenaline surges up through my chest, and my face gets hot as I look around to see who else is in the room.

"I'm scared and it feels hot back here."

There's nobody else in here, I'm thinking, looking around with a flush of heat crawling up my own neck.

"You know I'm afraid of fire, and there's a little fire down here inside this thing. And I feel like I'm back in that basement."

Well, I laugh right out loud as it occurs to me what's going on, and I reassure her that it's only a water heater, that there's one in probably every house she's ever lived in.

"I just don't like it, it scares me," she says, "Isn't there another place I could stay?"

We discuss it and decide that we both have to make these little compromises under the circumstances. I tell her that I really do appreciate what she's been through and that I'll do my best to get her out every day, to keep her safe, to maybe even find a home where we don't have to hide like this. Then I settle in for a little nap leaning up against the wall.

What a day, I'm thinking, yawning and stretching next to the water heater. I thought for sure Hoot would lose his temper and turn me in after finding Andrea like that. Most people would, I'm thinking. But now, as long as I bring her back and forth with me, we can still be together. I feel a little weird about talking to her, but she was the one who started it, talking to me the moment she died. What's the difference? I wasn't there then, at least in the flesh, and she isn't here now. That's balance, if you ask me, and I'm the king of balance. Some people pray to a dead God, I guess I can talk to a dead chick. And Andrea would be so proud to know that I think of her as a chick.

But my memory of her is slipping every day. It gets harder and harder to bring back exactly what she looked like. I have one picture in my head looking down at her in front of me, almost twice my age with waddles and bony ribs, but there's another with a face so young and proud, right there perched above the nicest chest the world has ever seen. Who wouldn't talk to a chick like that?

IT'S ALL ABOUT TRUST, I tell Andrea as we walk toward the parking lot at the bottom of the beginner area. I have her under my arm inside the trench, watching my legs moving though a loose and easy stroll. The tray ride up the T-Bar may be even scarier for her than bouncing down the hill next to it this morning. She's got to be a little spooked after that experience, I guess.

We cross the packed snow in front of the T-Bar shack and I reach in the window to turn it on. It jerks to life, T-Bars swinging wildly in every direction before settling down with the forward motion. I reach under the shack to pull out my tray. With the tray in one hand and Andrea under my other arm, I plop down hard on my butt and slip the tray underneath. I do a one-handed slide to the loading ramp where I, duck my head, carefully pull my knees up under my butt, Indian-style - which isn't, duck my head, likely to become Buck-style any time soon - so that I can get my heels up off, duck my head, the snow with Andrea snuggled in between my knees.

Just relax, Hon, I say, patting the top of the tin and wiggling it into place, duck my head, a little tighter. It's all about trust.

I grab the next T-Bar with my right hand and hug Andrea to my chest with every muscle in my left arm. We jerk forward and suddenly we are facing off to the left and my right arm is not doing a very good job of keeping us straight.

Hold tight, Hon, I yell, yawing left and right. I have to let go for a second, but we'll be fine.

I hunch my chin down tight against Andrea's lid to hold her in against my chest and let go of her with my left arm, committing us both to the maneuver. I flail forward and up, reaching by feel alone since I'm looking straight down at Andrea, whispering to keep her from screaming. I swing left to right, my arm flailing up and down, when the back of my hand hits cold metal. I flip my palm over and grab the flat of the bar, facing forward, the ride becoming smoother.

It's okay, Hon, I say. See? It's all about trust. You did it.

Halfway up I realize that I probably could have buttoned her inside my trench and used both hands from the get-go. But this is all so new to me. Anyway, it's working well like this as long as I keep my chin down. I've never been this scrunched up in my life, at least not since birth anyway. I'm all bent up and pulled in with my legs under me on the tray, my chin tight to the tin, and the bar pulled in under my armpits. We'll make it to the top as long as I don't move a muscle.

Relax, Hon, I say. We're almost home.

At the top I have to let go with one hand first, wrap the arm around Andrea, then let go with the other hand. With no extra hand to grab the tray, I have to roll off and let it slide into the fence at the bottom of the ramp, which also happens to me and Andrea. I stand, pick up the tray, and we walk to the shack where I hit the emergency stop. I reset the stop just like Hoot showed me, since I really can't get thrown out now that there's two of us living here.

Inside the shack I turn on the gas stove and tape up the window so I can light a candle. Andrea is sitting on the little cabinet next to the door and I sit down on the narrow bench to have a little tug at Hoot's whiskey. Cheers, I say, tinking the huge bottle up against the tin. Then I flip it up into the crook of my elbow and tip it up until it glugs three, maybe four times.

Aaaahhh, I say, wiping my mouth with the back of my Tweety glove. I wish you could taste this, Hon. But I guess she's okay since she doesn't drink anymore. And I'm okay because I don't drink any less, I guess. I laugh right out loud and take another tug.

It's been a long day, I say, my yawning stretch ending in a playful pat on the top of the tin. And a little scary for you, I guess. I've slept away half the day but I'm still very tired. I can't stretch out much in the shack where it's warm, and I can't sleep with my head down in the toboggan lately either.

I pull out my Kerouac and open it to the bookmark I've inserted, maybe at random. I don't remember what came before the section I'm reading, but I'm not following it very well anyway. I take another tug at the whiskey to get me closer to where Kerouac probably was when he wrote it. But it doesn't seem to help much.

So I reach into my pocket and pull out my wad of napkins and my girlie pen. I shake it to see if it still makes me smile – and it does, so I guess I'm still alright, I don't know. I smooth out a clean napkin and square up to start writing. I sit here for a minute pulling together the last three chapters in my head before I continue, but the thread is just not there. The Kneissl Kid has run out of ideas for the time being, I guess. He had a race in St. Myelin, somewhere in Europe, maybe France, when I last sat down to write, but I can't put it together at the moment. Maybe it's that I'm sitting on a flat board instead of one with a hole and water below me. I ought to at least be able to take some notes for the next chapter, Criminy. But I'm dry as a bone.

I shake the pen and watch the snow drift gently down across the spinning titties. I shake it again and hold it up for Andrea to see. Did I ever show you this? I ask, shaking again. Cracks me up every time.

I can't sleep and I can't stretch out. I can't read and I guess I can't write, either. I put down my girlie pen and look around the thirty square feet that have become my home, more if you include my bedroom downstairs. Some people might think it's depressing to live in a place like this, but not me. Not me. I've got four walls, a floor, a roof over my head, and a toboggan to sleep in. And I get one good meal a day. The only thing that depresses me is not being there for Andrea when she needed me. I just can't get that out of my head. But, now that we're together again, I actually feel a little better every now and then.

All I need is for the demons to go away for good and let me get a decent night's sleep. It's scary. Every time I lie down flat I hear them coming, twisting up every normal thing I think about. It's like I'm dreaming even if I'm wide awake. Who needs that? But, you know, it seems like maybe they're a little scared of Andrea, or something. Since she's been up here, I've actually been able to get a little sleep now and then. Especially when I bring her down into the toboggan some nights.

I take another tug at Hoot's whiskey and fish around in the cabinet for my last stash of quarters. It's still heavy enough that I figure I can buy another bottle without even bothering to count. I have to remember to bring about forty or so of them with me tomorrow so Hoot doesn't throw me out.

Whenever I get bored like this I usually go outside to look at the stars. So I take Andrea outside and we sit bundled up on the bench in the still air. I hear a pack of coyotes yipping as they run through the valley down next to the creek. An owl hoots up in the east bowl somewhere, same place I always seem to hear him. A snowcat's engine surges as it holds the machine from breaking off downhill grooming the ice up on Hilliard's Folly. A rifle shot somewhere across the valley tells me somebody's going to have another deer in the freezer by morning.

"You don't even know if he got it," she says, surprising me, probably smirking, "How do you know it wasn't some jerk shooting some other jerk over a woman?"

One shot, I say. One shot's all a good jacker needs with a deer in the lights. You never shoot just once when a girl's involved. He would have emptied his gun into the guy.

"No shit?" she says, "Learn something new every day around you."

That's the beauty of coming to a new place like this to live, to meet new people, I say. You ought to know about that, being from Montana, and all.

"You only need to know so much in Montana," she says, "People there know too much, and your kids disappear."

Disappear? Like invisible? I ask.

"Yeah," she says, "First thing you know, you come home from work, there's a fire, and there's no kids in bed next day."

Whoa, I say, shaking my head, tugging again at the whiskey. That's got to be rough.

"Yeah, I guess," she says, "I guess they just don't like mothers out making money at night."

Well, at least it's good you left that all behind when you came here from Montana, I say.

"Yeah, right," she says, more distant now, "I really sucked as a mother, no pun intended."

Well, that's all in the past, and the past just isn't here anymore, I say.

"Buck," she continues, "You know I didn't jump, right? I just need you to know that."

T...t...tell me about Montana, I say, more than a little uncomfortable with this conversation, shivering a little, gazing up at the same stars that hang in the sky out west. What's it like in the real mountains?

But Andrea doesn't answer this time. She must have fallen asleep or something, I'm thinking. I shake off a chill that has just crept over me and decide that it's time to go inside and warm up again. I pick Andrea up off my lap, stand up, stretch one arm out wide, transfer Andrea, then stretch out the other and yawn. We go inside and I set Andrea down next to my napkins.

Words, I'm thinking as I look down at my scribblings, just where do they come from, anyway? They seem to be just about everywhere - on my napkins, in my head, all over the *What's Up?*, on bathroom walls. The way most people talk, words are just little puffs of air coming out of a hole in the front of their faces. Criminy, talking is probably the world's stupidest waste of words. I mean, they come out as nothing but hot air, and they're dead as soon as they're born. The only words that ever get anywhere are the ones that get written down. Truth is, most of the others aren't worth the bad breath they ride out on.

For most people, talking is just like a dog scratching at his neck with his hind leg, or maybe sniffing around down below. Just something they all do without even thinking. No idea why.

But I'm not most people, and my words are different, at least they used to be. These days they all seem to boil around in a pool inside my head until they start to evaporate, right out into thin air inside there somewhere. Then, when I realize I can't even think anymore, they condense out on the inside of my skull and start dripping back down into the pool again.

Maybe that's why I have so much trouble with the demons when I lie down. Maybe the pool spreads out like a flooded river when I get flat, scares the demons and makes them start chattering, run for high ground or something. Once they start their yelling back and forth to each other, it's anybody's guess what happens next. Only thing you can do is sit up and make them run back downhill, maybe stop whatever it is they're planning.

But, everywhere you look, you see words. There's words on the front of the heater here, words on Hoot's picture of Cheryl Tiegs up here on the wall, words on the label inside my trench, words on this bottle here, words on my skis, my hat, my quarters, everywhere. The only place you never see words is in the air, the one place they all come from in the first place. Except maybe in the winter when I do sometimes see them coming out of people on those little puffs of steam. I see words spelling right out of their mouths sometimes. Little clouds, letters in the fog or something.

Inside my head, I see these words all the time. Other people waste their words in the air. Just hear them once, never see them, gone the second they get them out. Then they get old and die, if they're lucky, and they're gone, too - just like their dead, little words. Just like that, it happens.

Not me. My words will be around long after I'm gone, I'm thinking, unless the pool dries up completely, or just leaks out of my head for good some night when I lie down. I've got to get them moving again, get them all lined up in the right order in all the right places. I've got them in all the right places so far, but my story's not over yet. I've got to keep going somehow, even though Andrea's got me feeling pretty fucking low right now, 'scuse my French.

"Why do you blame me?" she says, surprising me again, making me wonder how long she's been awake listening.

It's not anything you did, I say. It's just that I miss you, I guess.

"Miss me? You miss me? You go to all that trouble to find me and bring me up here to keep you company, and you say you miss me? Words don't mean a fucking thing to you. I talked myself blue in the face trying to show you a good time, trying to give that dick of yours a reason to remember me, and you pushed me away. Just pushed me away like you didn't even hear me. You weren't there for me when I needed you, but now I'm here - right here, right now - and you say you miss me? What does that mean? Like it's my fault I'm gone? Or maybe my fault that you're stuck here with old, dead Andrea?"

I'm sorry, I say, tearing up, looking away in my shame. I'm so sorry.

"Words," she says, "Just words."

JANUARY 17ᵀᴴ

*AVE, AVE! YOU have to get up. You can't just lie there like this. Like some old bum who has nothing better to do with his life. You have to get out of there and go to work. You have to start thinking a little more cl...*ear as a bell and cold as hell, with the thickest frost that ever, that ever fell? Whoa, what's this? Morning? I pull my shoulders deeper into my four blankets and wish I could sleep forever. But I reach up to look at my pocket watch sitting on top of Andrea and find that it's 6:05 already. I'll be late for work if I take her to the lodge first. But I'll get thrown out of here forever if I leave her in the shack upstairs. And I may lose her completely if I leave her here in the toboggan and some beginner gets hurt down below.

Don't worry, I say. We'll figure this out. I pull back the cover and ooch my way out of the cubby with my four blankets and Andrea. I stretch and look east to where the sun will rise after we're gone. I yawn and make my way up and around to the front of the shack. I fold the blankets and stash them under Hoot's bench and turn on the heater so he'll be nice and happy when he gets up here. I pull out my tray, pick up Andrea, and it's off to work we go, we go.

Andrea is fine about the tray ride now. She doesn't scream anymore, at least not screams of terror. She seems to actually enjoy the feeling of speed, and it makes me wish she had been able to ski before she died. Then I think about her figure and how she would have to be careful about leaning forward, keeping her balance and all. Hoot would have loved helping her up off the ramp, that's for sure.

With my tray stashed back under the shed, I look at my watch and find that I'm already late - definitely no time to take Andrea to the lodge this morning. I'll have to take my chances at Sam's, I guess. I trot halfway down the hill holding her close under my right arm, then I break into skipping until I almost fall on some ice and have to bobble Andrea a bit to keep upright.

It's okay, I say. I'll try to be more careful.

"So, where are we going," she says, "It ain't Sunday, so I know we're not headed for church."

Very, very funny, I say, playful as a little pup this morning, really beginning to feel a little better for a change.

You be nice or I'll drop you off this bridge, I say. I swing her around and hold her on top of the railing, show her the drop. Whooo whooo, I say, swaying from side-to-side.

Then all the blood runs out of my face as I realize that this is the last bridge she ever saw, the one she was crossing just before she died underneath it. For all I know, this is the exact spot where she stumbled and fell to her, to her... My heart leaps in my chest and my eyes are glazing over, going a little blank. I suddenly feel how deeply hurt she must be, maybe wondering who I really am, whether I'm who she thought I was. I look back ten seconds and think about how easy it would have been to say something else, or just nothing. Nothing. If I could do anything in the world right now, I'd go back ten, more like twenty-some seconds now, and just do nothing. Just turn those words into nothing. Why is she so quiet? What do I do?

I'm sorry, I say. I just didn't think about where we were.

Silence. She isn't talking, probably hurt, but maybe playing hard to get. Anyway, I pat the top of the tin and tell her to lighten up, that we're going to be together too long for that kind of attitude. A car goes by on the bridge and the driver looks around watching me, nearly bumping up on the curb. He probably thinks I'm some kind of nut case talking to myself. Yeah, right. Like I have to talk to myself? Like I don't have enough going on in my life that I have to talk right out loud to myself? Certain people might do that kind of thing, but not me. Not the Kneissl Kid.

We get to Sam's and there's already a couple of early customers sitting at the counter. I walk in, nod to Marie, and hide Andrea up on the shelf above the coat rack where I hang up my trench.

Jimmy walks out with a broom in one hand and a mop in the other. "You sweep, I'll follow you with the mop," he says, "And if I catch up with you before you finish you can kiss your breakfasts goodbye, forever."

Yes, sir! I say, saluting, finding that I still have on my Tweety glove, which I stuff in my pants pocket. I'll be done before you start, Boss!

I spend the next five minutes stirring up quite a breeze around the dining room, sweeping up little piles of crumbs and napkins which I pick up as I go, making sure Jimmy doesn't catch up with me. I finish in plenty of time and begin scraping the grill and cleaning out the orange juice machine. Jimmy calls me over and hands me the mop to finish his job too. Criminy, I'm thinking, can't he see I'm busy. A deal's a deal, far as I can see. Why can't he just...But I act like a gentleman and thank him for the opportunity. He shakes his head and goes back into the kitchen.

"What's in the can?" Marie asks, gesturing in Andrea's general direction with her cigarette, like I shouldn't have even bothered hiding her.

What's it to you? I say, mopping my way around her stool.

"Fine," she says, adjusting her feet, looking back down at her coffee, "Knew I shouldn't have bothered."

211

That's okay, I say, patting her on the back. I was just being a jerk.

"I know," she says, without elaboration.

I'll tell you if you really want to know, I say, leaning her way, getting in a discrete pucker peek.

"Look," she says, "You tell me if you want, I really don't care if you do or you don't."

Okay then, I say. I'll tell you.

So I start telling Marie about my lifelong infatuation with tulips, about how Mom had literally hundreds of them planted all around the house, how she ordered the seeds from this famous company in Holland where they cross-breed the best in the world. I tell her about how my sister, Kate, was the high school Tulip Queen back in 1971 before she got knocked up, about how I spent hours and hours helping Mom plant the seeds, weed out the beds, water the young plants, help them grow into the beautiful flowers that people spend money on all over the world. I tell her that I found a mail-order greenhouse in West Virginia that specializes in seeds for the famous Grout Van Ness tulip that brings top dollar everywhere, and that I intend to start planting them all over Huntington to advertise the fact that I have the seeds to sell.

"I thought tulips grew from bulbs," she says.

"That's right. From bulbs," says Andrea, "Not seeds, you idiot."

I half-turn and hold a finger up to shush Andrea, then I tell Marie that she is technically correct, but that the Grout Van Ness is probably the most specialized tulip in the world and that it must be started from seed before it can get to the bulb stage.

"No shit," says Marie, looking at me a little funny, "I never knew that, and my mother's a tulip lover."

"Now, where do you go with this little story, Hon?" asks Andrea from up on the shelf, louder this time. "First you scare the living shit out of me on the bridge, then you start with your games, like I'm just another can full of your goddam lies."

No, wait, I say. I didn't mean...

"Mean what?" asks Marie, looking me square in the eyes now, no longer interested in the can on the shelf, which is probably a good thing.

Mean what? I repeat, with absolutely no idea what she's talking about.

Marie shakes her head and takes a sip of her coffee, a drag on her cigarette. "I'm just so confused when you're around," she says.

I'm standing here with her on my right side and Andrea up here to my left, and she's confused? You could take that one a couple of ways, all different. Might mean she thinks I'm a real jerk, kind of a squirrel. But just maybe she's beginning to see me as I am: a real alternative to the country boys and wife-beaters, the car fags and deer hunters, the bartenders and other lowbrows in her life, maybe even a husband. Now that would definitely be confusing. So I lean over toward her and playfully lay my head against her shoulder, telling her I'm confusing because I'm such a complicated person. I take the opportunity for another quick peek down the Gap, and suddenly I hear Andrea's voice booming that "something just awful could happen to that big dick if I ever see you doing that again". I jerk my head off Marie's shoulder and turn so the mop is between me and Andrea, just in case.

"You okay?" Marie asks, without empathy or sarcasm, looking straight ahead. "You seem tired or something."

Me? Tired? Well, I'm thinking, you can bet your sweet, little waitress job on that one, Hon. I stay awake until I can't think anymore, then my head flops back against something solid and I slouch there all night because the goddam demons, 'scuse my French, keep me out of the toboggan, upstairs in an apartment too small to stretch out my legs unless I'm sitting up straight. Tired? Yeah, I think so.

Got a lot on my mind, is all, I say. I hold my hand up to show her it doesn't shake, yet. When I can't pick my coffee up off the counter, or when you see me sleeping in the back booth, then you'll know I'm tired.

"Okay, fine," says Marie, looking hard down her nose at me. Like she doesn't believe a word of it.

Andrea's got me all tied up in little knots lately, even without the lack of sleep. I kind of like the idea of bringing her places with me - something I really never got to do when she was alive - but she's a bit of a package. I'm having enough fun with her that I haven't been thinking about Marie quite as much as I used to. And that's a big change. I still get all hot and bothered when I see her, as long as she doesn't have a puss on, but I sometimes even get the feeling that I could actually live without her. Then I look over at her and I know that she's still number one out of the girlfriends that I've ever had, ones that are still alive, anyway. Oh, Marie!

After breakfast we head down to the Mortar and Pestilence where I hope to be able to buy some aspirins before the owner decides to throw me out again. We stop at the laundromat first so I can test the bill changer again.

I'm telling you, I say, setting Andrea on the underwear folding table. It's always worth the time to stop in here. I got 25 percent on the dollar every time I fed one in. It worked all night until I guess I emptied it out, had to carry a huge load of quarters back to the apartment.

Andrea asks why it doesn't work anymore and I begin to explain how I saw the two guys working on it next morning, how it's been giving out exact change from that day on. So far, at least.

"Who are you talking to?" asks a woman dragging wet clumps of sheets out of a washer, muscling them into the dryer next to the change machine.

None of your beeswax, I say, winking at Andrea, picking up my quarters and the tin for the walk to the drug store. You have your secrets, I have my own. We'll just keep it that way, okay?

She stares at me as I lift the hem of my trench and shove Andrea up and under. I stick my left hand through the hole in my pocket and cradle the Andrea against my hip. I wave goodbye with my other hand in the Tweety glove and shove the door open with my shoulder.

Halfway down the block I take a quick peek at my reflection in a store window to square up my shoulders, to make sure I'm in balance. I generally make good use of every mirror, especially bar back mirrors, but I'm suddenly taken aback a little by my appearance. My hair has grown out very nicely since I arrived here, thank you, and my beard is looking pretty good, too. But my trench is definitely showing its age, without even considering the pocket, which I can't see. My pants have a couple of holes, but my longjohns keep everything in where it belongs, if you get my drift. I'm thinking that a real shower - something a little better than the sponge baths I get at the lodge - might be in order. Run hard and put away wet. But the funeral parlor is the only place I've been lately where I've run into a nice bathroom with more than just stalls for my novel and sinks for washing my face. And nobody around last time I was there. I could easily sneak back in and take a bath if I really felt like it, since I guess I can be invisible there easier than most places. Perfect opportunity, but there's no way I'd ever take Andrea back there. Nope. Maybe I'll get some handi-wipes along with the aspirin, I'm thinking, jingling the quarters in my other pocket.

"HOW BIG?" HE ASKS, LOOKING down at the tiny aspirin bottle and packet of handi-wipes.

I need something to carry this in, too, I say, holding Andrea up for him to see, but not to touch. What's the big deal about a goddam paper bag, anyway. I mean, it's not like they cost an arm and a le...*Get it together, Ave, before you find out the hard way. I just don't s...*uch a goddam tightwad that he can't give me a simple shopping bag? For Crissake, I mean, I'm giving him good money for them. It's not like I'm st... *ay calm, Ave. You're making him wonder about you. You sh...* ould fit in this one, give it a try," he says.

I stand here looking at him for a moment, then I take the bag and shake it open with a quick snap, just like I used to do bagging at Jake's Superette before I got fired for whatever it was they said I did there. I look up at him and smile that way I do when I do something that other people don't think I can do.

Okay, Hon, here we go, I say, as I carefully slide Andrea into the bag and put the aspirin and handi-wipes into my trench pocket. You'll be fine here. I pat the bag and he looks at me with his eyes bugging out of his head like he's passing a kidney stone or something.

Thanks, I say. Always a pleasure doing business at the Mortar and Pestilence.

"Asshole," Andrea says, and I have to open the top of the bag to shush her, glancing down the deodorant aisle for the Captain as we head for the door.

DUDLEY DOORIGHT PULLS UP ALONGSIDE before we get two blocks. He stops just ahead of us and sits there waiting. He gestures us over as we walk past.

"Well, if it isn't the Kneissl Kid," he says, adjusting the tilt of his sunglasses, "Where's your wheelie thing?"

It's a unicycle, I say, frowning at his stupidity, but smiling at the personal recognition. I've garaged it for the winter months.

"That a fact?" he says, adjusting the tilt of his hat above the tilt of his sunglasses.

Yes, it is, I say, smirking. I know that he has something

else on his mind, though, and I'm thinking it has something to do with the Mortar and Pestilence.

"What's in the bag," he asks, his eyes maybe glancing down at the bag but I can't be sure with the sunglasses on.

That's for me to know and you to f..., I say, but think immediately that I really don't need him to find out anything right here, right now. He might not appreciate the fact that I'm carrying a babe around in a can, especially in his town. He probably wouldn't understand the whole thing, or even the various little parts of it. He doesn't know what she means to me and how I'm the only person in the whole world who cares about her anymore. I mean, Criminy, he was probably right there that night pulling her out of the creek. Just another stiff on the way to the parlor, probably all he thinks of her. I'm certainly not about to let anybody take her from me at this point, let alone some cop who can't seem to give her the basic respect she deser...*very interesting, Ave. You still seem to get all worked up over the little things, I just don't know wha...*a look, please," he says, and I start to sweat a little more. What do I do now? He's got no right, I'm thinking. Why doesn't he just do his job, catch some criminals or something? Me, I'm just a very tired young man walking down the street minding my own business with my girlfriend, and...then we can both move on, okay?" he says, adjusting his stance.

I stand here wondering what to do next, wondering what it is he wants. I want to get away from here and out of this situation, but I don't have my uni with me. I'm sure he'd catch me right away if I ran, no help there. And he'd probably call somebody on his radio and they'd hunt me down or something anyway. Jack me like a deer. So I don't run, but I don't really know what comes next, either. I look back over at him and I clutch the bag a little tighter. I decide that I have to deal with him one way or the other to get out of this, so I ask him the one question that comes to mind at the moment, the epitome of all questions, the one that I've used hundreds, if not thousands, of times before to get me out of touchy situations.

Why? I ask.

Well, this takes him by surprise, I guess, because he doesn't say anything, just stares at me like I've asked him for the key to the universe, like I'm speaking European or something. And I really wouldn't expect Officer E. Y. Cotterly of Huntington, New York to know much about that.

"We've had a call about a possible situation, and I'd like to look in the bag, sir," he says, finally.

So I pull Andrea out of the bag and hold her up against my body as I turn the bag upside down and shake it so he can see I haven't stolen anything. See? I say.

"What's inside the can?" he asks, and my face goes pale as the shirt behind his clip-on necktie. I figure that I have to tell him or I'm headed for more trouble than I need. The truth will set you free, they say, or something like that. But I've never been convinced. In my experience, the truth makes other people follow me around, watch me. Makes me think hard about things that other people just take for granted, like walking. The truth, for me, has always been something else. More like hard, cold reality than something safe to fall back on. Not always what it's cracked up to be, you ask me.

Well, to tell you the truth, I say. There's something I do that I don't generally talk about. You know, I get a little embarrassed by the recognition sometimes. For a couple of years now I've been doing some volunteer work in the cemetery up the hill where my Mom is buried. She passed on awhile back and I visit every day to see her. Every day. Now, I don't know if you spend much time up there, do you?

"No," he says, "I have enough to do down here on the street."

Well, I continue. The whole place is just littered with dogshit, scuse my French, and I know how Mom feels about that! She used to get so worked up over the dogs coming and going in our front yard, even put a fence up just before she, before, before she died. It makes me almost cry to think about her being up there with some dog doing his business right in front of her final resting place. I mean, they never gave her any rest while she was alive, and...

At this point I turn away and wipe my eyes even though they are about as dry as the Sahara and there's no sink in sight. I turn back and tell him I need a moment, then wipe again before continuing. I'm thinking that I could do better if I could just crack open one of the handi-wipes and squeeze a little onto my cheek or something, without him seeing it. But I guess I should probably learn how those movie actors get the flow going. Might come in handy someday. I smirk at the quality of my little joke and turn around toward him again.

So, I've started walking around there every couple of days collecting all the piles I can find to keep the place a little cleaner. I don't know if you've got a Mom or anybody up there, but it's hard, very hard to visit under those circumstances. You never visit anyone up there?

"No, can't say that I do," he says, looking a little fidgety now.

Well, I say. I do. And I think it's important for somebody to take responsibility for...

"Okay, look," he says, "I don't need to get into the details," glancing at the can, "You mind if I check your pockets?"

Sure, no problem, I say, slipping Andrea back into the bag and carefully setting her on the sidewalk. I pull out my trench pocket with the hole in the bottom, telling him that he'd have to look just about forever to find anything in there. Then I pull out the other one with the aspirin and handi-wipes.

"You got a receipt for them?" he asks.

No, but I paid for them just now, I say. Down the street at the Mortar and Pestilence.

"The what?" he asks.

You know, the drug store, I say, wondering just how stupid you can be and still be a cop around here.

So, he asks if I'd mind taking a little ride back there so he can talk to Mr. Hamilton. I tell him that I've got nothing to hide, which isn't exactly true, but it works pretty well in situations like this. I get in the back seat with Andrea, and Officer Cotterly does a K-turn to go back down the street a block. Jesum, I'm thinking, he could have just as easily backed up. Or we could have just walked. But cops like to do things like that to show they're in charge, I guess.

Officer Cotterly pulls up at the curb and asks me to sit tight for a minute while he goes inside. After he's gone I try the door and find it locked. This doesn't seem right, since I'm not under arrest or anything, but I know everything is going to turn out fine since I've got Andrea and he isn't interested in looking inside this particular can any more. I set her on the seat next to me and stretch out, my fingers laced behind my neck, yawning.

When Officer Cotterly returns he catches me talking to Andrea but looks like he doesn't understand what's happening. I ask if everything is alright, and he replies that Mr. Hamilton verified the purchases I made.

So, we can go, right? I ask, realizing a little late that I maybe should have kept Andrea out of this sentence, put a little more thought into it. I hope that I haven't wasted a perfectly good story by spilling beans with a stupid off-hand comment. So I whisper to Andrea that everything is fine, that she should relax.

I hear a click inside the door and he says that I can go.

"Be careful who you talk to in this town," he says, and I salute with my Tweety glove as I climb out of the car.

JANUARY 22ND

THE BIG NEWS is all about the Olympics this year. Everyone at Huntington is talking, and a lot of people are planning on driving north to Lake Placid, up in my old stomping ground. The European instructors here all seem to have friends racing on the European team. I keep thinking that I could have been there, skiing for the good old USA if I'd stayed up north a little longer. Or turned down Marcy State. I know I'd be right up there with them, kicking European butt for Old Glory. God knows I can out-ski all these Nazis here on their best day, with my eyes shut, carrying Andrea under my trench, even. Pisses them off to see me ski right up to their little group lessons and pull one of my famous thumbs-up, spread-eagle jumps. I'd like to see them do that someday, I would. And I tell them so, right in front of their little chickadees, I do. Maybe that's why they get so aggravated, who knows?

I must be feeling better about things, because I've had three decent nights of sleep back in the toboggan without the demons. I lie here, close my eyes real hard, and count to a hundred. I sometimes hear them skittering around the edges in my thirties and forties, but I just keep on counting. Then all of a sudden it's morning, or at least not the middle of a night full of screeching anymore. Seems to work pretty well. Maybe they don't like math or something. Or maybe they're just afraid of Andrea.

Man, it doesn't get any better than this! A place to sleep, a place to eat, a place to ski for free. And I get to sleep with Andrea. I've picked her up behind the water heater after skiing every day, without fail, just like she deserves. Later today, I think we'll have a little drink at the bar while we wait for the sun to go down.

Andrea is such a comfort at night like this, especially when it's cold and lonely, which is pretty much all the time around here. She's not at all afraid to ride the tray anymore, and she even seems to look forward to it. I hate leaving her in a basement all day, but it's warm and we've discussed it for the last time. It's for her own good.

A BEER, I SAY. AND not that watery Milwaukee piss, 'scuse my French. She knows what I want, but I have to say this each time, just because it cracks me up. She brings me a Utica Club and counts out a pile of quarters. I chug the beer and signal for another before she drops the coins into the register. She rolls her eyes and brings me another.

"Now, before I go," she asks, "Are you going to want another right away?"

Probably, I say, winking large. But I won't know for sure until I drink this one.

I do this a couple more times and she's getting a little sick of me. And I'm getting a little drunk. I've got Andrea up on my lap now, leaving her stool empty for someone else – someone with buttons that face the right way, if you get my drift - except that nobody sits down. And now Andrea wants a drink.

Another beer, please, I say, winking large. And a nice, dry Manhattan.

"You sure?" she asks, arching her eyebrows.

Oh, yeah, I say, imitating her facial expression and the tone of her voice, staring her right in the left eye.

She shrugs and walks over to fill the beer and mix the

Manhattan. When she returns I have to pull another handful of quarters out to make up the difference. I take a sip of the beer and look her in the eye again until she's uncomfortable enough to walk away. Then I look all around - something I'm actually getting into the habit of doing - and quickly pry the top off Andrea's can. I look around again, pour the Manhattan over the top of the gritty ashes, and quickly replace the lid.

Cheers, I say, clinking my beer glass up against the side of the can.

"That went down quick," says the bartender, walking past with a sloe gin fizz for the hooker sitting down the bar, "Need another?"

No thanks, I say. We're fine.

She looks at me funny, then shakes her head as she delivers the drink down the bar. I know she didn't see anything, though, so I'm not worried about it.

So, was it dry enough? I ask. I know you have to tell them here, or you get one that's all syrupy the way *some* people seem to like them, I say, rolling my eyes at the hooker sitting four stools away.

We decide it's probably a good idea to leave now since I'm drunk and several patrons have started watching us for some reason. I pick up Andrea and ooch her under my arm. I say goodbye to the bartender who doesn't say anything at all in return. I wave to the hooker who toodles her fingers at me and winks.

We take the long way around the bottom of the beginner's area to make sure everyone has left for the day. We sit down at the edge of the treeline for several minutes until we are sure the coast is clear.

I reach in and fire up the T-Bar and pull out my tray. We have the tray ride down pat now. I set up, look back, duck my head, and wait for the next T-Bar to come around the bullwheel. I grab it and we're off again, on our way back home, jiggetty jig.

I miss Hoot's greetings at the end of a day like this. When I'm skiing, he yells something every time I come up here and I feel like I'm somebody, like I'm really somebody special. Andrea would be proud seeing me recognized for who I am, knowing her boyfriend is somebody famous. But I can't bring her up here during the day since Hoot's all funny about her for some reason. Anyway, she did get to read part of my novel before she died. At least she had some idea of who I am, who I'm going to be. That makes me feel pretty good, too. I only wish she'd stayed around long enough to finish it.

"Yeah, right. As if I had any choice in that."

Actually, I wish I could just finish it. I've tried hard enough, Criminy, I've tried. I've spent hours in the second stall in the Klondike, in the rest room at the laundromat, just sitting and staring at my napkins. Just staring at them. I just can't seem to get past the first word for some reason. Maybe I'm just looking for words in all the wrong places, I don't know. They came so easily in the Troubadour, in Gus's Gas, the lodge. Lately, I've had to scratch out half a sentence several times after getting sick of my style, or maybe lack of style. I need inspiration, even though I know exactly where the story is going and how it's going to end. But, for some reason, I just can't seem to put it together anymore. The words just won't line up.

We reach the top and I let go of the bar and drag my feet to stop the tray. I hit the emergency stop and we walk over to the empty shack. I set Andrea on the shelf by the bench, her usual perch, and I tape a few pages of the *What's Up?* over the window before lighting a candle. I light the pilot on the heater and turn it on, crackling and ticking as the heat begins to fill the shack. I look around and think that this has to be about the most romantic place you could ever imagine.

Sitting here with my back to the wall and my legs

stretched out about as far as they can go in here, I reach up and bring Andrea down to sit on my lap. I hug her and tell her how much I love her, and that I'll always be there for her. I pull out Hoot's whiskey and take a couple of tugs which I don't really need after all the beer. I'm getting a little sloppy and I'm hoping I don't do anything too forward, too unseemly, with Andrea.

You know, I say. You probably don't know it - or don't care maybe - I don't know, but you've been, uh, like a real inspiration to me since we met back in the Troubadour. You're the first woman I've been able to really open up to in a long time. Maybe you can help me with a little problem I'm having.

"Fat chance," she says, and I'm not completely sure it isn't Mom talking. But I continue anyway.

It's my story, I say. It's, I don't know, just harder and harder to get anything down these days. It's just not coming out the way it used to.

"That's been your problem from day one," she says, "Getting it out."

I'm trying, I swear, I'm really trying, I say. But it's just stuck somewhere.

"You had it out once, Buddy Boy, if you stop to remember," she says.

Buck, Buck Avery, I say.

"You had it out, and that big dick of yours was about to star in the best story of your goddam life, inside or outside of your little bathrooms," she continues.

That's a good metaphor, I say, thinking as critically as the beer and Hoot's whiskey allow. I'll have to think about that.

"A good what?" she asks. "Is that what you kids call it these days? You start thinking too long about something and all of a sudden something else is happening around you.

And you've got no idea what's going on. But you're done now, finished, a virgin for the rest of your life. End of story."

I cringe a little but I'm thinking that she's probably got a point. Life is just too short, and she ought to know. If I want to succeed, I guess I have to just start writing, get it out and over with.

"I was yours for the taking, but you're mine, now," she says, "Your little story is going nowhere because you're scared of the real story. You can't deal with my story, how are you going to make one up? Well, it's my story from now on."

You know, my biggest problem is where to go with my main character, a certain lady, this really beautiful lady, I say, glancing down at Andrea. This lady who lives over a little cafe in the Yalps, you know, over in Europe. The Kneissl Kid is winning everything he enters, but she's still cold and distant with him.

"So, does he ever give her what she wants?", she asks, "Does he ever act like she's got needs, too? Does he ever really think about her, take her seriously?"

Hmmm, I say. Maybe I'm not taking her seriously enough, too loose with the details. I need to give her something to do, a big piece of plot to work with. I mean, The Kneissl Kid loves her and all that, but he just got kicked out of the cafe where she works and he can't get in touch with her, and he...

"See," she says. "It's all about him. He's probably this perfect, superman-type of guy with nothing wrong with him, right? She needs to be taken seriously, too. Just give her some respect. And since it's me you're writing about – right? - I get to tell you just what I want in there. And I'll do you a big favor. Since it's all my story from now on, you got one hot ghostwriter, Hon."

Well, I say, feeling pretty sheepish right about now. It's all right there, written down. I mean, I've watched you walk, listened to the way you talk and all, and - this is hard, I mean, I've never told anybody this – but I've always been attracted to you. I mean, I keep thinking about how your sweater used to drape across your, uh, your chest like that saran wrap stuff, you know. There's some of that in my, uh...in your story.

"Isn't that sweet," she says.

I'm learning more about her every day, I guess. What she sees, what she doesn't. What she's thinking, how much she knows about my work, things like that. I feel like I should be completely open with her, but as long as she thinks she's the queen bee around here, I can probably keep moving forward with Marie. I'm pretty sure she doesn't suspect a thing. I wink large and pat my napkins.

"But you touch that bitch down at Sam's again and I'll have your balls dancing and sizzling on top of that heater over there, just try me."

Well, this is bit of a shocker and makes me wonder if we aren't on two different pages, which isn't all that unusual with men and women, especially in an unfinished story. My unmentionables suddenly feel tiny and vulnerable at the thought, but I'm not about to give her the chance to do anything like that to me. Criminy, my little story just made a big down payment on keeping her happy for years. I definitely know that a good story is always better than the truth, most of the time, anyway. Besides, she can't read it, especially if I don't bring her in with me.

No way, I say, crossing my fingers, just in case. You sound like I'm about to run off with some little bimbo, or something. Marie's a very difficult person to like, and she speaks way too much French. That's all there is to it. It's all I can handle just working there with her.

"Just keep your hands on the salt shakers and orange juice machine," she says, "And keep your eyes where they belong."

Yes, ma'am, I say, smirking a little, hoping she doesn't see it. I'm a one-woman man from morning till night.

"You just keep it in your pants," she says, "You had your chance and you blew it. You're done now, forever."

Man, she is one inscrutable babe. I can't keep track of her train of thought sometimes, even on a good day. But she's probably got good advice on my work, anyway. And it's not like I don't need help.

This has been really helpful, I say. And I think I've got a better idea of where this is going, like, what I've got to do from now on. I've got lots more work to do before that last chapter gets written in the stall at Sam's.

"You take that bitch into a stall, you're a dead man," she says, "Just try me. I see these things, don't you understand? I can do things you can't even dream of. I can take you out like a bag of trash, anytime, anywhere."

I suddenly feel like I've had much too much to drink at this point, and I'm getting very uneasy about responsibility, consequences, about things spinning out of control. Something like that. Which is exactly how I feel right now, anyway.

I feel like a good story never ends. The better it is, the longer it runs. But you have to work to keep up with it every day, stay right with it so you don't make some stupid comment someday that blows it all apart. I mean, they start out little, usually to get you out of some kind of trouble, then they just start growing. Growing and opening up like beautiful tulips. Some faster than others, some just die away on their own because you don't need them anymore. But you've got to - absolutely got to - keep up with them. Some of them get so beautiful as they grow. Just spectacular. But you've got to be careful about them, about them getting too far from the tru...I don't know, it's like, like a garden and there's weeds all over, and you just have to keep at it. Keep up with them. And somehow keep your fucking head, 'scuse my French, from blowing right out into space somewhere.

And I'm getting a little dizzy thinking about me, myself, and I, how my own little story has to end someday, somewhere.

Having Andrea here reassures me that there is something afterwards, that the story keeps moving forward as long as there's somebody else around to keep it going. She scares me a little, but she's got a real good story in there somewhere. I just have to pretend to let her help me, that she's my only inspiration. And keep my mouth shut.

But I bet she's still all confused, and probably not thinking at her best, either. It's a big change she's going through lately, and I bet there's things we don't know anything about. Things start happening that they never let you in on when you're alive. The dead have their little secrets just like we have our little stories. I feel kind of funny about it, but I bet she's got things she isn't telling me, either. But I'm feeling really, really drunk, and a little spooked, right at the moment.

But piss on that, 'scuse my French. I'm going to get moving right now – well, maybe in the morning - and I'm hoping that I can get the last couple of chapters down in the next few weeks or so. Then I can start telling everyone all about it. I know Andrea's bound to be putting her two cents in every time I sit down with her, every time I start a new scene. But I deal with quarters – a little out of her league, I'd say. She'll never know it isn't her I'm writing about. Spin one tale for the rest of the world, tell her another. She won't know. At least I don't think she will. She's dead, after all. But if she does happen to see things I think about, it's me that's dead.

Being dead must be something like being in a novel, anyway. Nothing but one metaphor after another once you start dealing with the ashes-to-ashes, rust-to-rust kind of thing. She must see things in a clearer light now. But, I don't know, maybe not. Seems like she bought my little story, anyway.

Okay, Hon, I say, picking her up, giving her a little bounce or two. Time for bed, or I'll be too drunk to get you down there. Andrea?

She must have dropped off while I was sitting here

thinking. So I stick my feet back in my boots and pull on my trench, buttoning it to the collar. I stick Andrea up and under, and we skid down and around the shack with my four blankets. I pull our toboggan halfway out of its cubby and pull back the canvas cover. I reach inside and set Andrea toward the front of the cubby where she'll be right next to my head once I'm back in and covered up.

It's really quite nice here, I'm thinking, as I nestle the sleeping Andrea in with me under the canvas. She seems so sweet and vulnerable when she's sleeping. But it sometimes makes me feel really, really bad for some reason. I don't know. I feel kind of dirty, like she deserves a lot more out of...well... more than I can give her, anyway.

All I have to do is keep up with my story, make sure I don't get ambushed by the future or anything. Keep it up for now and the problem's bound to go away as soon as I'm published and we start talking about something else for a change. Like a house and a car, for instance. But she sure seems comfortable right here, right now.

JANUARY 23RD

ANDREA, ANDREA, I yell, a little too loud I guess, shaking her awake. You're not going to like this at all.

A hard, cold rain is falling, windswept into sheets thrashing up against the side of the shack, into the toboggan cubby. The canvas cover isn't exactly leaking, but rain is finding its way along the folds and seams to drip into the toboggan somewhere and soak the seat of my pants. Andrea is high and dry, up next to my head, but that's about to change and she's not going to like it.

Andrea, it's quarter to six and we have to be up and out of here right now. I'll keep you as dry as I can, but you'll have to help.

I reach my arms out from below the canvas and pull the toboggan halfway out. I'm really getting pelted now, so I scramble up and out as fast as I can without dropping Andrea. I throw the canvas roughly back in place, grab my four blankets, and make a dash for the shack.

The rain is hitting the window in waves, and I can't see the lights at the bottom of the lift anymore. It would be so tempting, I'm thinking, to light the gas heater, settle back with Hoot's whiskey, and have a nice, slow cigarette if there was maybe one in my pocket. But this is crazy. We have to be out of here right now, rain or no rain.

I check to make sure everything is where it belongs, all hidden nicely in Hoot's shack.

He'll be up here in couple of hours and he'll need all the inside room he can get today, I say, tidying up around Andrea's perch on the cupboard. Then again, if he's sick and they send somebody else up for the day and he finds my stuff...I'm up shit's creek without a saddle, 'scuse my French.

These are the days, those stressful days, when you're more likely to leave something stupid just lying around here. So I make a really careful inspection before boosting Andrea up and under my trench, pulling my two hats over my head and ears, grabbing our tray, and heading out into what looks like the worst day of the rest of my life.

The snow is very fast under the tray and we bounce along, sending out waves of slush each time we land. My crotch is soaked through my jeans, two pairs of waffle weave, and my skivvies. My face is soaked from the bursts of water coming off the front of the tray, the ones that get past my crotch, anyway. Andrea is fine, though; safe under two wool shirts, three pages of yesterday's *What's Up*, and a trench coat, to say nothing of being sealed up nice inside the can.

I definitely don't have time to take Andrea over to her closet before work this morning. I'm on real shaky ground with Jimmy already. I can't risk another day being late, especially soaking wet. So we walk straight for the bridge in a steady, wind-whipped downpour. I have both hands in my pockets; my left one cradling Andrea through the hole in the bottom, my right one just keeping warm between trips outside to wipe rain out of my eyes.

I know she's awake, but she's awfully quiet this morning. No woman likes to be pulled out of bed this early, just to go out in the rain. There's just nothing I can do about that, though. She knows the rules just as well as I do. Maybe it's about crossing this bridge, I don't know.

We make it to Sam's a couple minutes early, and I would

normally get right in Jimmy's face so he knows it, so he can't ignore the fact. But today I'm a little concerned about bringing Andrea back in with me, and I just slip over to the coat rack where I pull my dripping trench off over my soaked wool shirts and hang it away from the others. I look all around, like I've been practicing more and more lately, before hoisting Andrea up onto the hat rack, hiding her behind a little yellow booster seat.

Hey, Jimmy, I yell, maybe a little too loud, as I pick the last inky pulp of what used to be the *What's Up?* off my wool shirt. Look who's in early today, huh? Look who's here.

Jimmy just points a long-tined fork at the clock above the grill and plunges it back into the rump roast he's checking. I guess I'm actually three minutes late with all the hoopla getting Andrea settled.

Don't worry, I say. I'll just be done three minutes early this morning. Jimmy rolls his eyes as I roll into action, dashing from table-to-table replacing condiments and butter patties, checking salt and pepper shakers, filling napkin dispensers, and leaving wet snail tracks everywhere I go this morning. It makes sweeping a bit of a task, but once I get it mopped everything will look normal.

I drop down on the stool next to Marie and wave to Jimmy for some coffee. He tells me to get it myself, and I do. I sit back down more carefully and set the mug next to my lighter. I yawn and pat at my mouth – since yawning is one of my best covers - and I sneak a quick glance down the Gap this morning. But I recoil, smacking myself in the lip, as I hear a loud bang up on the hat rack.

I'm sorry, I blurt, my face going suddenly pale. It was an accident.

Marie looks at me, staring for a moment, and replies, "Why? You do something?"

I mean, how do I tell her that I wasn't talking to her when she's the only person in the place at the moment, except for

Herb Dixon who just came in and tossed his hardhat up onto the rack. I look up there and it's still rocking and turning, upside down next to Andrea, who is now fully awake.

"What the hell is going on?" asks Andrea, her voice crackling with sleep and rage.

I didn't do anything, I say. It was Herb, he didn't mean anything by it.

"Mean anything by what?" asks Marie, leaning into the conversation now, "Did I miss something?"

It's hard to explain, I say, keeping my back to Herb Dixon, hoping he didn't hear the exchange. Let's just drop it, okay?

"Suit yourself," she says, eyebrows arching, going back to the reality of her coffee.

"We ain't dropping shit," Andrea booms, "First you wake me up in the rain, practically gag me under that stinking trench coat at six-goddam-o'clock in the morning, and hide me up on a hat rack like you're ashamed of me. Then some asshole throws his hardhat at me and treats me like I'm not even here. No, we ain't dropping shit, Buddy Boy."

Buck, Buck Avery, I say. Marie turns to look at me again. Thinking fast, I tug my season's pass out of my wool shirt on its lanyard and hold it dangling up in front of my face. See?

"Yeah, I see," she says, "But I'll never, ever understand." She turns back to her coffee as Andrea continues to rant from up on the hat rack. She's beginning to make me fidget, beginning to embarrass me with her inappropriateness. I mean, why not deal with this later, in the right place, at the right time? I do her the favor of getting her out every day, every day, so she doesn't have to endu…*Really, Ave, I'm, so embarrassed! You're in a public place. Just look at yourself! You've gotten all wet and smelly, you're talking to yourself again, and there's absolutely nothing more I can do for you! Nothing! You'll just have to think your own way through these things from now o*…nothing that other people in her condition have to put up with. I mean, she's really got it pretty good, on the

234

whole. Criminy, I take her out drinking. How many guys do you think would do that? C'mon, Hon, you've got all the answers, how many, huh?

How many? I yell, slamming my mug down on the counter, swiveling around and off the stool to glare at her. We're out of here.

Marie and Herb are staring now as I rip my trench off the hanger and shove my damp arms back into its own wetness. I pull Andrea out from in back of the booster seat, knocking it to skitter across the floor toward the kitchen. I pull my hats on and shove Andrea underneath the trench, reaching through the hole in the pocket to hold her, just a bit roughly this time, up against my chest.

Jimmy comes striding out of the kitchen with a huge roasting pan leading the way, his stomach right behind it, hiding his feet. He hits the spinning booster chair and trips badly, slamming the pan and its drippings down on the top of Table 3. He is on his knees now, looking over the top of the pan at me, maybe feeling a sprained ankle or something, I don't know. He stares and stares as I button my trench with one hand.

"Don't even think about coming back in here, ever," he says, wiping beef gravy off his forehead, "You're nothing but trouble. I don't know why I've been putting up with you. Jesus, just go!"

I wave to Marie, who doesn't acknowledge me at all, and feel a stab of pain in my side. Then it's out into the pouring rain again. I have the growing feeling that I can't come back here, even though I know that I have to.

The walk back up to the lodge is miserable, and Andrea does nothing to improve the situation with her constant complaints and accusations. There are only a few cars in the lot, but the lifts are running. A bank of fog obscures the top of the mountain from the mid-station up. I am soaked through and getting pretty cold, but the snow felt pretty fast and soft on the tray ride down this morning. I think I'll ski today since there's absolutely nothing else to do and I'm getting pretty sick of listening to Andrea.

She is really upset as we walk down the stairs. She knows where we're headed and she definitely doesn't want to spend the day behind the water heater after what she considers as pretty shabby treatment already. She just won't stop, and it's getting to me. Jesum, relax, I keep telling her. She keeps ragging on me from behind the heater as I search the closet for trash bags to use as rain gear.

"It's all about you, isn't it?" she says, her sarcasm every bit as wet and cold as the January rain, "Your job, your apartment, your ski season. Just where do I fit in?"

Look, I say, pulling a clear 30-gallon bag off the roll I find behind the mops, holding it up to check the size. I've got a life to live, too. Then I realize that may be a little insensitive under the circumstances.

"I can't believe you just said that," she says, "I'm starting to understand you a little better, I guess. It's just an I'm-alive-you're-dead sort of thing with you lately. You can really be a pompous prick at times, you know that?"

Listen, I say, carefully cutting head and arm holes in the trash bag, pulling it over my shoulders, turning left and right to check the look of my brand, new anorak in the little mirror on the wall. It's not about me, it's about us. Us. You and me. Satisfied with the fit, I pull another bag off the roll and cut the bottom open with my pocket knife.

"Just take a look at yourself," she says, "You're doing this and doing that, not even paying attention to me. It's always all about you, isn't it, Buddy Boy?"

Buck, Buck Avery, I say, stepping into my clear plastic skirt with my left leg, then my right. And just how many people do you know who would have done what I did to save you from a dark forever in that basement? Huh? How many people would bring you along everywhere they go, give things up in their lives, change their everyday routines for you? Huh?

"It's just words," she says, as I pull up the plastic skirt and tuck it in carefully under my belt, smoothing the upper bag over the lower one like shingles, "Just little words."

Look, Hon, I say. We'll talk later, I've got a lot on my mind and I've got things to do.

"Right," she says, "Like this skiing shit. The only reason you do it is because you walk funny, because you think you look better when you slide on those goddam things, because you think it distracts people. Well, let me tell you. This wheelie thing you ride around on? Same deal. You try to attract attention when you're on it because you're an bumbling idiot when you're not, and you know it. Just because you may be good at something doesn't distract me a bit. You've got quite a way to go with the rest of your sorry life, Buddy Boy."

Buck, Buck Avery, I say, sheepishly, but more than a little put off at this point. This is a little harsh, don't you think?

"More words, just little words. You just take care of Number One and leave old Andrea down in the basement. Where I belong. I understand."

Criminy, I say, smoothing out my skirt, squaring my shoulders in the mirror, winking large at my image. I just got fired, I just lost my only real meal of the day from now on, and I don't have time for this.

I slam the door closed and see a maintenance guy pretending to mop the hallway, maybe listening to me dealing with Andrea, I don't know. He watches me walk by in my two plastic bags, two hats, two wool shirts, waffle-weave longjohns, bluejeans that need washing, three new layers of soggy *Huntington What's Up?*, and a saturated trench coat. I'm ready to ski!

I'M SURE GLAD I DON'T wear glasses because I wouldn't be able to see a thing in this driving rain. I sit on the wet seat of the chairlift

- alone, because there are only two other children skiing today - and watch the rain pooling up on my plastic skirt, draining down off my plastic anorak, turning my wrist a dark blue where the dye is leaching out of my Tweety glove. A wave of rain plasters up against me and I turn my head to the side to keep it out of my eyes. I feel a small stream trickling down the back of my neck where the trash bag puckers a little, and I wish I had taken the time to duct-tape the bag tightly around my throat. I'm going to be soaked from armpit to asshole, as Dad would say.

I approach the top, raise the safety bar, and shove off for the next run of the rest of my life. I salute the liftie sitting warm and dry inside his shack and skate off down the hill, gaining speed on the fast snow. The faster I go, the harder it rains, or at least that's what it feels like. I swoop into a series of wide turns, my knees absorbing the little bumps, throwing waves to either side as I set my edges in the soupy softness. This is as good as it gets, I'm thinking, as I feel the wonderful combination of speed and softness below my feet.

The only problem is that I can see maybe ten feet in the fog up here. I don't have to worry about running into anyone, but trees seem to appear out of nowhere every couple of turns or so. The snow is so soft and fast that I just smile, close my eyes, and take it all in. The feeling is extraordinary, even though I'm about as wet as I used to get taking showers. I decide that I'm probably a lot better off squinting to keep the rain out of my eyes instead of closing them, even though that does seem to work much better.

As I reach the high meadow at the mid-station, I begin to come out of the fog, allowing me to accelerate a little down the lower mountain. I wave to the liftie at the mid-station as I whizz by, doing my trademark spread-eagle, thumbs-up jump off the big rock for his enjoyment. I soar like a hawk as gravity falls away, the rain hits me like a washcloth, and I close my eyes to relish the incredible moment. But, opening my eyes, I realize that I probably should have scouted the landing first. The rain has melted much of the snow below the rock, and all I see is gravel beneath me.

This presents a whole new set of difficulties, but I dig down deep into my imaginary pocket - the pocket where I keep all my Kneissl Kid tricks and attitude - and I find that it has a big hole in the bottom today, just like my trench. My jump takes me higher than usual which, on this particular rock, also means that it might be shorter than usual. I drop from the top of my arc and start down, ooching out as much forward momentum as I can by swinging my arms around.

I hit bottom, with the entire length of my classic Red Stars on the sharpness of gravel chunks, stopping them like a seatbelt. The extra forward momentum I fought for so hard sends my body straight ahead as my skis stop dead. The tumble begins and my face plants uncomfortably in the mud and gravel. I lose my Tweety glove and hats in the fall which I expect to end quickly. But I slide through the bare spot and back onto the snow, gaining speed on my belly, on the slickness of the trash bags covering me from armpit to asshole, and then some. I dig my skis in as best I can, and try to do a flip to get them downhill from my speeding body. I bounce painfully over several large bumps before slowly losing speed several hundred yards down the trail.

I lie here panting wildly, wondering if I've broken anything more important than my entire future, wherever that is. I shake my arms and legs and find that they are still under my control. I slowly look up and see a smear that looks like a cherry snow cone all the way from the rock I jumped. I reach up to find that my face is oozing pretty badly, and I plaster some snow on it to stop the bleeding and to keep the swelling down. Then I sit on my wet butt, in dirty clothing that smells a little different now that it's soaked, in the driving rain on a cold day in January, without a job, without a place to live, with a dead girlfriend in the lodge basement, and the rest of my life looming in front of me as mysteriously as the northern lights. Just beautiful. Can it get any better than this? And I have to wonder if things would have, or ever could have been any more beautiful – right here, right now – if a chick named Andrea didn't happen to be dead.

I shake off the memory of the fall and sidestep up to where one of my hats lies thirty yards from the other, which lies almost two-hundred yards below my Tweety glove. It takes a bit of effort to get to them, but it warms me up again and makes me even more anxious to get back to doing my turns. I squeeze out my hats and put them on. My glove drips a dark blue as I pull it back on my oozing hand. I sidestep up another twenty yards or so, pick up a ski pole, and push off to continue to the bottom.

THE BARTENDER ASKS IF I shouldn't go see the ski patrol as I order my beer and another Manhattan to keep Andrea happy, or at least quiet, for awhile. My face looks a little bit like luncheon meat, I guess, and my right hand looks a lot better with my Tweety glove on. But I wink large, telling her that only the good die young, that it's a actually stroke of luck if you get to leave a pretty corpse behind, but that under the circumstances I've got nothing to worry about, for awhile, anyway. She brings the beer and highball, avoiding eye contact, raking quarters off the bar so she doesn't have to touch my hand or anything.

I have Andrea on my lap since there are quite a few people in the bar, waiting out the rain. It's good that she's so upset and quiet, since there's an old guy next to me on the right and a hooker on my left. I can tell that this makes Andrea a little edgy, but she's taking it well. I'm pretty sure the Manhattan will help, but I've got to be a little careful with this many people around.

"So, looks like you've been outside today," says the

hooker, sipping at a Sea Breeze, "You look like you've been rode hard..."

And put away wet, I say, winking large, just like the picture on the pass hanging around my neck. Buck, Buck Avery, I say, extending my hand.

"What the hell happened to you?" she asks, recoiling from the oozing rawness,

Oh, sorry, I say. You forget about things like getting hurt when you're having so much fun.

"Out there?" she asks, "Today?"

Here, there, today, yesterday, I reply. What's the difference? Life is just so priceless.

"I suppose," she says, sipping. She takes out a cigarette and leans over for a light. I pull my lighter out of my pants pocket, light her up and ask if I can borrow a cigarette.

"No," she says, holding the uncomfortable silence for a moment, "But you can *have* one if you'd like." She breaks into cackling as she paws a cigarette out of her fake gold handbag.

Thanks, I say, feeling a stab of unfamiliar pain in my groin. I need one on a wet day like this.

"What's that?" she asks, gesturing at my wool shirt which I've unbuttoned in the heat of the lodge. It takes me a second to realize what she's talking about.

Oh, that, I say, pulling at a corner of the *What's Up?* sticking out at the collar. It pulls off into a smeared ball of pulp. That's the newspaper.

She sits there for a moment, just looking. I tape it on to keep warm, I say, unbuttoning my second wool shirt to the waist, showing her my handiwork. She sits there, just looking.

"Oh," she says, turning away to sip her Sea Breeze.

"Buck, we both know what she's after and you'd be a real fool to cheat on me like this," says Andrea, "And I'd like you to button up that shirt up right now."

Sure thing, I say, pawing at the buttons.

"It works that well, huh?" the hooker replies, "Looks a little weird, though."

Uh, yeah, I say, confused again.

"Feel like getting out of here?" she asks.

I turn her way and she's not bad looking, not bad at all. I reply, Sure, but you're not really dressed for skiing in this weather.

"I was thinking about a different form of exercise," she says, rolling her eyes and taking a big puff. She turns my way, leans in close, and blows a big, lewd smoke ring straight down toward my unmentionables, if you get my drift.

Well, all Hell breaks loose at this point and I feel an unbelievable pain in my, well, my unmentionables, as Andrea starts bouncing up and down, coughing and gasping. I'm grabbing at myself to stop the pain and the can is bouncing up and down in my lap. The hooker leans back with a big smile on her face, watching me paw at my genitals, writhing on the stool.

"Well, if that ain't the damndest thing!" she says, "I've been doing that for years and I've never seen anybody react like that."

Andrea hacks and gags while I squirm out the incredible pain I'm feeling. "Get that bitch out of here with that smoke or I'll twist them both off!" she yells, "Jesus Christ, You oughta know I can't stand smoke. Get her away from me! C'mon move! What the hell are you thinking!"

I shove the stool back away from the bar and grab Andrea, holding her away from the hooker as I scramble to the floor and run the length of the bar. Then, thinking again as the pain begins to subside, I set Andrea gently on a bench and run back to the bar to retrieve my quarters and Andrea's Manhattan. I scoop up the coins and, thinking again, shove my lighter over in front of the hooker as I take off at a dead run. She needs it more than I do at this point, I'm thinking.

It's going to be a cold day in Hell before I light up anything around Andrea again.

HERE, I SAY, PRYING OFF the lid in the safety of a men's room stall. I saved your drink. I pull out the cherry and pop it in my mouth before slowly pouring the Manhattan into the can.

I didn't think you'd mind, I say, chewing. You never used to eat them.

Silence. I hate it when she's so quiet at a time like this. I hope she's okay after the incredible fiasco upstairs. I should have known about the smoke, I guess, but I wasn't doing anything wrong.

I'm sorry, I say. But it wasn't my fault. She didn't know, how could she?

More silence. I sit here leaning back against the tank, wondering what comes next. Then I look up and see the back of the stall door: Twelve square feet of clean, varnished canvas ready for my indelible muse, ready to move my incredible novel forward toward completion. And I suddenly feel invigorated, the blood roaring in my ears as I realize in the pit of my stomach, without a bit of doubt – and perhaps for the very first time - that I really do matter as an artiste, that my work can indeed last beyond my own lifetime, that people actually do notice me.

I screw the lid back on Andrea's can and set it on the floor in front of my feet. I fumble around in my pants pocket for my girlie pen and marker, then reach in my wool shirt for my napkins. I find a wad of runny, ink-dark paper that I carefully open into separate sheets on my lap. I can barely read the smudges that are left there after my wonderful day on the slopes. But I have this feeling, this explosion of creativity, telling me that things have begun to move, that I might not even need my napkins to finish the story. I ooch forward on the seat and take my girlie pen in hand, shaking it first to watch the little titties spin, knowing it holds the key to my future. I begin my work, as a flood of images wash over me like the rain on the chairlift. My tongue curls against my bottom teeth like it does when I'm really into it, when I'm truly writing my heart out. I write faster than I've ever written in my life, the ink like a dark thread going back into the past, linking me with the timeless magic that connects the writer to the future every one of us craves. I begin to sweat under my skivvies, waffle-weave longjohns, undershirt, bluejeans, two wool shirts, a now-unreadable copy of last week's *What's Up?*, my tattered trench, and the glorious future that now lays upon me like a mink coat.

"Please, just get me out of here," says Andrea.

JANUARY 25ᵀᴴ

JUST DON'T KNOW, I say, passing the bottle back to Hoot. I'm really confused, I just don't understand what's happening to me. I'm finally back to getting my novel done, writing like a maniac. I feel like a million bucks in quarters, but my love life is going downhill faster than the Kneissl Kid.

"*You* don't understand," says Hoot, "I'm the one who don't understand shit when you're around, no offense." He takes a tug and passes the bottle back into the shack.

We're done with that? I ask, arching my eyebrows toward the door.

"We think we oughta give it a rest for awhile," says Hoot, "Besides, you'll probably knock it back considerably after I'm gone tonight."

I replace what I drink, I say. Just like we agreed, right?

Hoot knows I've kept to the agreement we made when I moved in, with a few setbacks here and there. All in all, it's been an excellent living arrangement. It would be a lot nicer if he could just accept Andrea, see her for who she is, so that she could spend a little more time up here with us.

"So, when are you gonna bring that book up for me to read?" he asks, "I can read, you know."

It's a little hard to carry around, I say. But you'll be one of the first to see it when it's done, which is going to be very soon.

"Well," Hoot replies, "I'm looking forward to seeing something else the Kneissl Kid can do. I seen some really weird shit since you come up here, that's for sure."

I think you'll like it, I say.

"Am I in it?" he asks.

Not really, I say, pointing at the door, raising my eyebrows. Bring that jug back out and we can talk about your future, though.

Hoot reaches back into the shack and pulls out the huge bottle. He looks around, uncaps it, and takes a good tug. He hands it to me.

Thanks, I say, wiping my mouth with the back of my Tweety glove, which isn't quite as colorful as it was back in November. But I never put my friends in my novels, just pieces of people here and there.

"Like the pieces in that can?" he asks.

I take a deep breath. I'd appreciate a little respect on that one, I say. And so would Andrea. You've got no respect for the dead?

"Respect's one thing," says Hoot, retrieving the bottle, taking another tug, "But sleeping with them is something else entirely."

Don't fuck around with me, 'scuse my French, I say, Somebody's got to take care of her and somebody else I know won't even let me leave her in the shack. Where else am I going to keep her?

"Where is it now?" Hoot replies.

That's none of your beeswax, I say. All you have to know is that she's safe. Criminy, you act like she wants to haunt your little shack forever. Well, I have it on pretty good authority that she hates this place and would rather live somewhere else.

"There you go again," says Hoot, throwing up his hands, "She don't live nowhere anymore. I got an idea your head ain't screwed on half as tight as the lid on that can sometimes." He takes another tug and hands me the bottle. "No offense."

You'll change that tune when you read my novel, mister, I say, wagging my finger for emphasis. This head is full of things you never dreamed of.

"I don't doubt that for a second," he replies, "You know, this year's been the most interesting one so far working up here. I got company almost every day, even if it does cost me. I got the heat turned on when I get here in the morning, and I get to read the paper you bring up here for the windows."

See, I'm not all bad.

"Buck," he says, "You're not bad at all, just crazy as a shit-house rat."

Hold that thought, I say, winking large. At least until you see what this rat's got up his sleeve in some of the shit-houses, 'scuse my French, around this town.

"You can spend your time anywhere you want," he says, "Long as you don't bring no bad smells back up here. Nothing you do could surprise me anymore."

We lean back on the bench with our legs stretched out in front, comfortable and lightly flushed with whiskey. Except for Andrea not being here, this is maybe the best place in the world right here, right now. Sitting here with my second-best friend, watching babes in stretchy pants fall down and squirm around, tugging at my favorite whiskey, thinking about Andrea - there's not much you could add to this priceless life, I'm thinking.

"So, what's on deck for the Kneissl Kid once the snow's gone?" Hoot asks, "You know, it don't last forever."

At the moment, that's about the farthest thing from my mind, I say. I've got a pass to ski on, a place to live, and a lot of work to do before I get to think about that.

"Well, once it melts, you got no way to get back and forth up here. That tray of yours ain't worth a shit on dry ground. Too far to walk."

I've never had a problem with a place to live, I say, wincing as a few passing images cross my mind. I always seem to have a roof, or something, over my head.

"Where do you go next?" he asks.

Where does the wind blow? I ask, "Where does the Pope shit, 'scuse my French?

"I don't know," he says, "But I'm sure you'll find it."

Actually, I say. This project's winding down and I'll be swimming in offers once it's done. I'm actually glad I didn't get hired as a Yellow Jack. Never would have had the time and energy to finish up my novel. Money's one thing, but there's nothing like being able to look at something you've done, something that really means a lot to you, seeing yourself in it, having other people see you in it. You should try it, Hoot.

"Hey, I can read pretty decent," says Hoot, "But I can't write worth a shit, not even a grocery list. Besides, I like the money better."

Hoot, when you spend money, it goes away forever. I got all I need, don't get me wrong, I say, jingling my quarters. But what's gone is gone and never comes back. I get to live forever.

"Not sure that's what I'm looking for," he says, "Once you get all crippled up with the arthritis and can't dip your wick anymore, what's the point?"

I think you're missing the point, I say. Being dead with nobody caring or knowing is the scariest thought a person can ever have. That happens, you're done. I mean, done. Where do you go next, what do you do? I been up in the cemetery on the hill over there. You ever ask any of them what's going on, what they've been up to lately? I can tell you. Nothing.

"I don't really talk to dead people," says Hoot.

Well, you're almost there, then, I say. The point is that I'm pretty sure dead people have a much harder time than we do with everything. It'd be pretty special if any of them could talk and tell us about it. Pretty special.

"You oughta know about that," Hoot replies, "What with carrying around that can and all. It talks to you?"

That's not the point, I say, squirming a little. The point is that once I'm dead, God forbid, I'll still be talking to all kinds of people through my work, my writing.

"So what? You looking for a big goddam monument up there just because you wrote some kinda book or something?"

Won't need one when I'm done, I say. I'll be noticed, don't you worry, dead or alive. You'll see.

"I do believe you'll get noticed," he says, rolling his eyes, "I do believe so."

I SIT IN THE LODGE with my oyster crackers and ketchup packets, hungry as sin and dreaming of butter. Things are definitely coming to a point where I have to make some moves, figure out some things. Like how to eat regularly again. Like how to get into Sam's to publish my last chapter. Like how to explain things to Marie.

I can't explain what's happened between myself and Marie since Andrea died. We've grown apart, I guess, though some days I think she never felt close to me at all. I'm still kind of in love with her, at least with her body, anyway. But then, I start thinking back to when I used to hang out with Andrea and how hot she used to look. But Marie's still my girlfriend, and I'm not talking. Not with Andrea around. No wonder I'm confused.

That's the problem; my words just don't seem to work with Marie for some reason. There are just so many things I want to ask her, tell her, find out about her. But I can't – especially now. But once I finish up my story in Sam's, my words will speak for themselves.

With Andrea, it's different. I've always been able to talk to her. Some people are a little uptight and closed-minded these days. But in my mind, she's still young and sexy, just like when we met that night in the Troubadour. Nice hair, nice skin, a nice figure like my girlie pen, and smart as a whip, too. She loved me for who I am, pure and simple, no second agenda.

I pick cracker crumbs out from between my teeth, listen to my stomach rumble, and begin to cry. Not tears of depression or bottomless gloom, but tears of joy at having such a wonderful companion, a woman who gives of herself without demanding anything in return. Except absolute fidelity for the rest of eternity, of course. I dab at my eyes and head for the stairwell.

I turn the knob on the closet door and nothing happens. I try again, then rattle it back and forth. Nothing. A cold sweat starts to break out under my six layers of tattered clothing as I realize that Andrea is in there, locked up and lonely. A series of terrifying thoughts cross my mind: the hopelessness of an afterlife hidden away from the rest of the world, the helplessness, the fear. I can hear her calling my name, crying in the dark.

Andrea, I whisper. Andrea, it's me.

All I hear is snuffling and the dry cough she has had since that frightening encounter in the bar earlier this week. I shake the door handle and kick at the bottom to no avail. I have to get her out of there before she, before she...I try to think, but there's nothing there anymore. Nothing. I slump down with my back to the wall. I stare at the door in front of me, looking for answers that just aren't there. Doors don't talk, and I shouldn't expect any help there. Walls have nothing to add, either. My own strength of purpose is all I have at the moment, maybe forever. Any solution has to come from within, from my own life experience. I sit in silence, listening to my breath going in and out, waiting for the help that just doesn't come anymore.

If I could make myself a quarter-inch tall I could slip under the door and rescue her. If I could make myself strong as Superman, I could open this door with a hand tied behind my back. If I was Einstein, I could think my way through this. If, if, if, I'm thinking. With no more than six feet or so separating us, I should be able to do this with no problem. But how? I'm sweating badly and not thinking as well as I should. No excuses, no excuses, I need to act, this is just wrong, do something, something, right now...cuse me, excuse me, sir, is something wrong, sir? Are you okay?", she asks.

She stands there next to a mop and bucket, sneakers below her swollen ankles, a set of fat knees, a dirty shift that has seen its better days, neck waddles, and - finally - a face looking down at me looking up at her.

Buck, Buck Avery, I say, making no real move to get up.

"Are you okay? Did you fall?" she asks, either genuinely concerned or interested in getting me to move so she can continue with her mopping.

I've fallen into a very, very deep hole, I say. And I'm hoping you can help get me out.

"Excuse me?" she replies, "Can you stand up?"

I can stand but I need your help, I say, scrabbling my way up to an upright, eye-to-eye position. There's someone locked inside this closet.

"Excuse me?" she replies.

She's in there and she's having trouble breathing, I blurt. You've got to help get her out.

"I'll get security," she says, sticking the mop back in the bucket, "They know CPR."

No time! I yell, rattling the door handle, clawing at the hinges. You got keys?

"I, I think so," she says, pawing at a huge ring hanging from her waist, "One of these, I think."

Quickly, please, I say, rattling the knob. She has asthma and I can hear her wheezing in there.

"I don't hear anything," she says, unclipping the ring, "And I don't know which of these works."

I grab the ring from her hand and try a key, then another, then a third. Shit, 'scuse my French, I say.

The twelfth key goes in like a hot knife through butter, setting off another pang of hunger. I turn it and the deadbolt retracts cleanly into the lockset. I pull the door open and paw for the light switch.

"It's on the left," she says, "Up above the shelf."

I know, I say, realizing that I probably shouldn't.

We both rush in and the maid starts peering around, looking confused. I make for the water heater and grope around behind it, pulling Andrea out into the light.

I've got her, I say, getting up off my knees, holding Andrea carefully against my belly.

"Excuse me?" she says, looking at the can, then back at me, "That's a, that's a, that's not a..."

That's not important, I say, squeezing past her bulk to get out the door. I have to get her out of here, fast!

And then we're gone. I glance back as we go up the stairs, two at a time, and see that we're not being followed, yet. I listen for the inevitable PA call for security, the sound of running feet, the command to stop. But all is quiet for the moment. I reassure Andrea that we've outwitted them, that she will never have to spend another day down there in the basement again.

"Where are you taking me?" Andrea asks, as I scoop up my trench, hats, and mismatched gloves off my table by the window.

That's for me to know and...I say, realizing too late that I've made another big mistake.

"I understand," she says, coughing twice, "It's all about you, all about you."

JANUARY 29ᵀᴴ

IT'S GETTING HARDER and harder to get a decent meal in this town, especially without any money. I keep trying the machine at the laundromat, but it keeps giving me exact change, and dollar bills are getting harder and harder to come by. I've lost twelve pounds in the past two weeks and I wasn't exactly plump to begin with.

I haven't seen Marie since getting fired, and Andrea is hardly talking to me anymore. When she does, it's a rough ride for awhile. Actually, I can't say that I haven't seen Marie, since I've been sneaking peeks into Sam's front window and I even followed her home once. I have to leave Andrea somewhere when I go looking for Marie, and it's tough explaining to her that nobody ever looks in back of the underwear folding table. I hardly spend any time in the lodge anymore, except for putting on my boots, gathering crackers and going through the coin returns. And I'm certainly not leaving Andrea around there anymore.

It turns out that Marie lives only about five blocks down and two blocks up the hill toward the cemetery. She seems to have an apartment - not a house - and I haven't seen anybody who looks like kids or a husband. But who knows. It's hard to see everything from twenty feet up in a pine tree.

If Andrea knew what I was thinking about up here, she'd be talking a blue streak. I guess it's better this way. All she needs to know is that I'm not going to do anything with Marie, especially when my unmentionables are on the line. I think about her, but I don't understand her most of the time. And I know that if I touched her, I'd never hear the end of it, forever. Andrea's like that.

So far, though, she has no idea my novel isn't really about her. And as long as nobody spills those beans, I'll get to keep my own a little longer. I feel like I'm cheating on her every time I go in a bathroom, though. Whether I'm writing or not, I get this grim feeling whenever my butt hits the seat. I should probably tell her the truth, but I'm just not ready for that yet, and neither is she. Once I'm done and people start recognizing the value of my work, I'll be able to explain it, read it to her from a real book, maybe even fold a couple pages into the can with her. Who knows? But for now, I just have to continue my story.

I had this dream about Marie last night and Andrea got all worked up over it. She can apparently dream just what I do when she's in the toboggan up next to my head. It wasn't even a sex thing; Marie was just serving me a big dinner of corned beef, cabbage, potatoes, onions, carrots, horseradish, mustard, rye bread, lots of butter, apple pie, vanilla ice cream, and Royal Crown cream soda. It's not like we were doing anything except chewing. Jesum, though, was Andrea ever pissed off. She started right off in the middle of the dream, waking me up and ragging on for over an hour. I'm starting to get sick of her jealousy, though I have to keep in mind the fact that she's dead and probably can't help it. I don't know how to break it off – or even if I really want to – but I don't know where the relationship is going anymore.

Women! Criminy, you can't live with them and you can't live without...food. I am so very, very hungry. The ski patrol sangwiches I used to occasionally grab are now under lock and key since they saw me with a bag under my trench last week. But by the time they asked me about it, the sangwiches were in my belly. Find them now, will you? Ha! But when times are tough, the tough get time, so I'm being real careful about getting caught stealing anything around the lodge.

I'm signed up for the Huntington Cup race next weekend, but I don't know if I can make it that long without decent food. I plan to win it and take the five-hundred dollars, but I'll need my strength to show them that I'm still maybe the best there ever was, anywhere. I've been practicing to see how fast I can go, how far down Tamarac before I have to turn. I've been warned twice by the patrol, but they can't even catch me on foot with a bag of sangwiches. On skis, I'd be gone before they get out three words. Excuse me, sir, he'd say,... hey, where is he, anyway? Crack me up.

The five-hundred bucks will set me up like a king for the rest of the season. I'll be able to eat regular meals and probably move out of my apartment into something a little more roomy. I'll be able to get my uni back and keep it in my bedroom, just like the old days. I'll be able to sweep Marie right off her feet and figure out some way to deal with Andrea. I'll have a nice, warm place to leave her, at least. I mean, I can't just dump her, can I? It wouldn't be civilized, after all we've been through together.

"DO YOU HAVE ANY JOB plans?" she asks, actually trying to be helpful, "A paycheck would make it a lot easier buying food for yourself."

No, I say, looking away sheepishly. I'm kind of tied up finishing my novel at the moment.

We sit here with the heater going and a nice fat candle on the shelf above my head. I had to search all over for Hoot's matches since giving away my lighter last week. The glow spreads out across the entire shack, giving a feeling of even greater warmth. I have a nice, full belly for a change, thanks to the pack of hotdogs I stuck inside my pants down at Don's Deli this afternoon. I did a masterful job of fooling them into thinking I was stealing a steak in my trench pocket. When they followed me out of the store, I stopped and acted really cooperative while they found out I had nothing in there. Then I acted really put out and made them apologize like the dickens. Then I walked back up to the lodge eating hot dog after glorious hot dog, right out of the cellophane. Life is good.

Andrea has been humming a little tune this evening, finally relaxed for the first time in a while. She likes the warmth as much as I do, and we're both getting a little sleepy. We're getting along a lot better lately, and I'm beginning to think we might even have a real future together.

We decide to turn in early tonight, maybe lie out in the toboggan and look up at the stars for awhile before dropping off. It's clear as a bell, cold as hell, with the thickest frost that ever fell. I remember how Dad would always say that on cold mornings, just like I do. Nice ring to it. I untape the *What's Up?* from the window, turn off the gas heater, have another tug at Hoot's whiskey, tidy up a bit, have some more whiskey, and head for the, little more whiskey, toboggan downstairs.

My four blankets keep us toasty as can be down here. I have just my face sticking out from the canvas cover, with Andrea tucked in next to me, both gazing out at the blazing firmament overhead.

I could stay here forever, I say, looking over at her. It's so incredibly beautiful out here.

"You smell anything?" she asks.

I didn't do it, I say, smirking. But if I do, you'll be the first to know.

"No, not that," she says, "Something smells funny."

I sniff away and smell nothing unusual. Just the pine and cedar trees, the scent of roughcut lumber, my four blankets, and my clothing. Nothing out of the ordinary.

"I smell it," she says, "I swear to God, I smell it."

I look up at the sweep of stars, a beautiful curtain of

aurora borealis waving back and forth above the roof of the shack, a few high clouds, and the little plume of smoke curling from the top edge of the window.

Andrea suddenly starts shrieking like two cats doing their damndest, and I almost pop out of my skin. My heart is doing jumping jacks and I paw at the canvas cover to see what's the matter.

"Aaaaaaiiiiiiigggghhhhheeeee!" she screams, "Get me out of here! Help me! Help me!"

I look at her and see that the cover is still on nice and tight, nothing looking out of the ordinary. But she continues to scream at the top of her, her...well, she just keeps on screaming. I wiggle half-way out of the toboggan until I can sit up and look around. That's when I see the glow through the window.

You stay here! I yell, as I wiggle the rest of the way out to look around, find out what's happening. I leave Andrea sounding like the two cats are now up on a hot tin roof, as Dad would say, and I immediately find out that's not too far from the truth: the shack is on fire.

Well, it's too late to do anything about it, like blowing out the candle we forgot about an hour ago. And I've found out the hard way, several times lately, that you can't go back to fix things like that. Flames are licking up the inside wall and spreading out across the ceiling. Andrea screams louder and louder out in the toboggan.

"Get me out of here," she yells, "Oh, my God, I'm, I'm gonna, I...Holy shit! Fire, Fire, Fire!"

I grab my tray and start scooping snow through the door, but it's too little, too late. I reach in and grab my Kerouac from the bench, along with my second pair of jeans, three socks, and my wool shirt with the blue and green houndstooth check pattern. One of my sweaters is already well ablaze, spitting sparks and smelling like it did back in Utica the day I burned my mustache real bad lighting up my hash pi...but I'm not talking. Andrea continues to scream uncontrollably, and I watch as my wad of napkins bursts into flame. I sweep them off the burning shelf and kick them into the snow, stepping on them to put out the fire. I stuff the still-smoking wad into my pocket and try to figure out what comes next on what I hope is the worst night of the rest of my life. I'm pretty sure, however, that a Huntington Cup win next week is no longer a part of that future.

I run around to the cubby and pull my four blankets out of the toboggan. I throw them clear and run around to save my duffel from behind the door.

"What about me? What about me?" she screams, "Get me out of this goddam thing!"

Well, I guess she's more uptight about fire than I thought. Maybe it's about her kids, maybe it's just since being cremated, but who would know? How could I know this? Should I know that people remember these things? I drag out the duffel and run back around to the toboggan. Flames are now licking around the edge of the window frame, and several pieces of burning wood have dropped onto the top of the toboggan.

"Aaaaaaaaaiiiiiiiiee! Oh, my God, get me out!" she screams, as the top of the shack drops into the conflagration below, sending a cascade of sparks and smoke into the clear night air. I grab Andrea and dive away from the cubby as the floor of the shack begins to burn through, dropping its flaming debris onto the toboggan.

Andrea's screaming continues unabated, and it chills me to hear her like this. Then again, it's cold as hell out here except for the heat of the fire, which is probably why she's still so upset. I guess it must heat up the sides of the can, making her more sensitive or something. One of my sweaters, a pair of jeans, a sock, a tee shirt, two pairs of underwear, my broken sunglasses, my Swiss Army knife, my pocket watch, and my hash pipe are gone, probably more.

Suddenly I start patting at my pockets, pulling things out,

and I'm not sure why until another surge of adrenaline tells me that it, too, is missing. My scream blends with Andrea's and I rush back to the front of the collapsing shack. There on the edge of the collapsing floor, beneath the shelf which has dropped from the wall, about to fall through the hole that lets me look down at the smoking toboggan, lies my girlie pen.

There's fire - and a good deal of it - between me and the pen, between the writer and his muse, but I have to do what I have to do, I guess. I pull my Tweety glove up as high as it goes on my wrist, pull the sleeve of my trench down over it, ooch forward on my belly, and reach into the inferno. I can't see a thing for the smoke, and it takes me a while to locate the pen by feel through the insulation in my Tweety glove. But I find it and grab and hold it like I'm a fireman rescuing a three-year old. I pull back and roll down the incline in front of the shack, afraid to see whether my one and only chance has saved my most valuable possession. The sides of the shack fall in as the rest of the roof drops, and the flames and smoke billow higher and higher into the night sky.

I open my smoke-filled eyes and look at my singed and melting Tweety glove - the back now looking more like a cloud-mottled sunset than a cheerful cartoon character - unable for a moment to open my hand, afraid I'll find it empty. But as I uncurl my fingers I see the pen; flattened on one side, its plastic casing smudged and melting. I drop it into the snow and roll it around and around to cool it off. I pull it out of the snow and hold it up in the eerie light of the fire as Andrea's screams continue to pierce the night air. I shake it, and the snow inside - the glorious, beautiful snow of so many winters past - begins to fall again. And the little titties – right here on the second-most beautiful girl I have ever seen - begin to spin again inside the smudged and heat-sloughed plastic barrel.

My eyes brim with tears of joy as I carefully pocket

the pen and clamber to my feet to reassure Andrea, who is wailing louder than ever.

Andrea, Andrea, I yell, shaking the can. Andrea, it's over, get hold of yourself.

"No, no, no, no," she screams, "I can't do this again. I'm, I'm, Aaaaaaaaaiiiiieeeeeee!"

I cradle her in my lap, rocking with my back to the fire to console her, to keep her from looking at the one thing that scares her more than I can imagine. There, there, I say. It's better now, you're calming down, everything's okay now.

I reach into my pocket to show her my girlie pen, how I've saved the two things most dear to me at this point in my life. See, I say, shaking up some snow. She's still here and so are you.

Well, this is one of those good news-bad news situations, because Andrea immediately goes bonkers over the little titties spinning around and accuses me, again, of gross insensitivity, infidelity and my so-called inability to think about anybody except myself. Jesum, Andrea, relax. On the other hand, she's not screaming quite as loud and I can see that she's headed back to her old self again. I carefully pocket the pen and continue to rock her back to more normal composure.

But the future seems to be coming at me pretty quickly, even though I'm basking in the thought that we have all escaped with our lives, that there really isn't anything more important than that. I hear the distant whine of a snowmobile coming up the liftline and I know we have to get out of here fast. I stuff my four blankets into my singed duffel as quickly as I can, along with my extra sock, my Kerouac, my extra pair of jeans, my sweater, my wad of wet and charred napkins, and Andrea. As the whine of the snowmachine approaches, I reassure Andrea that this is only a temporary solution, that she just has to be quiet for a while. I run for the edge of the woods where I toss the duffel behind a tree and hunker down next to it. Then I notice the tray lying next to the bonfire, and I run back to grab it.

The two Huntington maintenance men jump off the sled and stare at the column of flame and smoke that used to be Hoot's office. I shush Andrea and hunker down a little flatter as they walk in aimless circles trying to figure out what to do.

"Oh, man," he says, "What the fuck we do now, Ray?"

"Shit, Billy, I dunno, roast some weenies?" He leans over and spits a brown oyster on the virgin snow next to his boot.

"Well, I ain't got any," says Billy.

"I sure hope fucking Hoot wasn't in there."

"What if he was? What do we do?"

"Well, he wasn't. Couldn't a been," says Ray, "I saw him at the Klondike drunker than shit on rye, before I come up to work."

"You don't think he might have come up here instead a going on home? You don't know where he went."

"Fuck you, Jack," says Ray, spitting brown, just like Billy now. I guess he must have picked up that disgusting habit since we first met. "Only a goddam nutcase or crazy-ass lunatic would sleep up here on a night like this. Hoot's a drinker, but he ain't crazy."

Well, this gets Andrea all riled up again, and she starts in ragging on me for turning her life into such a piece of shit, without 'scusing her French, and for making her live in a place that only a lunatic could love. I shush her and flatten out a little more, hoping they don't hear us. She continues, though, and I roll on top of the duffel to keep her voice muffled.

"Guess we better get down and call Barnacre."

"I'll let you wake him up," says Ray, "Pleasure's yours."

With that, they straddle the snowmobile, yank the starter cord, and whine off down the hill. I sit up and pull Andrea out.

It's time to move, I say. They'll be back with a bunch of people in no time.

"And just where do you plan on moving to?" she asks, cattily, without the joy I feel at surviving such a catastrophe.

I've got just the place, I reply, stuffing her back into the duffel and picking up the tray for our last ride, on what was very nearly the last day of the rest of our lives.

I MAKE MY LAST TRIP under the bridge, this time without any skis, boots, poles, or unicycle. I arrange what's left of my stuff below the little ledge I have made to keep us from rolling down into the creek. It took a while to calm Andrea down again once she heard the creek burbling and saw where she would be spending the night. But she seems okay now as long as I keep her on the uphill side, keep her occupied and talking. I pull out my four blankets and put on all my extra clothing for the night. I drop my tired head onto the duffel and pull Andrea in close.

We'll be fine, I say, stroking the outside of the can. It's all over now.

JANUARY 30ᵀᴴ

THE CAR SLOWS in the early morning half-light, the driver eyeing me carefully before pulling over. I gather up my duffel and Andrea as I approach the back door.

"Where you headed?" asks the driver. I toss what's left of my priceless life into the back seat and walk around to sit shotgun.

West, I say. Same as you.

"Okey dokey," he says, "We're off."

I look over at him, sizing him up, and decide to ask.

Do you mind if we make one fast stop before we get headed?

"Nah," he says, probably figuring this involves a bathroom, "I might get some coffee for the road."

I've got just the place, I say, winking large.

HERE'S SOME MONEY, I SAY, dropping a dozen or so quarters into his hand outside the door. Order me a regular coffee to go and if anything happens I'll meet you out by the car.

"Holy shit! You gonna rob this place?" he asks, "I seen this on TV once where some guy..."

No way, I say. Got money in both pockets. I love this place, only there's something I have to do before we head out.

We walk in and he heads for the counter as I bolt for the

263

room with my name on the door. Marie catches a glimpse of me as I make my way across the dining room. I wink large and barge into the men's room.

I lock the stall door and sit down with my pants up. I locate my girlie pen in the pocket of my wool shirt and gaze down fondly. I shake it and watch the snow falling on spinning titties, like I have for so many seasons past. Then I begin work on my last chapter on the last day of the best winter of my entire life.

When I come out, I am no longer uptight about Jimmy seeing me, or Andrea getting pissed off anymore. I have a big, shit-eating grin, 'scuse my French, on my face as I walk tall and proud over to the counter where Marie is sitting three stools down from my new friend. I sit down next to her, take one last peek, and unfold the napkin in front of her, setting it next to her coffee cup.

"It is finished," I say, as she squints at the list of local bars and businesses. I pull my Huntington pass from around my neck and drape it around Marie's. "Just a little something so you don't forget me."

"That ain't fucking likely," she says, looking at the picture.

I lean over and kiss her tenderly on the cheek and stand up to leave. I wave over at my new friend.

"Got that coffee?" I ask, "Let's boogie."

EPILOGUE

Huntington What's Up? - April 3, 1980
What's Up With That?

YOUNG FREDDIE JACKSON got a big surprise this week when he decided it was time to get his bicycle out of the shed for his first ride of the season. Instead of his old Schwinn, he found what he thought was only half of it - a unicycle.

Fred Jackson scratched his head when our reporter asked him about it. "Dunno," said Jackson (Sr.), "I never seen nothing like that before. Almost like his old bike had a baby in there or somethin."

How the unicycle got there in the first place is a matter of speculation at this point. The only clue, according to Jackson (Sr.) was a pile of saltine wrappers on the floor of the shed.

Well, we're all scratching our heads on this one. But young Freddie Jackson seems pretty happy as he spins up and down the street. How long did it take him to learn to ride it?

"Not long," said Freddie (Jr.), "I can balance on it real good! And I'm gonna be the best there ever was."

* * * * *

Missoula Herald - May 21, 1980
Good Sam Closes a Circle
by Jill Johannson

Last week, County Department of Human Services Director, Anne Shuttleworth, was astonished to see a young man from New York appear in her office with a dented and rusty can under his arm.

"I have to say," said Shuttleworth, "I thought for sure he was another applicant, the way he was dressed, just another young victim of the recession down on his luck."

But, when the smoke cleared, he began to tell his story, which was far from the tale of woe she expected. Young Buck Avery, a professional ski instructor from the east, had come to Montana on a mission.

Avery, an experienced instructor at prestigious Whiteface Mountain - recent host of the winter Olympic games - had been hired for a private lesson by a woman who hailed from Missoula. Avery said that she had been working as a licensed masseuse in Lake Placid and catered to the needs of the elite athletes who train there. "She had magic in those hands," according to Avery.

But the story doesn't end here. She intimated to Avery that her life had not always been so professional and fulfilling, that she had a past that she would rather forget...but could not. This past involved Missoula and two young boys who happened to be her sons.

Andrea Collins - well known to the Department, according to Shuttleworth - had a bit of a checkered past before turning her life around on the east coast. She had told Avery about her two sons, her only living kin, who had been removed from her home by the Department in 1977. It turns out that Collins had also been a very busy working girl out here in Big Sky country.

According to Shuttleworth, Avery had broken down in

tears telling the rest of the story. He and Ms. Collins had dated and were scheduled to be married when she was killed in a tragic automobile accident. Avery said that he had been wearing his seatbelt and had survived with relatively minor injuries, though his Mercedes was flattened out "like a pat of butter".

Avery had paid for a proper funeral with a catered dinner for all her friends and associates, telling us that, since he had the means, it was the very least he could do. He arranged for a cremation, but was constantly plagued by thoughts of the two young boys out west and the way Ms. Collins had cried talking about them. So he made it his mission to return her ashes to her sons. "So that she could finally rest in peace", in Avery's words.

He started out with no idea where she had lived or who and where her sons were. He said that he simply drove his brand, new Cadillac Fleetwood west until he entered Montana where he began to make inquiries in every little town he drove through. He finally hit pay dirt here in Missoula.

Ms. Collins' sons, who have since been adopted by Mr. and Mrs. Olaf Ferguson of South Hazel Street, were too stunned to comment, or even look at the ashes when Avery presented them in a ceremony in the Department's Blue Conference Room, according to Shuttleworth. Our own photographer, Bill Williams, took pictures of the event and gave Avery several as keepsakes.

This goes to show: All's well that ends well. Avery, when asked about his plans, replied, "Europe's next, maybe France. I have an instructor job lined up for next season: Assistant Ski School Director at Grenouille des Yalps, as soon as my new skis arrive." We know where we'll be going if we ever decide to learn how to ski!

* * * * *

Marcy Comings and Goings - November 3, 1980
by Jean Cummings, R.N.

Doctor James C. MacIntyre of Building 7 has just announced his retirement, effective December 31st. "Big Jim", as he is affectionately known by his patients, has been an institution here since the early 1950s. Watch this column for details on his retirement party (and we sure hope it doesn't conflict with Santa's arrival this year - rumor is that he's going to parachute into the D Ward exercise yard!).

Talk about comings and goings! Averell Harriman Avery, whom we all know and love, has done it again! He turned up at the front desk (again) on September 15th - this time as a voluntary admission - with nothing but a duffel bag, that wink, and a grin that hardly fit through the front door. He was assigned (again) to B ward, where staff say he told the most incredible stories...and they've heard some doozies over the years. They thought something was up when he came back from Commissary last week without that beard of his, and sporting a nice, crew cut. Did he ever look different! Next thing we knew, he had disappeared...again! Good luck out there, Averell!

Betty Treadwell (C Ward Charge Nurse on nights) has finally had that baby! We thought it would nev...

"...*Valereeeeeeee, Valeraaaaaaaaaaah, Valereeeeeeeeeeeee,*

Valerah-ha-ha-ha-ha-ha-Valereeeeee..."